BACK FROM HELL

BACK FROM HELL

REVENANT FILES™ BOOK 1

D'ARTAGNAN REY

MICHAEL ANDERLE

DISRUPTIVE IMAGINATION

LMBPN Publishing
PMB 196, 2540 South Maryland Pkwy
Las Vegas, NV 89109

Version 1.00, September 2021
eBook ISBN: 978-1-68500-498-9
Print ISBN: 978-1-68500-499-6

THE BACK FROM HELL TEAM

Thanks to our Beta Team:
John Ashmore, Erika Everest, Kelly O'Donnell, Larry Omans

Thanks to our JIT Team:

Zacc Pelter
Wendy L Bonell
Peter Manis
Dorothy Lloyd
Jackey Hankard-Brodie
Jeff Goode
Angel LaVey

If we've missed anyone, please let us know!

Editor
SkyHunter Editing Team

CHAPTER ONE

The Wicked Easy. The easiest place to sin in Sulfur, Louisiana.

The large sign held the attention of a young man in a long, dark trench coat who stepped out of his car into the dark, rainy night and adjusted the strap on his eyepatch. He certainly hoped it proved to be so. He strode to the entrance but a large bouncer blocked his path.

"You look a little young to be here," the man said and noted the long blond hair, thin skin, and sharp features of the new arrival. With the eyepatch and the resolute look in his other eye, he did briefly question his deduction. Still, rules were rules.

The young man held his coat open slightly with one hand and slid the other in to retrieve his wallet and show him his ID. The bouncer read it somewhat skeptically. According to the card, he had turned twenty-five a few months earlier and his name was Jack House.

"IDs are easy to fake," he said and tapped the bottom right of the card before he produced his to point out that the young man's was missing the intertwining pattern.

"True enough," he admitted with a sigh, took his wallet out, and produced a collection of twenties and fifties. "This seems real enough though, don't it?"

The bouncer studied the stack—which appeared to be around three hundred dollars—and decided there were times when it was in his best interest to fuck the rules. "Welcome to The Wicked Easy," he proclaimed as he took the stack and opened the door for him.

With a nod of thanks, the customer walked inside and looked around. The venue was bustling for a seemingly sleepy town. Tables were stacked with drinks and an abundance of smoke had already formed almost a haze throughout the room. He nodded, moved to the bar, and grinned at a couple of barely clothed ladies who all but purred at him as he passed.

Still smiling, he sat on possibly the only empty stool but it took a few minutes for one of the bartenders to approach him. The thin, tanned, mustachioed individual greeted him with a wily grin that revealed one gold-capped tooth in place of his right canine. "Good evening. Are you looking for some debauchery?"

"Is that the special?" he asked and studied the man. He was very well dressed in a black vest over a red shirt with some kind of swirling black pattern and black slacks with a golden chain. The outfit made him wonder if the proprietor was originally from Las Vegas. He should probably have checked into that before he came.

"Every night," the bartender said with a laugh before he looked quizzically at him for a moment. "You seem a little young to be here."

"I already settled it with the good man outside," he responded. "Can I place an order?"

"Sure thing." He propped his elbows on the bar. "What'll it be, my friend?"

He slid his hand into his coat again and retrieved another bundle of cash with a deft hand. "I need some information," he explained and placed the notes on the counter. "And I'm looking for the proprietor of this bar."

The barkeep looked at the money for a moment and pursed his lips before he chuckled as he tapped a finger against the wood surface. "Well, you are certainly no cop since that would be a badge and not a bribe. And even if you were, you would merely be returning what we already paid you."

"True enough." The customer rested his hands on the bar and looked into the man's eyes. "But that's not the information I'm looking for."

In response, the other man chuckled and followed it immediately with a sharp whistle. "Hey, big guy. Clear the table!" he ordered and another large bouncer nodded silently as some "woos" and "ahs" erupted around the bar. The barkeep picked the cash up. "We'll consider this your entrance fee into our game," he said as he began to walk out from behind the bar and gestured for the young man to join him.

He stood casually from the stool and followed, his hands in his pockets as the many gazes in the bar watched him stroll to a round red table the bouncer had cleared before he placed a black box on the surface. The bartender rolled his sleeves up and opened the box to reveal a deck of cards with shining red-and-black designs on the back, reminiscent of a demonic face. "You've played blackjack, I presume?"

The young man took his seat, slid his hand into his pants pocket, and produced another small black box, which he opened to reveal cigarettes and a lighter. He lit one and took a puff. "I certainly have." The bouncer placed an ashtray next to him. "Appreciate it."

"Good," the bartender-turned-dealer said with a devious smile. "Then there is no need to explain the rules except how the bets will work." A stack of ten black chips was placed in front of the dealer and the gambler. "We don't play for money here, only special prizes." He gestured to his ten chips. "We play one chip for one chip. If I lose all my chips, I'll tell you anything you want."

"And if you win?" the young man asked after another drag and let the smoke slide out between his words.

The dealer's smile turned to one of mockery. "I'm damn sure you know," he said with a hissed laugh. "You aren't the first to come in with...interesting orders."

"I had to ask." He gestured to the cards and shrugged. "I guess with the motif you have there that the wager is 'my soul?'" he asked and gestured theatrically with his fingers.

The dealer shrugged casually. "In a manner of speaking. Let's simply say you'll be indebted for a favor owed. That's how things work around here." He pointed to the party behind them in the main lounge. "It's not like it's anything too bad. Some of them owe favors and they don't look too sad about it, huh?"

"What about him?" he asked and pointed to the silent bouncer. "He doesn't seem to be having a fun time."

The dealer shrugged. "He'll loosen up after a while,

trust me." He placed his hand against his chest. "Now, to officially get this started, let's take a moment to introduce ourselves. My name is Lucien and I'll be your dealer." He pointed across the table. "And you are?"

"My name's Johnny and I'll be your player," the young man replied with a small smirk of amusement. His stare became determined when the other man extended his hand to shake.

"Well, Johnny. My information against your soul. What do you say?" The dealer picked one of the cards up and held it beside his face as he mimicked the demonic grin on it. "Are you up for a little sin?"

He chuckled at the man's overt theatricality, nodded, and shook his hand firmly. "It might be a sin but I'll take your bet and you'll regret it."

The other man laughed as his hand grasped Johnny's and shook it hard. "That's the spirit!" A white shimmer encased the chips for a brief moment before it vanished. The dealer shuffled the deck. "All right, what will your first bet be?" Johnny gathered all ten of his chips and placed them into the pool without comment, much to the other man's surprise. "You aren't very patient, are you?"

"More than you might think," he responded with a shrug, "but in this case, I still have things to do so let's hurry this up."

Lucien leaned back toward the bouncer. "This is gonna be an easy night," he declared with glee before he straightened and dealt the first two cards—a jack for Johnny and a seven for himself. The young player's next card was an eight and the dealer placed his second card face-down. "So then, what will you—"

"I'll stay." The young gambler said and waved his hand over the table. The dealer pressed his lips against his teeth to stop himself from laughing. This boy might have played blackjack but he did not know the real rules—one never let the dealer dictate the game and more importantly, shuffle the deck. He flipped his card, prepared for the nine he had snuck to the top of the deck, and stared at the queen in surprise. Seventeen. He couldn't hit again.

Johnny leaned closer as both Lucien and the bouncer gaped at the outcome in shock. "I guess that means I win," he stated flatly and pointed at the dealer. "Now, tell me where Ciro is."

"Ciro?" the man asked, utterly gobsmacked. "How do you know about—ah!" He spilled the chips as he lurched across the table. Everyone nearby looked at them in surprise as he stared at the other man and tried to clench his teeth to stop himself from talking. "Ciro is in the... baasemeent..." His words strained as he attempted to hold them back. "S-sssecret entrance... I-i-in the k-kitchhen. P-pull the chain."

"I appreciate it." Johnny pushed from his chair and turned to leave but his path was blocked by both the new bouncer and the one from the entrance. "Huh. I thought we had an understanding."

"Play again," Lucien demanded and used the table to support him as he stood, his slicked-back hair now as wild as his eyes. "You cheated!"

"Can you prove it?" the young man asked as a large hand settled on his shoulder. He sighed and nodded. "Well, since this seems to be for pride, all right. One more game." As he turned to face the challenger, he slid his hand inside his coat. "We need a new bet, though. I don't have anything else I want from you so if I win, I get to shoot you."

"Do what?" the dealer asked in disbelief.

"You heard me." He pulled out of the bouncer's hold and moved to the table, where he thumped his hand onto the surface. "Deal the cards."

"Like hell will I accept a bet like—" A card flew off the top of the deck to settle in front of the player's hand. "What?" Lucien gawked at the king of diamonds as another card landed beside his hand that now clutched the table even more desperately. He tried to move past the unfortunate truth that it was a two while the deck dealt the player the ace of clubs.

"Well, would you look at that?" The young man slid his eyepatch off slowly to reveal a pure white eye with a glowing white iris, something that caused dread in the other man when he saw it. It seemed the boy knew the real rules of the game after all. A silver revolver clicked against a button on the long coat when Johnny drew it and Lucien stared down the barrel at a familiar blue light. "Blackjack."

CHAPTER TWO

The partygoers yelled in shock and anger when Lucien was shot but their outrage was tempered by confusion when they realized it was certainly not with a normal bullet. A blue light pierced his chest but left no wound, and a red humanoid figure emerged from the dealer's back with a shriek of pain before it vanished.

Johnny turned to fire at the bouncer who stood next to him and tried to catch his comrade's body. His shot struck him in the head but again, no injuries appeared before a green figure slid out and faded away. He spun and unleashed two more shots when the two bouncers behind him tried to tackle him.

Both stopped in the middle of their rush and a red figure was cast out of one and a blue out of the other before both disappeared. Many of the patrons rushed outside, but a few stayed to try to deal with the trigger-happy gambler. Some held knives or broken bottles or while others simply used their fists. He made short work of them, which confirmed that he wielded no ordinary revolver as he did not need to reload. Not only that, he was damn accurate with it too.

Some bottles clinked near the bar and Johnny noticed that two scantily clad bar girls had retrieved machine guns. "Oh, well shit." He dove into the private room as they fired and the barrage ripped through the flooring, tables, and walls as they tried to catch him in a hail of lead.

"Take care of them," he ordered his invisible companion and ducked as a few bullets whistled over his head and flung himself prone behind one of the walls. "No, I don't care that they are ladies. They have guns." After the firing stopped, he peered through one of the holes in the wall to see them reloading. "Now would be a good time."

Behind the two gun-toting women, two bottles of vodka elevated sharply and swung down on their heads. This made them stagger a little but did not knock them out. "They are resilient, aren't they?" Johnny muttered as he scrambled quickly out of the private room when the women turned toward him. He fired two shots and struck one in the head and the other in the ribs.

A blue figure burst out of the first woman with a horrifying shriek before it departed with a hiss. The red figure that emerged from the second tried immediately to return to its host. Unperturbed, the young man walked forward and fired several shots in succession until the entity finally released its hold and disappeared and the body slumped heavily.

"That one was clingy. Yeah, it was a nice grouping, though," Johnny commented but was distracted from that thought when someone stirred behind him. He leaned back into the private room. Lucien had pushed to his knees and now clutched his head.

"What happened?" he gasped and tried to get his bearings when the young man approached. "Who are you?"

"Johnny, but the better question is who are you?" he asked as the man groaned again, still holding his head as if he thought it might explode.

"Uh...James Shelton." He dragged in a deep breath. "Where am I?"

"At a bar that will be out of business soon," he replied. "What day do you think it is?"

James took a moment to think. "Isn't it Friday?"

"What month, day, and year?"

"First of November, Twenty-Nineteen?" the man asked and the young man whistled, surprised by his answer.

"Damn, three whole weeks. Well, at least you won't be possessed for Christmas."

"Wait, possessed? He recoiled. "I was?"

"Yep." The bouncer began to awaken along with the others behind him. "You and everyone else who is waking up. Do you mind giving them the details? I have something else to attend to at the moment."

Johnny marched out of the private room and into the kitchen where two cooks attempted to slice him with butcher's knives. He blocked their attack, kicked one in the knee to topple him, and twisted the arm of the other to force him to drop his weapon.

Before his opponent could recover, he placed his revolver against the man's chin and had barely fired before a green figure darted out. He let the body drop and turned to the other chef, who attempted to retrieve his knife. A headshot ended his efforts and with a hissed groan, another green figure disappeared.

"Green, red, and blue. We have quite an assortment of ghosts in here," he told the invisible shade beside him. "Wait, what do you mean they aren't ghosts? Spirits? I thought a shade had to be... Oh, okay. Well, that's a pain but you wanted to take care of him anyway so have fun with that."

Johnny noticed a silver chain close to one of the fryers and when he pulled it, something chimed. He searched for the secret entrance he needed to open but found nothing so he pulled on it a few more times with a frown. "I think this is for orders," he muttered. Something rattled in the corner of the kitchen and he looked in that direction. A fridge moved aside to reveal a doorway that accessed a staircase.

He sighed as he approached it. "Show off," he snarked quietly before he noticed an iron pan and picked it up. "This will probably be useful in the next few moments," he said and descended the staircase.

Judging by their footprints and the way these suddenly ceased, he estimated that at least two guards awaited his arrival around a corner at the bottom. Before he took the last few steps, he stopped and studied their shadows and was almost certain that they held guns ready.

After a few moments during which he remained utterly motionless, they began to creep to the side so they could see up the stairwell. A loud clang made them swivel to the lowest stairs and they jumped when they caught sight of the bouncing pan.

Using the advantage of their surprise, he bounded down, kicked one of the bodyguards away, and fired into the stomach of the other. He nodded with satisfaction when a red spirit vanished and he fired almost immediately into the head of the man who had fallen. Another red spirit joined its friend.

Once he'd scanned the short hallway to check for others, he approached a pair of doors and kicked them in, his weapon ready. The room contained a large ornate desk and a brown leather chair that faced away from him in what had been designed as an office with several drawers and a few expensive-looking decorations.

"Who the hell do you think you are?" a gruff, irate voice demanded as the chair turned slowly. "You come into my home, expel my people, and point that little peashooter at me?"

When the figure finally faced him, he revealed an appearance different than the spirits Johnny had dealt with thus far. He seemed to have the appropriate skin to be one —or at least what looked like skin, although it was thin and an odd shade of red. His wispy hair was brushed into a coif and his white eyes had no irises. He wore a black silk shirt, black slacks, and well-made black leather shoes.

When he raised his hand, the bone could be seen through the flesh but appeared to be made of white light rather than calcium. He pointed a pistol at the intruder— one that was regrettably a much larger caliber. "You had better answer me. I can make this fast or very, very slow."

"Are you Ciro Corallo?" the young man asked while he

held his much smaller revolver trained on him. "Former small-time mobster in the New Orleans Mafia?"

"Small-time?" the shade roared and pushed to his feet. "You little bastard. I was in charge of keeping the family running while—"

"Yeah, you were a bookkeeper. Congrats. I'm sure you'll get a movie someday," Johnny mocked. "The thing is, I'm not here for who you were in life. I was sent to deal with you for what you've done in the afterlife and for what you have done in the living world after you escaped Limbo."

Ciro clicked his tongue in disgust. "The best they can send against me is some punk kid playing like he's an FBI agent?"

"Make that detective, and I'm twenty-two, you husk," he retorted. "I'm surprised you were even able to become a shade. That takes strong attachments and a hell of a lot of phantasma. I guess being a pen-pusher gave you some skills, although with how easy it was to get past all your goons, you certainly don't screen them well, do you?"

The shade fired his gun but his intruder was ready and dodged easily. "Don't you disrespect me." His growl was a warning. "I was simply minding my own business and creating a new organization. I certainly don't intend to let a little rat bastard like you stop me."

"Oh, I won't." The young man smirked for a moment as he straightened, holstered his revolver, and nodded at the space beside the shade. "He had already called dibs."

Ciro was confused for a moment before he turned his head and was immediately thrust into his desk by a skeletal hand. He dropped his weapon when he was caught by the throat and lifted off his feet. A figure formed beyond the hand. The skeleton glowed with cyan light, his whites eyes illuminated in their sockets. He was dressed similar to Johnny in a dark trench coat, white shirt, and pants and wore a dark trilby.

"Vic?" The shade gasped and clutched the skeletal arm. "Vic Kane? What the hell? You're dead!"

Vic drew him in. "So are you, dumbass." His voice was gravelly and full of menace.

Ciro seemed caught off-guard by this for a moment. "Oh, right." His assailant thumped him into his desk again, picked him up by his shirt, and continued to deliver a sound beating.

Johnny stood for a moment and looked around the room. "So how long will this take Vic? Should I look around or something?"

"Give me a minute, kid," his partner demanded and ceased his assault for a moment to turn toward him. "I'm getting reacquainted with my old pal." He turned to deliver a solid blow but his adversary deflected it and tackled him. They fell in a tangle and continued to try to gain the upper hand.

The young man sighed and looked at one of the desks. "Yeah, it will be more than a minute." He took a pair of black gloves out and slipped them on. "Let's see if there's something interesting in the study to steal."

Ciro brought both his hands together, chopped them into the back of Vic's neck, and managed to stop his assault briefly enough to kick him off. He ran to his desk, drew a knife from a sheath that lay on top of some paperwork, and spun to slash at his adversary with more fury than skill. His ineptness allowed the other ghost to catch his hand during a bad swipe and swing him into a wall before he flung him face-down and began to stamp repeatedly on the back of his head.

Johnny looked admiringly at a gold watch on the desk, then noticed Ciro's gun on the floor and picked that up too. He placed both on the desk as he took a moment to look through the papers.

The proprietor grasped Vic's leg and flung him aside before he raced toward his gun on the desk. Utterly calm, Johnny drew his revolver and shot him in the face. The shot didn't cause him to react like the possessed ones on the ground floor had, but he was catapulted back. His left eye and a piece of his face were blown away but began to repair themselves a moment later. Vic lunged into him and when he fell, trapped him between his knees and began to batter his wounded face with a flurry of punches.

The young man opened one of the bottom drawers but found nothing interesting. He checked the others and finally opened the top one and noticed a manilla envelope —those which, in his mind, usually contained something important.

While the battle between the shades continued, he opened it and a letter slid out, which he read quickly. Some kind of emblem or symbol that looked like an ax on the bottom caught his attention.

Ciro pushed Vic off of him again. Johnny collected all the items including the proprietor's gun and wandered to the door as his partner stood and the shade staggered past him to his desk. "Are you done yet?"

Vic cracked his neck and put his fists up. "I could beat this jackass for eternity."

"I know. You told me that before but we have to deal with him now. So how about a real solution?" He aimed his revolver at the small-time gangster.

The shade laughed. "Do you think you can stop me with that?" he asked while his red flesh oozed down the side of his face.

"I think I could, and very, very slowly." The young man twirled the gun in his hand. "This is a deadeye revolver, one of the few weapons that those of us who breathe can use to hurt the dead. Admittedly you'd probably heal after a while, but you'd be wounded enough to have to return to Limbo."

"And you think I'll go back there?" The shade wiped some of the sludge from his face. "Not on your life." .

"Or yours," Johnny replied with a smirk. "They don't want you back."

"You're a criminal in Limbo, Ciro, exactly as you were in life. You didn't even try to be different." Vic spat his disgust. "Then you returned to the living world after you busted out of Purgatory. And since you aren't anyone special, you're merely a liability."

Ciro laughed but a trace of fear was evident in his bravado. "So what? Do you think you can finish me off with that?" he asked and pointed to the smaller weapon.

The young man shook his head. "No, but like I said, he called dibs." He tossed the gun to his partner, who caught it easily. Flames the same color as his bones poured out of the barrel.

His adversary froze for a moment. "Wait, you can't be serious."

Vic pulled the hammer. "You die in death as you did in

life—forgettable." He fired as the other man cried a protest and the bullet emerged as a small orb of cyan light that struck him in the head. His body was filled with slivers of the light, erupted a moment later, and turned into a smoky substance before it vanished completely.

Johnny watched it until it dissipated. "This is the first time I've seen a ghost obliterated," he commented as he slipped the envelope into his coat pockets. "Do you think it hurts?"

The ghost looked at the gun before he slid it into a holster beneath his coat. "I hope so."

"What the hell did he do to you?" The young man rolled his eyes. "Sleep with your boney girlfriend?"

"Shut it, pretty boy," Vic snapped with a trace of humor. "Let's return to the bar. I need a drink."

"Which means I need a drink." He sighed and rubbed his temple. "Although honestly, that sounds all right."

CHAPTER THREE

Vic sidled behind the bar while Johnny studied what remained of the lounge. It seemed that all the previously possessed individuals had left as fast as they could—the smart decision, all things considered. The number of people who stood around to gawk after such an event was annoyingly high.

"Do we honestly have time for this?" Johnny asked as he slid onto one of the stools while the ghost perused the unshattered bottles of alcohol on the wall. "The cops are probably on their way."

"If they ain't here yet they ain't coming," his partner retorted with a disgruntled expression and examined a half-full bottle of whiskey before he threw it on the floor. "Ciro had them paid off. They most likely have orders to stay the hell away and let his men take care of any disturbances."

Johnny took a fresh pack of cigarettes out and frowned at them before he beat the top in his palm to force one out. "And how long before they get curious?"

Vic pulled a long-necked bottle off the upper shelf. It contained an amber liquid, which had an eerie glow to it in the low lights. He smiled as he picked a glass up. "Long enough. I found the good stuff."

He bit on the top and pulled the cork out, spat it to the side, poured himself a shot quickly, and downed it. Johnny felt the burn in his throat—a damn strong one that almost caused him to cough his unlit cigarette out as it snaked downward. He shook his head as he took a silver lighter out and lit his smoke. "Why would he keep any of that stygia liquor up top if all his boys were in host bodies?"

"They probably had some ghost patrons from time to time," Vic responded as he poured another round for himself. "Besides, phantoms or any other dreck can't help other ghosts possess bodies without the right amount of stygia to stabilize them. He probably had to get his operations established first before he could build his ranks up."

The young man took his smartphone out and looked at his notes. "The guy's probably been running around the breathing side for a while then, huh?"

The ghost downed his shot and his companion's face contorted for a moment. "Longer than he should have been. If I can give that bastard one thing, he's certainly wily. How the hell he was able to escape Purgatory is beyond me. That place locks down some of the toughest ghosts around. How a pencil-pusher slipped through is a question for the ages."

"Or maybe the clerk when we turn our bounty in," Johnny suggested and looked at the device again before he stowed it in his pocket. A thought came to him that made him rub his head. "Shit, I never got my money back."

Vic chortled and poured another shot. "Well, it's a good thing we fixed this. That was a few hundred bucks you lost, right?"

He nodded solemnly. "A fair amount more than that if you factor in gas and the informants."

"It wouldn't have taken so long if you had simply come in with guns blazing," the ghost noted with a tilt of his head. "Like I suggested originally. It came to that anyway."

"I thought we were detectives, not commandos," he retorted.

"You play the field," Vic snarked. "We're not hitmen either, technically. Sometimes, sneaky is good but at other times, loud is preferred. I mostly prefer it anyway."

"And look at what that got you." Johnny snickered and glanced at his cigarette. "With all these vices you passed on to me, the thing that killed you was a nine-millimeter."

"A .357," the ghost countered and took another sip. "Give me some credit. I could have shaken a nine-millimeter off."

"Isn't that worse? You should have seen a Magnum coming." The young man chuckled once he'd adjusted to the trail of the last mouthful down his gullet. "Still, it's been almost two weeks of footwork. If you weren't so pushy about getting this gig, we could have found one closer to Austin."

"Sulfur ain't that far," his companion chided and swished the glass. "That was maybe four hours at most."

"Closer to five," Johnny corrected and pointed at him with his cigarette. "By the way, you don't get control of the radio on the next ride."

"Try to stop me," Vic challenged and downed his drink

as Johnny took a puff, which made him almost spit the liquid up. "I can't listen to that electric junk you blast constantly. I'm dead and I have more life to me than that so-called music."

"And your rodent pack doesn't exactly thrill me, not for hours on end." He took a more cautious drag. "The time I was almost thrown in jail when you pinched a couple of greatest hits albums still irks me."

"It didn't please me either and I still don't have a vinyl player." He took the box of cigarettes off the table, helped himself to one, and lit it. "And it's rat pack, you moron."

The young man waved him off, slid his hand into his coat, and removed the letter. "I found this in Ciro's desk." He placed it on the counter. "Take a look. He might have had help on this side."

Vic unfolded the envelope, withdrew the letter, and read it in silence.

Dearest Friend from hottest Hell.

I am writing to you with a proposition, one I will not fully explain in this letter, but you should know it can be of benefit to you, me, and many others. I have already begun to act and your actions in this wretched plane have caught my attention. Should you wish to prosper further, I recommend meeting me in our unofficial southern capital if you wish to return to the big time exceptionally easily.

The ghost tapped the emblem on the bottom of the letter and tried to recall if he'd seen anything similar to what appeared to be a hatchet or ax made of red wax punched into the paper. "So he did have friends. Well, that is surprising."

"Is that the only thing that interests you?" he asked and took another drag. "Not the telltale words of a psychopath trying to get in good with ghosts?"

His partner shrugged and downed his shot but this time, Johnny had grown accustomed to the hit. "Eh, what can you do? It's not like that is a shocking turn of events nowadays. Hell, even in my day." He flipped the glass and placed it on the bar before he refocused on the letter. "There is something familiar about this, though. The salutation ends with 'hottest Hell.' Do you think that's a club or organization?"

"It could be. Honestly, it's a pity they simply didn't spell everything out like those guys in Houston." The young man chuckled. "That was an easy gig."

Vic slid the letter into the envelope and folded it before he pushed it across the counter. "So, are you thinking of heading there?"

He shrugged. "I merely thought it might be of interest to you. We took this gig because you wanted it so badly. I thought you might want to tie up some loose ends."

"Aw, you do think about me." The ghost chuckled and took a drag and the smoke drifted into his skeletal frame and disappeared. "But this doesn't matter to me personally. I was after Ciro. He was a loose end I wanted to burn."

"So you simply settled for shooting him in the face?" Johnny asked, took a glass from above the bar, and filled it from a bottle of red wine. The ghost sighed as he took a sip and shook his head. "This is too sweet. Liquor ain't good unless it fights back."

The young man shrugged and put the glass down. "So what's the plan from here?"

His partner leaned against the bar and the lights in his sockets rolled up as he thought. "Eh, I'm open. If you want to head to Austin and veg, we could probably use the break."

"I guess that all depends on what the clerks have for us," he reminded him as he took another sip. "We are quite popular over there."

"They don't get much work from the living side of things," Vic said with a dry laugh. "It cuts the middleman out. We may get good money from them, but that's because they save a bundle working direct."

"It keeps us in business," the young detective said with a nod. "So unless they have another gig that sets fire to your boney ass, maybe we can shop around."

"Yeah…" His partner took another drag and stared him in the eye. "I know I was probably somewhat irate during all this. But thanks, kid. You did me a solid letting me finish that rotter off."

"No worries, Vic," the young man replied, finished his cigarette, and stamped it out on half of a broken ashtray. "It wasn't like there was anything more interesting. I still have to get through what I owe you."

"Heh. It's less than you think." He rapped the bar with his skeletal knuckles and put his hands in his pockets as he continued to take drags of his cigarette. "All right, are we heading to the clerks?"

"Tomorrow," Johnny said as he slid off the stool. "All that diving around got my chest bruised and this ringing in my ears won't stop."

"You might wanna get used to that," the ghost advised as he floated next to him. "I've already told you that it will be a thing."

"Yeah, yeah," he mumbled. "Either way, I want a nap before we head to the clerks."

They walked out into the darkened night still illuminated by *The Wicked Easy* sign. The young man opened the driver's door, sat, and drew a deep breath before he rolled his neck and turned the car on. A heavy roar came from the engine. "Speaking of loud..."

"It always fires me up!" Vic declared as he appeared in the passenger seat. "Much better than those mewling electric shavers you have nowadays."

Johnny adjusted his mirror and could barely make out red-and-blue lights in the distance. "It isn't great for sneaking away."

"That doesn't mean it isn't great for getaways." The shade reached his arm through the glass window and dropped his finished cigarette. "Floor it."

He complied and they roared out of the parking lot and into the dark night. Behind them, the police finally reached the now still and silent bar. They would doubtless see only the shattered remains and perhaps a couple of people who had begun to regain consciousness in the cellar, all of them looking like they had lost their bonuses.

CHAPTER FOUR

The next morning, the two partners entered a swamp near the city of Breaux Bridge, Louisiana. Johnny trekked through the muddy terrain and grimaced when he noticed the bottom of his long jacket getting soggy.

"Why do these places always seem to be in the sticks?" he muttered as he stepped cautiously around a patch of mushy grass. "Can't we ever cross to a place that's located in a hotel or something convenient?"

"Don't you remember our third case?" Vic asked and floated casually at his side. "That took place in a hotel."

"Oh, right." He recalled the spectral blood bath that had turned into. "Those geists haunting the thirteenth floor. You'd think breathers would have learned to adhere to superstition sometime in the last couple of hundred years."

"No kidding." The ghost chuckled, took their shared pack of cigarettes out, and lit one. "Although these places aren't exactly controlled by us either. They simply pop up when they feel like it." He retrieved a compass attached to a chain on one of his belt loops, clicked it open, and looked at the arrow. "We only have about another forty minutes. That's enough time but let's not dawdle at the clerk's. We might end up teleported to another city."

"How much farther then?" Johnny asked as he took another step and his boot sank into a pit of mud. "Dammit."

Vic chuckled, closed the compass, and pointed at two trees. "Over there. Do you have the door?"

"I'll simply use my jacket," he stated, pulled his leg out of the muck, and shook it. "That works, yeah?"

His partner nodded. "But make sure to swap it quickly. All that matters is that we cross correctly." As they approached trees, he nodded to the young man and handed him his cigarette before he drifted closer to layer himself over his body and disappear.

Johnny removed his eye patch as a chill ran through his body like his blood had been replaced by ice. He removed his jacket quickly when he saw an orb of white light and smaller wisps surrounding it between the trees. With the jacket raised in front of him, he held it taut as he took a long drag of the cigarette, spat it out with the smoke, and stepped forward. He flipped the jacket hastily behind him as he closed his eyes.

When he opened them, he was no longer in the swamp but stood in front of a large wooden building and watched in silence as a few ghosts dressed in both modern and older southern-style garb walked in.

Vic popped out of his body and now stood normally on the ground. "Let's see if Angie is in. She won't talk our ear off."

The young man rubbed his arms against the feeling of cold now outside his body before he donned his jacket again. He looked at a dark sky with white lines streaked through, similar to the northern lights of the living world. A line of buildings stretched from the clerk's office, older in style from the 1920s to maybe the early '50s until more modern buildings began to appear farther up the road.

He checked his smartphone. It wouldn't turn on, which was typical of live electronics coming into the ghost realm. The street wasn't too busy at the moment, although he noticed a handful of ghosts gawking at him. Real flesh was rather exotic there after all.

Ignoring them, he popped the collar of his jacket and walked toward the building. Big Papa's Gigs and Deals was one of the more shady businesses they got their work from, but they were consistent and paid well, at least.

Johnny opened the door and a small bell rang as he entered. The security guard—a darkened skeleton with a long beard and white, glowing eyes—seated a few feet away looked up from his newspaper. He nodded to them and pointed down the hall, where another ghost with long, coiled red hair and blue bones wearing a pin-striped dress was talking on a rotary phone.

"I appreciate it, Saul," Vic said with a nod as they wandered to the clerk.

"We ain't paying for information," she stated to the person on the other end in an irate New Jersey accent. "We're paying for the job getting done. So get it done or stop bothering me."

She slammed the phone down and tapped her temples in annoyance for a moment before she opened a small black purse, removed a small bottle, and poured the contents into the mug on her desk emblazoned with *Dead and loving it.*

"Hey there, Angie," the shade greeted her as Johnny sat in one of the two seats in front of her desk. "Are you having a rough day?"

"And it is only getting started," she muttered and sipped from the mug. "I wondered when you two would get back. Do you have good news for me?"

Vic sat next to his partner, nudged him with his elbow, and nodded. The living man retrieved the watch he had taken from Ciro's office and placed it on the table. Angie took it and studied the clock face. "This is that old bastard's memento, no doubt about it." She tapped the device. "It isn't running anymore either. Is he gone?"

"Dusted," Vic said contentedly. "His buddies should have been sent here some hours ago."

"Yeah, I heard we had a load of missing spirits forced back into Limbo at gate Forty-four. All former mafia goons." She took a box out and placed the watch inside it. "I assumed you'd come by after they appeared. I'm surprised it took you so long."

"The kid needed to get some sleep." The ghost snickered and nudged Johnny again, who merely sighed and rolled his eyes.

"The disadvantages of being alive," he said and leaned back in the chair. "Ah, well. At least I can taste real food and I still have my jewels."

This time, Vic rolled his eyes. "Seriously? You gotta hit below the belt like that?"

He shrugged and looked at Angie. "So are we good?"

She nodded, motioned a guard forward as she jotted something on a piece of paper, handed it to him, and shooed him off. "Everything looks in order. Thanks for taking it on such short notice."

"No problem," the shade assured her and rested an arm on the back of his chair. "I wanted to finish it anyway."

"It's more convenient sending us rather than having to clear all the paperwork to send a ghost troop in, huh?" Johnny commented.

"No kidding. The amount of stygia needed to make that happen would be a pain. And our living associates are a little reluctant to give us bodies to possess."

Vic laughed. "I wonder why after that blunder in Chicago."

"Yeah, yeah." Angie grimaced as she looked at the monitor of her Data-Dasher. "Do you need another job while you're here or do you simply wanna keep razzing me?"

"Can't we do both?" the ghost asked.

Johnny slid his hand into his jacket pocket and felt the envelope he had forgotten to take out the night before. "Angie, is anything going on in New Orleans right now?"

She turned slightly away from her monitor and gave him a look that asked, "Did you seriously ask that?"

"There's always something going on in New Orleans," she stated flatly. "Most of those gigs go through other companies, though, like Heartman and Bloodgood. The Abaddon Company also gets their share, but that's different fare from what you are used to." She turned the screen to show them at least a couple of dozen offers. "We get the smaller gigs. They don't pay great but many turn out to be bunk anyway so could be easy."

"Can you cross-reference with the other companies or is there a database for that?" he asked. "I'm looking for something on a larger scale—maybe a gathering or cult or something like that."

Angie made a noise somewhere between a huff and a snicker. "Are you looking to go full-on bounty hunter? I wondered when you would drop the detective schtick."

"Can you or not?" he demanded.

She shrugged and turned the monitor again, typed quickly, and scanned the results. "Nothing like you're asking for. I have some possible possessions, a hell of a lot of hauntings, and a handful of murders but no cults. They are more a Maryland and California thing." She smiled wickedly at him. "Texas too."

"Uh-huh." Johnny deadpanned and scratched his head. "So if one were to say...stumble upon such a thing, there would be a finder's fee connected to it, right?"

"Sure," she agreed uneasily. "But you would need definitive proof. A finder's fee is a big payout so something like words on the wind or a letter won't cut it."

He frowned and took his hand out of his pocket as the guard returned with a sack that he dropped on her desk.

"Ah, our hard-earned reward," Vic said with glee as he reached for it, only for Angie to whack his hand with her pen to stop him. "Hey!"

"The kid has gotta hold it, remember?" she chastised and handed it to Johnny. "Otherwise, it doesn't turn to cash on the other side."

The young man took a handful of silver coins and passed it to his partner. "Here's your cut."

"This pittance?" he asked sourly as he fumbled in the back of his jacket for a small sack and added the coins to the contents. "Ah, well. I have enough to have myself a good time for a few days at least."

"You certainly drink expensive liquor for someone who says I have 'froo-froo' tastes," Johnny chided.

"The liquor is one thing. It's the women who rob me," Vic admitted and craned his neck. "Sometimes literally."

"It's nice to know our earnings are going to a good cause," the young man muttered as he pushed from his chair. "Thanks, Angie."

"No problem. See you again soon." The phone rang again and she picked it up and yelled, "What?"

As the two partners left and began their return to the glowing orb, the ghost detective looked around. "So are you taking some time off?" he asked and jangled his sack of silver. "If so, I'll stay here for a while."

"I might but I have a proposition," Johnny responded as he removed his jacket. "I need some lunch first, though."

"What? Can't you spit it out while we're here?" Vic asked, slightly annoyed.

"It'll take a while and I'm hungry. If you aren't interested when I tell you about it, we can find another crossing point for you." He smiled and his unnatural eye sparkled. "There could be a lot of money in it."

His partner frowned for a moment before he shook his head and smirked. "You sweet-talking bastard. All right, I'm in for now—wait, do I have to wear the suit?"

The young man nodded as he held his jacket out. "I don't want to look like a lunatic talking to nothing."

Vic clenched his jaw as he began to fade into Johnny. "Which means I get to look like a moron. Let's get out of here already before I change my mind."

CHAPTER FIVE

"And what will your...friend have?" the waitress asked as she looked at the gentleman across from Johnny decked out in a large black coat and a winter cap with a scarf over his mouth and shades on his face.

"He'll be fine with the coffee," he stated and handed her their menus. "Sorry, he's not too chatty—sore throat."

"Uh-huh." She took the menus and checked her notes quickly. "Right...one lunch special with a Coke and one coffee. I'll be back soon." She hurried away to the kitchen to hand in the order, no doubt gossiping to her coworkers about the odd man in the layers of clothes on the way. Still, given the area, maybe it wasn't the oddest thing they'd ever seen.

"I hate this, Johnny," Vic mumbled and adjusted the jacket. In reality, he wasn't wearing the clothing so much as possessing the mannequin below them. This was the third one they had gone through and they used one whenever he needed a physical presence. Sometimes, they used it for plans in which one needed to be a distraction for the other.

At other times, it was simply to chat in a public place so Johnny didn't look like he was talking to himself and draw unwanted attention.

Despite the mannequin being his idea, the shade grew to despise it. He said it always felt off and just because he was in control didn't mean it was any more maneuverable than it normally was. Seeing him waddle around in it always amused the young detective, however. "Shut up and enjoy your coffee," he said with a smirk as he drank some of his cola.

"You know I can't drink anything in this plastic prison." Vic grunted and slid the scarf up. "Hurry up and give me your spiel so I can take my mind off this."

"I'm surprised you haven't thought of it yourself yet." Johnny took the envelope out again and placed it on the table. "I think we go to New Orleans and poke around to see if we can't find anything related to this note."

"You got me into this get-up to suggest what could merely be a wild goose chase?" his partner demanded in genuine irritation.

The young man whistled. "You seemed more interested in the note last night."

"Yeah, well, I was in a better mood." The ghost sighed and used a bulky hand to pick the envelope up and shake the contents out. He picked the letter up and read it slowly. "It makes sense why you were asking about the finder's fee back there, though. To give you some credit, even if we find out that this 'cult' has only four members, one of which is a small dog, it would still be good enough to earn us a heap of pay as long as they were plotting something."

"That's my thought." Johnny opened the bag from Angie

and looked inside. "We got about six grand all in all for the last job. It's not bad but that was almost two weeks of work, and given the money lost in that time, we made about three and a half thousand. A small finder's fee is still usually in the lower five digits so if we stumble onto something good, we are looking at a nice payday. Maybe enough for you to have a whole week to yourself in Limbo."

Vic placed the note on the table and tapped it a few times as he thought. "We wouldn't even have to solve the crime, only report it. But if we do both we could probably take a nice long vacation."

"I like where your thinking is going." The young man chuckled.

"That's if anything turns up," his partner reminded him cautiously. "If we do this, we can't dawdle too long. That'll cost us potential cases that would bring in definite money. We have our usuals at Big Papa's and The Exorcist, but we don't have our foot in the door at the big organizations yet."

"That's the price of working for yourself, isn't it?" Johnny stated and sipped his drink. "That's something you've hammered into my head often enough."

"Too true," Vic admitted and folded his arms. "Still, until you're ready to start your own agency, this is the circuit for now."

Johnny decided to add to the offer now that his companion seemed somewhat interested in the idea. "Along with the vacation, maybe we'll have enough time left to look into more personal jobs."

The ghost went silent and tilted his head when the words struck home. "We have become cold with that, haven't we?" He began to tap both hands on the table. His partner had learned over the years that this was a habit when he was nervous or lost in thought as if he wanted to make sure something filled the silence.

"Life and death have gotten in the way," the young man remarked as the waitress returned and put a plate containing a meaty sandwich with fries and ketchup on the table. He thanked her as she took his glass to refill it and he began to dig in. "We don't know if that thing is still in Limbo. It had to be getting all those souls for something."

"Yeah...had to have been," Vic muttered, his head bowed as he went through his memories and the start of their memories. "I give us three days starting from now. If we can't find nothing, we grab the next gig we can, understood?"

"Agreed," Johnny said with a nod. "I'm thinking of getting some pie. Do you want anything?" His companion's response—which only he could see—was that his eyes flared beneath the darkness of his shades. "I'll get it to go."

Johnny set his box of apple pie on the roof of their black 1985 Z28 Camaro IROC before he popped open the trunk and placed a hand on the mannequin's chest. "Go ahead."

"Thank God." Vic sighed as he left the plastic body and his partner scrambled to catch it. "It's nice to have elbows again."

"I forgot how heavy this can be." The young man grunted as he tossed the body into the trunk and slammed it shut. When he turned, a family walked out of the diner and stared incredulously at him. He scratched the back of his neck and shrugged. "Don't worry, that's his favorite place!" he called before he scrambled into the car and turned it on.

The ghost entered and passed him the box of pie. "You forgot this."

"Oh, I appreciate ya." He placed the box on top of the center console. "Although it makes me wonder if the family was weirded by the body being thrown in the trunk or the floating box."

Vic shrugged as he picked the pack of cigarettes up and lowered the window. "Either way, it's probably a more eventful day than they had planned. Let's get going."

Johnny looked over his shoulder as he backed out and grimaced when he realized that the family still stood and gawked at them. "Agreed," he stated, turned away, and eased the vehicle out of the parking lot. He turned left and toward one of the most haunted cities in America.

For them, of course, it was always a place of potential business.

CHAPTER SIX

At Vic's suggestion, they roared down a backwoods road on their way to New Orleans. His northern upbringing was showing because the tougher it was to drive, the more he admitted that he'd thought they would be able to go faster without worrying about cops. While there might have been fewer officers to ticket them, however, their vehicle wasn't exactly equipped to handle the rougher terrain at high speeds.

"I still can't believe you talked me into buying this." Johnny grunted as they hit a rough patch. "I could have gotten something more modern that would have made traveling through these areas a little easier."

"What are you complaining about?" his partner asked casually and leaned back in his tilted seat. "I got you a great deal."

"Why were you so insistent on this car?" he asked as he checked the speedometer and frowned when he realized they were barely pushing fifty-five mph. "You weren't even alive when this model was out."

"Nope, fourteen years dead at that point." Vic agreed. "I thought it was a good compromise—somewhere between my era and yours."

"Except you were dead and I wasn't born yet," he pointed out and finally had a chance to accelerate when they reached a long stretch of empty road. "Still, it does feel nice when you can open her up."

"Her?" Vic asked with a snicker. "You are growing attached."

"Humph," Johnny muttered and turned the headlights on as the sunlight was beginning to fade. "It looks like a paved road up ahead. I'm taking it."

"Do what you like, kid," his companion said and stretched his arms. "We shouldn't be too far from New Orleans at this point."

The young man turned onto the paved road, which stretched for miles with only grassland on either side. "Do you have any idea where we should start once we get there?"

"I thought this was your plan," Vic replied somewhat jokingly. "I have an idea or two, but you are taking the reins on this one for the most part. That way, you'll get all the credit when we—"

"Hey, what's that?" He slowed the car slightly and leaned forward. The ghost straightened in his seat and they both focused on a dark spot in the distance that was coming toward them.

"Is that a person?" Vic asked as the object got closer. "Running in the middle of the road?"

"Wait—" The young man's eyes widened in shock. "He's bleeding." He braked sharply. The man was dressed in a blue dress shirt and jeans, both covered in blood with a large tear over the shoulder of his shirt. Johnny got out and ran to him as he collapsed. "What's going on here? Are you all right?"

"T-thank God," he said, his voice hoarse. "P-please, don't let i-it get me."

"An animal attack?" he asked both the man and Vic who appeared at his side.

The ghost leaned down to examine him. "Not unless animals have smartened up enough to use equipment."

"I-it had an ax," the man responded, raised his head, and looked directly at the ghost. "It's still coming!"

"You can see him?" Johnny asked incredulously.

"Question that later," Vic ordered and his gaze searched the road ahead. "Who are you? What's coming?"

"F-Frank Rossi! We need to get out of—"

His words died in his throat as the wind picked up. The young detective only now realized how dark it had become and he looked up when he felt a familiar cold presence. He removed his eye patch and was able to see a dark-green glow heading down the road. The wind continued to strengthen and became a howl while the three watched as a dark figure hidden under a long cloak and hood emerged from the light holding a bloody ax.

"O-oh, God!" the man babbled and forced himself to his feet. "We need to go!"

Johnny let go of him, drew his pistol, and fired as he walked toward it. The first couple of bullets didn't seem to do anything to it and he hoped for the first time in his life that he had missed. It staggered when the next few struck home but pressed on despite the shots in its chest.

"Vic!" he called and tossed the gun to the ghost.

His partner lined up a shot and fired a spectral bullet at the approaching maniac. This one seemed to affect it as it fell and green light burst from its chest. Before either of them could celebrate, however, the being simply sat and pushed to its feet.

"I second that guy's idea." Vic grasped his shoulder and pulled him away. "Back to the car, Johnny!"

"Try shooting it aga—" A hatchet whistled past his head and when he looked back, it brandished another. "Good idea—let's go!" The three of them ran to the car. Johnny scrambled into the driver's side seat and accelerated at the being.

"What are you doing?" the shade demanded. "That is some kind of ghost. You can't run it down!"

The young man swerved to the left a second before they made impact. The being turned and slashed at the side of the car with its ax as they drove past and the weapon gouged the metal noisily. "What the hell?"

"The bastard ruined the finish!" Vic growled, held the pistol up, and leaned out of the window to fire as they fled but his quarry had disappeared. "What the hell? He's gone."

"Keep driving!" the man hollered in the back. "Get into town. We can find a place to hide there!" At a loud thump above, the man, already pale from blood loss, somehow grew whiter. "Oh no."

"Vic, he's on the roof!" Johnny yelled. "Blast him off!"

His partner tried to shift position to fire but the back window shattered and spewed shards of glass inside the car. The young man braked as he tried to cover his face. Vic cursed vociferously and he turned to fire behind him as the wounded man was hauled out and the being jumped down with him in tow.

When the car stopped completely, both partners pushed out. The ghost detective fired at the attacker and a bullet caught it in the back. It hissed angrily, turned, and launched the hatchet, which struck Vic's hand and knocked the gun out of it. They looked at the ax buried in his hand with astonishment before Johnny snapped back to reality and lunged to snatch the gun up and fire. As before, his bullets did nothing.

The being held its victim down with one foot as it raised its weapon. The man cried out in terror for a brief moment before the blade drove into his chest to unleash a burst of blood and end his life. It reached into the wound and white light poured out of it and into its hand.

"It's taking his soul," Vic said as he pried the hatchet out of his hand.

"What the hell is it?" Johnny asked but his partner had no answer.

The being finished his theft of the man's soul and to the young detective's horror, the body crumbled to dust. It uttered another angry hiss. "Not the one." Its voice sounded like a heavy smoker gargling gravel.

He moved his hand to the back of his belt, unclipped a sheath, and drew a dagger. "Your other hand is good, right?"

"Yeah, give it here," Vic said and he threw him the gun. The ghost fired on the being and drew its attention again. It began to race toward them but he held his ground as Johnny moved to the side. It raised its ax to strike at the living man, but Vic shot it in the side and deflected the attack while his partner thrust the dagger into the being's eye.

It howled in pain and rage and thrust the young man off. The shade was knocked down at the same time, a surprise for both of its attackers. It yanked the dagger out of its eye to reveal a dark-green glow within, folded its arms across its chest, and turned into an orb of green light. Vic stumbled to his feet and fired at it, but the orb simply moved out of the way of the shots before it glided away toward New Orleans.

Johnny stood slowly, picked the dagger up, and sheathed it as he walked to his companion. The wind began to die down around them. "What in both worlds was that, Vic?"

"I have no idea, kid." The ghost detective holstered the pistol and sighed. "It's like it was three different types of ghosts in one. I've never seen anything like it."

"What ghost can take a soul like that?" he asked.

"Wraith, demon, geist." He listed the names quickly after a moment's thought. "But it didn't act like any of those. Maybe a wraith but I've never seen one that can travel that freely or possess a body like that. It should have been knocked out by a shot or two."

Johnny sighed and scowled at their car. "Well, I guess we have our evidence. I should have got it on my phone."

"Well, you have me convinced, at least," his companion muttered and put his hands in his jacket pockets. "This seems like something for the bureau."

"Should we bail?" he asked and folded his arms as he awaited his partner's answer.

Vic took his good hand out and adjusted his cap. "Probably." He looked at Johnny. "That's not how we work, though, is it?"

The young man looked down the road. "It was headed to NOLA and we were heading that way anyway."

"Back to the car." His partner nodded and they returned to the vehicle. Johnny threw some of the broken glass out while Vic looked at the horizon. "Always something going down in New Orleans indeed."

CHAPTER SEVEN

"Man, he scuffed it good, huh?" Johnny muttered unhappily. They were in the motel parking lot and took a proper look at the damage in the morning light. A long slice had been gouged through the right side of the car, along with a dent on top and the broken back windshield.

"Not only the body damage," Vic commented. "Take your eyepatch off and have another look."

He complied and saw traces of the dark-green glow in the huge tear. "Man, what the— Why can't I see this with my eyepatch on? I can see ghosts fine normally."

"It's phantasma, Johnny. You're not used to seeing it outside of me and the ghost world, huh?" his partner explained. "It's the pure ghost…blood, for lack of a better word, that I'm made of—what the cranks used to call ectoplasm back in the day. The reason you can see ghosts normally is…well, because of me. But what you see is the stygia in their bodies, which enables them to sustain themselves in this world. Well, that and the ether you have, but you mostly use that to shoot things."

"So the fact that this guy glowed like the one light remaining in a blackout is what?" he asked with a frown.

Vic took a drag of his cigarette. "Bad, for one. It means he's a stocky bastard. Did it seem like he was possessed when you touched him?"

"He felt solid." He leaned against the car. "But Ciro was solid too, wasn't he?"

"Yeah, but that's because he was so chock full of stygia that he might as well had an IV bag full of it on him at all times." Vic patted the gun under his jacket. "Plus, he was obliterated by one shot. We blasted that guy with dozens and he still flew off."

"My shots did next to nothing to him." Johnny sighed as he recalled the previous night. "I need to go back over that guide you gave me."

"Yeah, then maybe I won't have to repeat myself as often," Vic agreed and rolled his eyes.

"Yeah, yeah." The young detective grimaced. "I probably need to take the car in for repairs first thing."

"No kidding." His partner took one last drag and stamped his vice out. "It's not exactly an inconspicuous ride now with that cut running through it. If this baby turns heads, we want it to be for the right reasons."

"Do you have any idea where we should look after we do that?" Johnny asked. "I assume it will lay low for now, at least. There isn't any glowing green stuff in the distance."

"We might have to look around and check on any killings in the area," Vic suggested and checked his wounded hand. "What gets me is the fact that it drains souls. You saw what it did to that guy. I would think there would be more reports about people turning to dust."

"It probably doesn't leave witnesses," he reasoned. "We were an exception because we could hurt it. So maybe we should look into missing persons."

"Agreed." The shade floated to the car and settled into the passenger seat. "Do you have any thoughts on the ax?"

"It glowed green like he did, although I can't tell if that was the ax or him." He checked the damage again before he sighed dejectedly and moved to the driver's side. "It was also strong to be able to tear a hole in a car going sixty without breaking apart."

"It's probably a memento," Vic muttered as Johnny turned the car on.

"His ax?" The young man chuckled. "You have to have a special attachment to something in life for it to be a memento, right? What, did he cuddle with it at night when he got scared?"

"It doesn't have to be his ax necessarily," his partner stated. "Merely that he has some connection to axes. Mementos have unique properties and how he feels about the ax plays a part in that."

"So he has some kind of super-ax and Ciro's watch was what? Always shiny?" Johnny asked as he put his seat belt on.

"And it probably also never stopped working."

The young man chuckled again as he pulled the car out of the parking lot. "Remind me to have strong feelings about something worth a damn, like a gun."

"Speaking of which," Vic began and looked at theirs. "When we're done at the shop, I want to visit the market."

Johnny gave him an odd look. "What, do you have a hankering for Beignets?"

"Not the food market, dumbass," his companion chided, turned to him, and waved his bag of coins. "*The* market."

He stopped the car in front of the exit and thought for a moment. "Oh… Do we even know one we can get into around here?"

The ghost nodded and put the bag down. "Trust me, I'll get us in."

———

At a repair shop, Johnny came up with a story about an accident that they didn't seem to buy completely but he paid up front and the questions stopped. He had taken a streetcar from there into St. Charles and Vic led him to a parish house a couple of miles from their drop-off.

"How did you find this?"

"I learned about several Limbo markets when I had my agency," the ghost explained. "If you know the right people, you can get maps, although it's better to commit them to memory. I could never remember where I put the damn things."

"You can memorize shady market locations but not where you put the maps?" The young man hung over the fence and studied the off-white house. "You know, you don't talk about your time in Limbo much."

"There isn't much to tell. My afterlife was very similar to my normal life." He looked at one of his boney hands before he adjusted his cap. "Well, there were some differences but that's neither here nor there."

"I gotcha," Johnny stated and opened the front gate.

"We're heading in but don't we need a password or something?"

"It's down the stairs on the side, kid." They moved through the weeds and tall grass to a somewhat hidden alcove with a stairway. "And a password? What pulp have you been reading?"

"My life," he retorted and knocked on the heavy door at the bottom. "So any curious passerby can get in?"

Vic moved in front of the door. "Not exactly." A panel on the top slid open and a pair of glaring eyes turned to wide, shocked ones as they studied the ghost. "Hey there, buddy. Do you wanna let us in?" He took his sack of coins out. "We wanna make a few purchases."

"Uh…what's the password?" the doorman asked. Johnny chuckled and his partner clenched his jaw and passed him the bag.

"Hold onto this for a moment, would you?" The young man took it with a small grimace because it felt like ice in his hands. The ghost suddenly flung himself through the door and surprised shouts and pained grunts ensued inside, together with arguing and demands.

After a few minutes, the door opened and a bouncer with blood trickling down his head waved him in. A couple of bodies—one ghost and the other human—lay sprawled on the floor and Vic straightened his jacket while he and another ghost bickered. Johnny looked at the bouncer and motioned to his eyes.

"Are you a specter?" he asked, although the man still seemed to be reeling from the blow to the head and merely stared at him. "Come on. It's an easy question, man. Specters can see ghosts. You can see them, right?" The man shut the door and nodded before he slumped into a nearby chair and closed his eyes. While he probably shouldn't nap on the job, this maybe wasn't the time to judge.

Johnny heard the jangle of coins and turned to where Vic handed some to the ghost he was talking to. He checked the sack and it seemed a little lighter than before. His partner beckoned him closer, tipped his hat to the ghost, and descended another flight of stairs. "I smoothed things over with them. We're good."

"With your usual charm, I see. How much did that cost us in real dollars?"

"Don't worry about it," his companion assured him. "The password is 'spicy mama' by the way."

He laughed. "Well, I wouldn't have guessed it."

The stairs continued for a while—much longer than expected—and the young detective began to feel uncomfortable. "You're sure we're going to a Limbo market and not Hell, right?"

"Shut it," Vic retorted and pointed below. "See that light? We're almost there."

An amber light was hidden behind some drapes at the exit at the bottom of the stairs. When he didn't feel the telltale chill of death, he had to assume it was merely a normal light. Once at the bottom, they moved the drapes to the side and scanned the sight of a few dozen stalls, several grills cooking food, and humans and ghosts perusing the area. The light at the entrance came from several lanterns hanging above, but the underground market was illuminated by many different ones, including purple, gold, and green, a nice NOLA touch.

Johnny marveled at all the ghosts who floated around

the area and identified normal spirits and phantoms talking amongst the crowd. "I'm surprised by the number of dead around," he muttered and slid his hands into his pockets. "I thought the market was for the living looking for Limbo products?"

"Breathers are more common, but for those ghosts hiding in the living world, they want goods from home like anyone else who has homesickness," Vic explained, took his box of cigarettes out, and frowned when he realized he was down to his last two. "I wonder if they sell any down here."

A few ghosts were dressed in suits or large coats and some held guns. "How many do you think are on the run?"

"I'm sure a handful, at least. They aren't too selective about their clients here. I suppose they can't be, not if they want to do business." The ghost lit a cigarette. "Don't stare, kid. It's rude, but keep an ear out. Maybe we can come across some info for a future gig if nothing else." He took a drag and moved down one of the lanes. "Now, let's see if we can find ourselves a big popper in case that freak appears again."

CHAPTER EIGHT

"Good Lord. Take a look at this!" Vic exclaimed as he held out a large Magnum pistol in black plating with a skull emblem on the grip. Johnny took it and nodded. It had a nice heft and he could feel a good portion of his ether drain into it. The gun would certainly have a kick.

He looked at the stall where his partner had found it and his eyes bulged at the price. "Vic, we can't afford that, man, not unless you have a secret stash somewhere."

"I have a fair amount saved up from my jobs," the ghost said but when he looked at the price, he lapsed into silence for a moment. "Maybe I can haggle."

"For less than half the price?" the young man remarked as he replaced the gun on the display. "Be my guest, but if you try anything funny, at least give me a heads-up." The red ghost behind the counter eyed them suspiciously.

"He's kidding," Vic said hastily and approached the counter. "But let's talk, my friend."

As he and the salesman started their negotiations, Johnny wandered off to look at some of the other stalls.

Most were selling weapons, potions, stygia supplies for the ghosts, enchanted trinkets, and many other novelties one could not find unless one got lucky at antique shops in normal society.

He smelled something familiar in the air—the aroma of grilled meat—and walked on until he found a stall serving burgers. He bought one and a Coke and ate as he continued to peruse the wares. His partner might still have hope, but he could tell from the handful of stalls they had looked at that they wouldn't find anything better than the gun they already had.

Still, given the value of the other guns he saw and the detail on Vic's gun, they could probably demand a good price for it, although he was well aware that the ghost would never trade it in. He had given it a name and every-thing—Nancy—although he tried not to mention it out loud. Johnny had only learned it from a night when Vic was good and sauced up and he was sober enough to remember.

When he turned the corner and scanned the suited and weapon-wielding ghosts and breathers who wandered around, one of the patrons stood out. He couldn't tell exactly why, however. It was probably her posture or that she was better dressed than the other customers. For a moment, he wondered if she was part of the gang or orga-nization that ran this market, perhaps a secretary or accountant. As he studied her, that thought was cast aside. She looked around her with curiosity and examined the items like someone who had knowledge of them but was not used to being around them all that much.

He estimated that she was probably a little younger than him, maybe twenty or so, and wore a dark blue jacket and pants and a wide-brimmed hat in the same color. She had dark skin and wore her hair in a braid that draped over her left shoulder. With a casual gesture, she picked up what appeared to be a compass or watch, studied it, and asked the attendant questions about the item. Johnny was about to look away when something caught his eye. A deadeye revolver hidden in her jacket was visible only briefly from his angle as her jacket moved when she and the clerk grew more animated.

His gaze wandered to some of those in suits. Three of them were looking at her. The human seemed to be gawking but the other two talked quietly to one another and nodded at her. It seemed she had drawn more than only his attention.

"Well, no luck." Vic sighed as he appeared beside him. "Did you find anything interesting kid?"

"Nothing worth spending the doubloons on," he admitted and gestured to the woman. "But have a look at her. Does something seem a little off?"

"Who, the rookie cop?" his partner asked and surprised him.

"A cop? How can you make that out? I haven't seen a badge."

The ghost shrugged and straightened to stand in a similar posture to hers. "It's how she stands. She's probably fresh out of the academy and still has the rigidness that gets drilled into you there. Plus her gun is standard issue for the police forces that work in the supernatural."

"You caught that too, huh?" Johnny looked at the suited

men again. "You aren't the only one. I think she's been made."

"That isn't good for her, then," he stated and glanced at the armed guards. "These markets usually pay for protection or a blind eye but that doesn't mean they like cops here, especially if it's a rookie trying to make a name for themselves by exposing their precinct's secrets."

The young man frowned and tapped the side of his leg nervously with a finger. "Do you think that's what she's here for?"

"I would say it's what they believe she's here for if they don't like her being here. They probably won't bother to try to get the real story if it's something different."

"We need to get her out of here," Johnny declared under his breath.

Vic tilted his head at his protégé. "What for? If she's a cop, I'm sure she can handle herself. Besides she walked in here."

"Well, if she's green she certainly can't take them all on. It doesn't look like she even realizes she's aroused suspicion," he stated. "Besides, even a super-cop falls to enough lead. And if we can't get a weapon, getting information is the next best thing right? Having a cop owe us could work out well."

"That's a fair point," his partner agreed. "How do you wanna do this?"

"You simply pull the vaudeville act," he recommended. "I'll get her out."

The ghost detective nodded. "The classic. All right, I'll head in." Vic sauntered to the men who still watched the woman suspiciously and waved a hand. "Hey there, fellas!"

he greeted and shook the living guard's hand, much to the man's surprise. "I gotta say, great market you have here. It's hard to find one that's run so efficiently—and those suits!" He patted one of the ghosts good-naturedly on the chest. "It's a nice look and makes that phantasma sparkle, I gotta say. I wanted to ask you if there is any way I could join this organization? I just got back into the realm and finding work has been a pain." He continued to talk to them, although their annoyed or uncomfortable looks indicated that they weren't particularly amused. Still, they were focused on him for now.

The young man strolled up to the woman, downed the last of his Coke, and tossed it into a bin as he took her arm. "Hey, honey, we gotta leave."

She looked at him in astonishment. "What the hell are you—"

"Yeah, I know it's sudden, but your boss called me. The contractors are coming in today and all eyes will be on you," he said in an attempt to provide her with a hint. However, in his little ruse, he didn't account for one thing.

"Wait, I thought you said you were single?" the salesman asked and looked from one to the other. "What was that about?"

Johnny's face fell and he tried quickly to come up with something, conscious that the lady on his arm was equally as bewildered, but they were interrupted by another ghost guard who stepped close and tapped her on the shoulder. "Pardon me, but we need to speak to you," he said, his voice almost a growl.

"Called it," the young detective muttered and turned to her. "We gotta go." He twisted and punched the guard in the face, shaking him, the salesperson, and her as he dragged her between the stalls to the exit. "Let's go, Vic!"

His partner turned to see them running, then glanced at the guards he was speaking to, who seemed ready to rush in pursuit. He grabbed one of their chairs and thumped it against the living guard's head before he drew his revolver and shot both ghosts in the leg. The limbs exploded and they collapsed. "You'll live," he said and spun away to catch up with the fugitives. "Metaphorically, at least."

Johnny and the girl raced through the aisles. "Who are you?" she demanded.

"Someone with more self-awareness than you, apparently," he retorted as Vic appeared next to him. "Gun if you would!"

When the ghost handed him the gun, he fired at the two guards at the exit and both disappeared in a blast of smoke. They raced up the stairs and were close to the top when they heard furious steps coming up after them.

Vic was the first out of the stairwell and he pointed at the guard he'd paid off. "You tried to stop us but couldn't." When the ghost shrugged and fell dramatically to the floor, he pointed to the guard by the door. "Open up!" he ordered, but the man was still unconscious. "That can't be good for his head."

"Get the door, Vic!" Johnny yelled as he and the girl reached the top.

"I have to do everything around here." He pushed the door open and his partner snatched the keys from the guard and handed them to him as he and the woman ran out. The ghost detective shut and locked the door before he flew through. "You do know some of them can do that too, right?"

"Back away," the girl said as she slid her hand into her jacket, took a circular device out, and planted it on the door.

"What's that?" Johnny asked as ghostly hands reached through. The door, wall, and entire house above lit with white light and the hands were stuck inside, leading to yells of surprise and pain.

"It's an ether blockade," she stated. "It stops them from getting through. but doesn't last long. Do you have a ride?"

The partners shook their heads. "We took a streetcar here."

"Then we'll use mine." She bounded quickly up the stairs. "Come on. I don't know what happened there but it seems like you did me a solid. They'll be after us in a few minutes so let's get some distance."

"I like her thinking," Vic agreed. "Let's move, kid!"

The trio rushed down the path from the house and ran a few blocks before she stopped at a blue Chrysler 300. She opened the doors and they scrambled in, Vic in the back, before she accelerated away.

"It's a good thing you're a cop," Johnny muttered. "Otherwise, we would probably get pulled over."

"Cops can get pulled over too, kid." Vic reminded him.

"How could you tell I was a cop?" she asked as she took her badge from her jacket pocket. "My badge wasn't visible."

"You had...a certain presence," the young detective offered charitably. "Anyway, my name is Johnny and given that you were down in the Limbo market, there's a good chance you're a specter so that's Vic."

"Charmed," his partner said and tipped his hat.

"My name's Valerie," she replied. "I would like to ream you out for interfering with an investigation, but it wasn't exactly official so..." She shrugged, her focus still on the road ahead.

"Under the table?" Vic asked.

"More like a personal job," she confessed. "We can talk later."

"How about some coffee?" Johnny asked.

She looked questioningly at him. "Your heart isn't racing enough after all that?"

"It's more to go with my cigarettes—wait, I'm out. Can we stop at a gas station?"

"Don't you know those things will kill you?" Valerie asked sharply.

He sighed and nodded. "Trust me, it honestly wasn't my choice."

CHAPTER NINE

Johnny plunked down at one of the tables outside the front entrance of the café, patted his new box of cigarettes, and undid the wrapper.

"Are you simply gonna let a lady take care of the order?" Vic asked as he appeared in the chair on his left.

"Hey, man. She offered," he replied, took one of the cigs out, and put it to his lips. "Besides, it's only two cups of coffee." His partner stretched for one, but he shooed his hand away as he lit the cigarette. "We're out in the open, Vic. A floating cigarette is gonna arouse suspicion. Besides, it seems NOLA already has more specters than normal from what we saw."

"So why deny me a cig?" the ghost demanded. "They probably used to weird stuff in this city."

He took a drag and blew smoke into the air. "I don't even like these damn things," he bemoaned. "It's 'cause of you that I have to smoke. Don't you get a buzz off them anyway when I smoke?"

"A little, but it's not like we're that intertwined yet," Vic muttered and leaned back in his seat.

"Thank God." Johnny looked over his shoulder when he heard the jingle of a bell over the café door. Valerie came out with two cups of coffee and handed him one. He nodded in appreciation.

"Sorry about you, Vic," she began as she pulled a chair out and sat. "There's nothing for ghosts in there."

"Eh, I'm used to it," the detective said with a shrug. "I'm sure I can find my people elsewhere."

She chuckled as she took a sip. "There are more around than you know."

Johnny looked down an alley across the street where two ghosts talked to one another. "I've noticed," he remarked and sipped what he thought was black coffee, only to realize it was colder than anticipated. "What is this?"

"New Orleans' style cold brew," she answered after another sip. "It's a local specialty. Don't you like it?"

Johnny considered it and finally decided it wasn't bad. It had some weird spice or something in it but the flavor was pleasant. "It's all right. I expected something hotter, I guess."

Vic clutched his hands together as he regarded the woman. "So Val—can I call you Val?"

She shrugged. "It's nice to get acquainted so quickly."

"No kidding." The ghost chuckled and gestured to his partner with his thumb. "Jonathan here wouldn't let me call him Johnny for months after we first met."

"Jonathan?" She smiled and the young man scowled at

him before he shrugged and took another sip. "So, what brings you two gentlemen to the big easy?"

Johnny placed his cup down and took another drag. "You don't have a guess?" he asked and let the smoke drift out of his mouth. "Or is this vetting?"

She swirled her cup. "Can you blame me for being curious? I'm a cop so I have a reason for being in a Limbo market, but what you were doing there is still a mystery."

He scratched his chin and looked at his partner. "Should we plead the fifth?"

"I wouldn't worry about it too much," Vic stated while he observed her. "She was the one driving. If she was truly suspicious she could have simply driven us to her precinct."

"It's nice to see one of you is reasonable." Her gaze shifted from one to the other. "So, do you care to tell me the details?"

Johnny sighed and leaned back. "We're here for a…kind of unofficial investigation," he told her. "We had some info that something is going down in New Orleans."

Valerie laughed and nodded. "Yeah, that's about right, but you hardly need evidence to make that assumption." Her lips pressed together for a moment. "Although, out of curiosity, what did you find that made you come here?"

"Well, a note we found on a ghost gangster we obliterated," he revealed and her eyes widened for a moment. "But beyond that, I think the real suspicions started when we were heading into town and were attacked by a ghost of some kind that slashed our car with an ax and drained the soul of some poor bastard running down the road."

She almost spilled her coffee. "You're kidding me."

He shook his head. "Granted, I haven't had the best

sleep for the last week or so, but that's what it looked like to me."

"That might be the creepiest thing I've heard this week," she admitted.

"To hurry this story along, that's why we were in the market," Vic continued. "We were looking for a bigger gun as whatever we ran into could take a beating." He looked at his revolver and sighed. "It's all right, baby. I know you tried."

"And that's the creepiest thing I've seen this week," Valerie quipped, which drew a snicker from Johnny as the ghost flipped his jacket shut.

The young detective took another drag. "That's our side of the story, so how about we hear more of yours?" He folded his arms as he waited. "You already said your visit was a personal one like ours, which makes sense. You're too young to be sent on undercover missions, I would think. And since specter cops are so rare, I can't imagine they would waste you by sending you into the lion's den alone like that. But what I don't understand is why you would risk going in alone when you have more experienced people you could rely on."

She shifted uncomfortably in her chair. "I suppose fair is fair," she began and stirred her coffee with a straw. "I'm Valerie Simone of the NOPD, supernatural division, but like you said, the only reason I'm working there rather than traffic or something basic is because I'm a specter."

"Whoa, now," Johnny interrupted and held his hands up. "I didn't mean anything bad by it."

"I can vouch for him," Vic said with a nod. "That's merely his typical charm at work."

He frowned and flipped the ghost off under the table, but his partner paid no attention. "So Val, how long have you been able to see ghosts?"

"Since birth, I guess," she stated. "But can't say for sure. It runs in the family on my mother's side, but I didn't see my first ghost until I was about seven—my grandmother visited me just after she died and helped me to understand the ghost world and my ability before she passed over."

"Aw, that's sweet." Vic tilted his head. "She must have had tremendous willpower to not be sucked directly into Limbo after her death."

"I don't think she went to Limbo," Valerie said quietly. "When I finally said goodbye, she disappeared in a bright light. I think—I hoped—she went to Heaven."

"A ticket straight to the big time, eh?" the ghost mused. "I would believe it. She's from the good generation."

"Uh-huh," Johnny said dismissively and finished his cigarette. "Because nothing bad happened in your day. No sir, not the fifties and sixties."

"Quiet, you," his partner muttered. "So, is it only the sight or do you have any other tricks up your sleeve?"

Valerie's eyes closed and she shook her head. "If you are talking about those special powers some specters have, I can't say that I do—or at least they haven't manifested yet."

The young detective put his cigarette out in an ashtray. "So you're a specter but not an empath?" he said thoughtfully. "I guess you don't need to be one to work in the supernatural, but it must bite to not have that little extra something, eh?"

"You have no idea," she admitted with a huff. "I take it you do?"

He nodded. "Technically speaking, yeah." He pointed to Vic's jacket. "I can use ecto weapons without those special bullets everyone else has got—exorcist rounds." He adjusted his eyepatch strap. "A few other things as well, but I guess the most interesting one is I can enter the ghost world on a whim."

"Seriously?" Valerie thumped the table with her hand and stood. "Can you take me?"

The partners looked at each other in surprise. Most people Johnny had mentioned this to found it both fascinating and frightening. Tales abounded about what happened to a living being inside the ghost world, none of them great, so someone who wanted to go in willingly was certainly a first.

"I said I can, not that I like too," he stated and backtracked quickly. "Besides, it's a little more complicated than I made it out to be. Sure, I can cross over as long as I have something to 'enter' it like a door or even a sheet—some kind of divider—but where I end up is a mystery unless I go to certain locations."

"It's basically a fast-pass version of what ferrymen and shamans do, although we have a one hundred percent success rate so far," Vic clarified. "We haven't tried it with another breather coming with us so maybe you don't want to be the first."

Valerie hesitated for a moment before she nodded and sat again. "It does sound a little sketchy," she admitted with a look of disappointment. "I've always wondered what the ghost world looked like. I guess I shouldn't be in a hurry to find out, huh?"

"I wouldn't suggest it," Johnny replied. "You're more

likely to end up there permanently if you aren't careful, if you catch my drift."

"Yeah, maybe." She sighed and finished her coffee.

Vic scratched his skull. "You know, you never answered our question." He tilted his head. "You know, why you were at the market?"

"Oh, right." She bit her lip. "Like I said, it wasn't exactly an official investigation, and given that there are people on the force who know about it and don't do anything, I can guess why they leave it alone. But beyond that, I was looking into weapon purchases during the last few weeks."

"What for?" Johnny asked and set his empty cup down.

She paused for a moment as she considered her answer before she leaned closer. "I'll only tell you the basics. You can probably find it in the papers or online so it's not like I'm giving away secret information, but you didn't hear it from me, all right?" They nodded and eased closer. "We've had murders over the last month, which are unfortunately not too surprising in and of themselves. But the way the bodies were left is what's weirding people out."

"The bodies?" Vic questioned. "I assume ritualistic mutilation or something? That generally gets lips flapping."

Valerie shook her head. "Even weirder than that. The bodies are left like...husks. Like corpses left out for years in the sun or something. In fact, a couple of the more recent bodies that had been reported had begun to turn to dust before we could even get there to investigate."

Bodies turning to dust? They stopped themselves from looking at one another but that sounded very familiar—less than twenty-four hours familiar.

"No rotting corpses and none of them dug-up bodies?

Maybe a seriously macabre prank?" The ghost detective tried to think of anything else that might explain it.

She shook her head. "Homicide already considered something like that. But we have a few positive IDs, at least, and in some cases, their friends or family who called in or talked to us said they had seen them only hours before. I can't think of a natural way for a killer to turn bodies into something like that in such a short space of time."

"I can't either but then again, it's not something I think about in my spare time." Johnny tapped his finger against the table as he considered what she'd said. "Do you think you could give us an address of one of the victim's houses?"

"Do you intend to go and take a look?" she asked. "You know, I guess I assumed you guys were detectives but you look about as young as I am. Who are you really?"

"Technically, we're supernatural bounty hunters," Johnny confessed reluctantly. "But we aren't merely lugs with guns and a desire to hunt abnormal game. We bring a more sophisticated approach to our investigations."

"And you would be right. I was a detective in both life and death and taught this kid everything he knows." Vic rapped his knuckles against the table. "Even if he forgets chunks of it."

Valerie pursed her lips again and they could almost see the wheels turning in her mind. "So you guys don't have an agency?"

"Not yet. We're working on it, though." Johnny folded his arms again as he frowned. "Look, we want to help. We're not exactly here on a gig but this has turned into something and we're looking for evidence. As part of the supernatural division, I would think you wouldn't mind a little help."

She leaned back, dejection visible in her eyes. "Yeah, you would be right. The department is looking into the murders, but New Orleans has no shortage of supernatural cases so we're stretched thin. I've worked on this case out in the streets instead of on whiteboards and computers, mostly on my own. I can't get clearance for many things because of how green I am—plus, you know, not being an empath means I'm more of a liability to some." She removed her phone from her pocket. "What's your number?"

Johnny gave it to her and retrieved his phone. She sent him a text with an address. "And whose home is this?"

"Jessy Thompson, possibly the first victim. I'm not sure if you will find much as I'm certain we picked it clean, but you might turn something up or at least find things out for yourself." Valerie stood and the other two followed suit. "I'll head back to the precinct. Thanks for your help at the market and if you do find anything else, let me know, all right?"

"No problem," the young detective promised with a nod. "A favor for a favor, and we always pay those. Besides, it'll be nice to have someone on the inside."

"And it'll be nice to work with someone who's willing to do a little legwork." She waved goodbye and they separated. He stepped into the street while she headed to her car.

"So these killings have been going on for a month, huh?" Vic said thoughtfully as his partner waved down a cab.

"At least," he replied as the cab pulled up. "It seems we stumbled onto something seriously screwed up this time, Vic."

"Isn't it exciting?" The ghost chuckled. "A real case and a potentially big payday."

Johnny opened the cab door. "Assuming whoever is doing this doesn't turn me into something that looks like you," he said as he slid into the back seat.

Vic floated in and adjusted his cap. "You wish you would look this good when you're dead."

"1202 Canal street," the young detective instructed as the taxi began to pull into the traffic. "I also wish I won't find out for a while."

CHAPTER TEN

Johnny tipped the driver and watched him drive away before he turned toward the small light-blue house across the street. "Is this the place?"

"It's the right address," Vic replied, took a cigarette out, and looked around to make sure no one was nearby. "It doesn't look like anyone is home, though. Do you have the lighter?"

The young detective dug in his pocket and handed it to his partner before he stepped into the street and crossed to the front of the house. He took a couple of minutes to study it carefully and quickly came to the same conclusion as the ghost had before he stepped onto the walkway that led to the front door. "No yellow tape. I guess the blues are done here?"

"Most likely. Val said they had picked it clean, at least to their knowledge." Vic tapped him on the shoulder and handed him the lighter and pack. He put them away and retrieved a pair of gloves before he turned the knob. It only allowed a quarter-turn before it stopped, infuriatingly locked. He looked at the side of the door and the small, decorative glass windows there.

With a furtive glance in both directions of the street, he walked onto the lawn and found a rock. He used it to break one of the small windows before he reached inside and unlocked the door.

"You know, I could have simply flown through and unlocked it for you," his partner pointed out as he pushed the door open.

"I didn't wanna hear you whine about having to put your cig down." He looked at the ghost. "Besides, how much energy did you waste doing that little stunt at the market? Maybe chill with the interaction for now."

Vic mulled it over for a moment before he nodded in agreement and the two entered the home. As Johnny walked from the entry into the hall, he noticed how barren the area was. Either most of the small objects and decorations had been taken as evidence or this lady had lived a rather spartan life. As he approached the bedroom, he saw that the left side of the doorframe was damaged. He knelt, examined the hole, and noticed a faint, glowing light within. "Vic, take a look at this," he said as he removed his eyepatch.

The ghost detective peered into the hole. "That's phantasma, all right." The lights in his eyes narrowed. "The destruction was caused by either a hammer or a very blunt ax."

"Given what he did to our car, we can't call that a blunt ax by any stretch of the imagination." The young detective peered into the crevasse. "I don't see any stygia. Do you think there could be more than one of them?"

Vic took a drag. "I hope not. One is enough of a pain in the ass if we're trying to catch them." He clicked his teeth together. "Val said this was the first victim."

"That NOPD is aware of, at least." He stood and looked at his partner. "What are you thinking?"

"I said before that the ax being used was probably a memento." Vic peeked into the bedroom. "Mementos are tied to the ghost using them, which means that if the ghost was weak or not all here, the memento would also not be in the best state. It is entirely possible that this killer was in an exhausted or possibly emaciated condition and his ax therefore wasn't as deadly as it was when we encountered it."

"So 'it wasn't all here' means it was a ghost possessing a body it didn't have complete control of?" Johnny looked at the damage again. "I didn't notice any stygia marks but they would have disappeared after a couple of weeks anyway."

"Val didn't mention seeing anything like this when we talked to her, although I guess we never asked how involved she is or was with the case until now. Even to me, those traces of phantasma looked weak. How about you?"

He nodded. "Yeah, but I was able to see it with my patch on." He placed said patch in his pocket. "I needed to take it off to see the stuff on the car."

"That's probably because it was controlled." Vic turned and pointed his cigarette at him. "I'll forgive you not knowing this part, kid, mostly because I'm very sure I haven't explained it to you yet. Strong ghosts, whether through their power, a good supply of stygia, or having a damn strong connection to their host, are able to exert control over their phantasma—within reason. The stuff naturally seeps out of their bodies and mementos but with proper control and a calm mind, they can make sure it doesn't spill everywhere."

"So you're saying that because he was weak or agitated when he came for this victim, he spilled it everywhere?" Johnny asked. "Wait, are you saying that if it is the same guy from the road, that was him when he was calm?"

"Well, it's not what I would call it, certainly." The ghost floated to a dresser and a small framed picture of a young black woman with curly hair and a black man with a big beaming smile. "But it was powerful enough to survive multiple shots and a gouged eye. Whatever it is, it seems to not need stygia—or not anymore, at least. It's found something else to fuel itself with while in the living world."

"The souls," he stated solemnly. "I've thought about the options you tossed out earlier. Wraith's don't possess, they puppet, and they contain souls and don't drain them. Geist devour souls to keep themselves functional, but they don't gain any power from them—or, at least, it doesn't last long and they aren't particularly sturdy. That leaves demons."

"And if there is anything that will push both the ghost world and living world into hysterics, it's a demon running around," his partner concluded. "And it doesn't seem like this one is doing a great job at hiding. But we can toss that out as well."

"Because if it was a demon we'd already be dead?"

"That, or chained in some dark pit having our insides torn out slowly—or your insides, at least—depending on how playful the demon is." The ghost picked the picture up and threw it to him.

"If this picture is recent, she was in her late twenties or early thirties," Johnny deduced. "Do you think this is a boyfriend or sibling?"

Vic shrugged and drifted across the bed. "It could be either but he didn't live here. From what little décor there is, nothing suggests that a man lived here. I suppose I could be going by stereotypes but this is a queen-sized mattress. If they were a couple or siblings, they certainly cared about personal space."

"There are other rooms," the young detective pointed out as he placed the picture on the dresser. "So she was a black woman and the man we ran into on the road appeared to be in his forties and was white. It doesn't seem like he has a preference."

"Maybe not gender or race." Vic had moved to the other side of the bed and examined the window and more specifically, the curtains. He pointed at the rod. "But the guy could see me. Bring this down, would you?"

"The curtain?" Johnny asked as he walked over, stretched, and lowered the rod. His partner gestured for him to pull it apart and when he did so, a small cylindrical container popped out and fell to the floor. "What the— How did you know there was something in there?"

"There's a small gap between the rods. I've seen many a hidey-hole in my time. It's not exactly a classic but still somewhat common," he explained.

The young man picked it up and examined it closely. It was black and in the shape of a lipstick container, but a familiar smell emanated from it. "Stygia."

He opened it slightly and his eyes widened for a moment before he shook his head and capped it quickly.

"Uh...like smelling salts and gasoline. What would she need with this?"

"It could be any number of things," Vic postulated. "If she was an empath, stygia increases their abilities and even a tiny dose does it. She could have been selling it too, although such a small amount would last a ghost maybe half a day." Johnny handed it to him and the container fell into the ghost's hand. "I'm not tangible and I can still hold the container so it's probably coated in the stuff. That means she used it often."

"And it also means that whether she used it for herself or another ghost, she was a specter." Johnny folded his arms. "All empaths are specters and if she was selling it to ghosts, she would need to see them in the first place."

"I see you're finally bringing all those lessons on deductive reasoning together." The ghost detective tossed the container to him. "One of these days, I might feel a tinge of pride to call you my apprentice."

"If you feel that bad, I wonder how you feel calling me partner," he retorted snidely as he studied the container again.

"It's an existential crisis mostly," his partner replied and chuckled at Johnny's disapproving look. "This is something to start with. We still need to look around but if we can find the person she bought that from or who it was for we might get somewhere."

"It was for me." The two partners turned quickly toward the unexpected voice. Vic drew the gun and aimed it at the new arrival. He was a ghost but unlike most of those Johnny had seen, he was not skeletal. He still had the odd color that ghosts did, in this case bright green, but he had a human body and wore simple jeans and a shirt. He didn't have flesh but the appearance of it, and the young detective could see straight through him unlike Ciro, so he wasn't a phantom. He studied his face, which seemed familiar. "Wait—you're the guy in the photo?" he asked and gestured to the picture on the nightstand.

The ghost nodded. "My name is Dwayne. I was Jessy's friend." His fists clenched and he began to tremble. "Are you here to help find her killer?"

CHAPTER ELEVEN

After a few minutes to allow the tension to ease, the trio relocated to the living room. Johnny and Dwayne sat on the sofa and Vic stood in the center and observed the other ghost. "Now that we've cleared the air, can you fill us in, Dwayne?" he asked. "Jessy died over a month ago. I assume she was the one who brought you over, so how are you still here?"

"She didn't," the newcomer stated, folded his hands together, and leaned forward. "She was supposed to. Every year since I passed on, she would bring me over. It was her gift."

"She's an empath, then?" Johnny asked and received a nod in response. "She could bring you over at will?"

"Kind of." Dwayne took a moment to compose himself. "She had the ability to peer into the ghost world but only for brief periods. When I died, she found me and we would talk to each other while I got used to the other side. Eventually, she found out how to make a portal—well, mostly.

She began to use stygia so she could keep the windows open longer, then learned about portals and how to make them, although she could never get it quite right. But with enough stygia, she learned to hold the window long enough that the rest of the ritual would start and open a portal for a few seconds. That's all you need to get through when you know where it will open."

"That's the kind of thing that gets empaths arrested or risks bringing seriously bad things over." Vic folded his arms disapprovingly. "The kind of things even the dead want dead."

"I know." The other ghost sighed. "I...I never got over my death in a car crash a little over four years ago. It was sudden and violent. When I arrived in Limbo, I was in shock for who knows how long." He rubbed his head and the movement drew attention to a long scratch running from the top of his head down to his neck.

"I wandered to this forest one day and I heard Jessy's voice. That was the first time she opened a window and I saw her again. I was so relieved. She said that even after I died, she could still feel me and had been searching." His voice shook with emotion. "She helped me to adjust and find the final feeling of closure and know that everyone else—my friends and family—were healing." He looked at the two partners. "Ghosts need closure too, sometimes."

Vic gave him a comforting nod. "So if you got used to the afterlife, you were probably caught up on the rules. Getting permission to cross over is rare for new spirits."

"Yeah, I know. The risk of going back means I might become too distraught to return or keep my form and get obliterated." He leaned forward even more and rested his elbows on his knees. "I only wanted to see her again and maybe feel her. She had found a stygia supplier and pawned some of her jewelry to get it. After all that, I felt I should at least try. She wanted to see me too."

"Were you family or boyfriend?" Johnny asked. "Husband?"

Dwayne chuckled and shook his head. "Nah, I was a close friend since childhood. She was always dear to me but when I started to have romantic feelings, it wasn't for her."

The young detective nodded. "Still, to have a connection between life and death is something else."

"So how did you end up here if she didn't bring you over?" Vic asked in an attempt to get to the meat of the matter. "If you had this connection, could you tell she was dead?"

"It took me a while to feel that connection." The other ghost straightened, his lips pressed firmly into a grim line. "I wasn't used to being a ghost so everything felt strange and I couldn't pick up on it at first. But after some time, I learned to recognize it—like this warmth or jolt that would go through certain parts of my body when I was close to her, or as close as I could be across the divide."

He looked at his hands. "Even if it was faint, I always felt it but one day..." He balled his fists. "Nothing. It was gone but a second before it disappeared, I felt that jolt stronger than I ever had, except it was cold. I had almost forgotten what cold felt like at that point." He placed his fists on his knees. "I thought something had happened so I went to the places where we would usually talk, but she never came. I checked with the ferrymen and attendants at the new arrival gates and asked if they had seen her. One of them told me she was listed as dead but hadn't come through yet. When I died it was instant—one second I could see the front of my car crushed and the next, I was in Limbo. They couldn't tell me what it meant that she hadn't arrived yet."

The partners kept their thoughts on this to themselves. "So how did you get permission to come topside?"

"I didn't," he admitted. "I had done several odd jobs to get doubloons over the years and Jessy had bought some from the market for me as well. Whenever I came through, she would send me back with more." He looked around the barren living room. "She did so much for me." He shook his head. "I used every coin I had to get a load of stygia and pay a ferryman to bring me back.

"I had to find her. If she hadn't arrived, she was still stuck in the world of the living. After everything she did for me I had to help her, even if I risked Oblivion." He began to tremble again. "We traveled through the river to a bridge and a door with a dim light around it. I stepped off and walked through it to cross over. I ended up in a bar— the Carnivale—and when I came out of the bathroom, the first thing I saw was a news report talking about the killings and how the body was left.

"A few other ghosts were in the bar and some were talking about it. One of them said it was because they had their life sucked out of them and their soul stolen." He thumped a fist on his leg. "I haven't found an answer yet. Can you tell me?" he asked and looked at Vic. "Does that mean they are gone? If Jessy's soul was taken, does that mean she was obliterated?"

The ghost detective clenched his jaw and the lights in his eyes darkened as he pulled his hat down. "I'm not trying to be a fence-sitter here, but I honestly don't know. What we're tracking isn't something I'm all that familiar with. Of the types of spirits that can take a soul, most simply trap them, use them like batteries, or take them as a compulsion. If you get rid of them quickly enough, everything is fine except the trauma. Geist and demons can obliterate a soul, but this being? We have no idea what it is, does or even why it wants the souls in the first place."

Dwayne processed this for a moment and nodded before he leaned back. "I see. That's the closest I've come to an answer."

"I'm sorry it ain't much," Vic apologized but the other ghost held a hand up.

"That's all right," he said, his voice a whisper. "It's something. Maybe—possibly—a little sliver of hope that it's like the former and not the latter."

Johnny nodded and rested a hand on his shoulder. "Dwayne, I have to ask—your body...the only way a ghost can get like that is by using a hell of a lot of stygia at once. How long have you been up here?"

"A week," he answered and looked at his hand. "When I saw the report and Jessy's name as one of the victims, I was so angry I forgot I had my bottle of stygia in my hand. I broke it and spilled it all over me." He sighed and lowered his hand. "I probably have another day, maybe two before it runs dry. I've looked around all week and came here on the first day but the police had already moved on. Now and then, I come to check in case…maybe she would be back." He leaned forward, pressed his hands to his lips, and closed his eyes. "You said you're investigating this case. Are you a part of the NOPD?"

"Nah," the young detective replied. "We're private investigators on a gig. But we are looking into this…being, whatever it is."

"We came here looking for leads," Vic stated. "Do you have any?"

Dwayne tapped his foot. "Not that I haven't checked myself. But I've kept a low profile. There are too many dead gangsters, cops, and the like running around." He pointed at his neck. "I don't have one of those pendants that says you are cleared to be up here. Many don't, I guess, but I kind of stand out right now. I've checked the Limbo market and haunts to see if anyone had any clues, but they either didn't or wouldn't tell me."

Johnny nodded and removed his hand while the ghost took a moment to compose himself. He looked at one of the walls and when he noticed a picture, he pushed off the sofa and took it down. It was another picture of Jessy with a friend but the face of the other person was ripped out. "Dwayne, do you know who this is with Jessy?" he asked and brought the photo to him.

The color in the ghost's hand darkened and he was able to hold the photo as he studied it. "I think this is Annie," he said and tapped her hand. "Annie Maggio—that ring is hers and the clothes seem like her style."

"Were they good friends?" Vic asked. "I'm not sure why she would tear her face out like that."

"Yeah, Jessy and Annie have been friends since the

eighth grade," he said and handed Johnny the picture. "She didn't say anything about them having a fight or anything. No one had problems with Jessy. That was one of the first things I checked—no jealous boyfriend or anything, living or dead."

"Then this probably wasn't done by her." The young detective looked knowingly at his partner.

The ghost detective nodded. "Do you know her address?"

"Why? What's wrong?" Dwayne asked and stood quickly. "I can take you to her."

Vic shook his head. "No, you need to get back to Limbo."

"But if this could lead to finding out who—"

"If it's the being we think it is, you can't do anything to it and you would simply end up obliterated or as food," the ghost detective interrupted and placed a hand on his shoulder. "I understand, Dwayne, but if you don't get back to Limbo and they catch you here, they will send you to Purgatory or fine you. Since you said you spent all your coin to get here, you will still go to Purgatory—or the Big Dark which ain't any better."

"We can cross into the ghost world," Johnny said, took the photo out of the frame, and zipped his jacket. "I promise that once we take care of this bastard, we will tell you."

"Hey." Vic squeezed the other ghost's shoulder and handed him the vial of stygia. "What good does that little sliver of hope do if it turns out she is alive and you are gone, huh?"

Dwayne clenched his jaw but nodded slowly a few

times. "All right. They live in a shotgun house, 1446 Tulip Lane." He relaxed. "Thank you."

"No need. We're doing our job." He patted him on the shoulder and turned to Johnny. "Let's go, kid," he said and drifted quickly to him. "And let's hope we find more clues rather than bodies."

CHAPTER TWELVE

"I texted Valerie," Johnny stated as the cab pulled up to the house, "to see if she could give us anything about Annie. She hasn't replied yet."

"It's not a surprise," Vic replied as his partner paid the driver and they stepped out. "They might already have her on another case or dealing with paperwork. She said she was still low on the totem pole at the moment."

The young detective shut the cab door and looked at the pearl-colored shotgun house. He scanned the yard and noticed that they had neighbors but were spaced fairly far apart. With a small shiver, he frowned at the dark clouds rolling in to announce imminent rain. "I checked news sources. Annie Maggio's name never came up," he said as they approached the door.

"It means she's either still alive or hasn't been reported dead yet," the ghost detective replied thoughtfully. "And if she's alive, we might wanna play this more sensitively than normal, so try to not destroy anything quite yet."

"Yeah, yeah," Johnny muttered, knocked on the door, and waited. "Do you think she's a specter too?"

"So far, that's all we have in terms of similarities among the victims." Vic shrugged. What I'm trying to answer is why the police didn't notice the torn photograph."

"Maybe it wasn't torn at the time," Johnny reasoned. "Didn't you once tell me that phantasma can linger if the ghost is around often and leaves a larger imprint?"

"Yeah. So you think it came back?"

He nodded. "Maybe it was also looking for something it missed." He slid his hands into his pockets. "Back on the road, it said 'not the one' after it sucked that dude's soul up. It's not simply going on a rampage but is looking for something specific."

His partner stroked his chin. "Yeah, it's on some kind of mission." They could hear steps coming toward the door. "Let's stop it from getting any more objectives for now."

"Agreed," he replied as the deadbolt was unlocked and the door was yanked open. Surprisingly, it did not reveal a woman.

A man in his mid to late twenties with slick black hair stood at the entrance. He was dressed in a striped bowling shirt and jeans and regarded his visitor curiously. "Can I help you?" he asked with a hint of an Italian accent.

"My name is Johnny. I'm a supernatural detective—bounty hunter...uh, supernatural detective bounty hunter. I'm looking for Annie Maggio."

The man leaned casually on the door frame and pointed at Vic. "Do you know there's a spook with ya?"

"Well, I guess that answers that question," the ghost stated plainly.

Johnny nodded. "Yes, sir. We're a package deal."

"Uh-huh." The man frowned. "What do you need with Annie?"

Vic drifted closer. "Sir, there's a good chance she might be in danger." The young detective took the photo from his jacket and handed it to him. "We found this at Jessy Thompson's house. It makes us concerned that whoever attacked Jessy might have plans to target her."

The man took the photo and traced the area around the missing face. "Are you serious? What could the bastard who did that to her want with Annie?"

"We're still trying to piece that together," Johnny replied. "Is it all right for us to come in and speak to her? You as well?"

For a long moment, the resident leaned against the frame and stared at the photo. He drew a breath, nodded, and motioned for them to follow as he handed it back. "Yeah. Shut the door behind you, would ya?" The partners entered and did as requested. "Annie!" their host called. "Come on out here. We've got guests! They got something important to talk to ya about."

"Are you her boyfriend?" the young detective asked.

"Huh? Nah, I'm her brother." He grinned. "Don't you see the family resemblance?"

Johnny flashed the photo at him. "I haven't seen her face, man."

"Oh, right." He turned and extended a hand. "I'm Marco —Marco Maggio."

He nodded and shook the proffered hand. "Like I said before, I'm Johnny and that"—he pointed to the ghost—"is Vic."

"Pleasure," his partner said quietly.

"Is your sister a specter too?" Johnny asked.

"Huh? Oh, yeah. It runs in the family." He looked at the ghost. "No offense if she jumps when she sees ya. Just because she can see ghosts doesn't mean she's all that used to them."

Vic shrugged. "It comes with the look."

The back door closed and a woman appeared wearing a tie-dye blue shirt and white pants. She had long black hair and soft features and dusted her shirt off hurriedly. "Who is it, Marco? I'm still doing the garden and look like—" She glanced at her brother and Johnny but more importantly, caught sight of Vic. While she didn't jump, she did utter an audible "eep" and froze in place for a moment.

"It's all right, Annie," Marco said calmly. "These are some…uh, detectives. They need to talk to you."

Johnny stepped forward and extended his hand. "Hey, Annie. My name is Johnny—Johnny Despereaux—and this is my partner Vic Kane." The ghost removed his hat and held it against his chest as she shook hands gingerly. "We need to talk about Jessy Thompson and possibly about you."

"Jessy?" she asked with a small frown. "So you are looking into— Come on into the living room." The group followed her and she motioned to the sofa where the two partners sat while she and Marco each chose a chair on either side. "What do you need to know?"

The young detective handed her the picture. "We first need to confirm—this is you, right?"

She took the picture and looked at it, her eyes

sorrowful as she nodded. "Yes. We took this at the park a few months ago." She bit her lip. "Was it damaged in the attack?"

"We're not quite sure," Vic admitted. "But we think there's a chance that whoever targeted Jessy could come after you."

"Me?" she asked, surprise on her face. "Why would they target me?"

"Again, we're not quite sure." He looked from her to Marco. "The only thing we can deduce so far is that they are focused on specters. You both fit the bill but since he tore your face out of the pic, we thought it would be better to come and speak to you directly."

"So you know who's doing this?" Marco asked and balled his fists. "I've kept up with the news and this guy has killed at least five people now. New Orleans is a beautiful place but it has a dark underbelly. I'm used to hearing about killings but they are usually gang-related or crimes of passion, things like that, but this guy is a serial killer."

"And what he does to them—" She shivered slightly. "I've heard the reports too. How he turns them into skeletons."

"I can't tell if the news teams are that good or the public relations is that crap," Vic muttered. "You'd think they would want to keep details like that out of the press, especially in this city where there are more ghosts than normal."

"Hey, I got my fair share of spook friends, all right?" Marco protested. "I don't think they are all bad or anything, but many people are still iffy on the whole subject. And not everyone can see them so they have nothing to go on but their fears. I've heard that those old bars and hotels they hang out at—those haunts or whatever—have been ransacked and defaced. Hell, even that rickety warehouse in ninth ward. I heard it got torched not too long ago."

"That sounds about right." Johnny nodded. "Even with everyone knowing ghosts are real now, superstitions still run rampant and many people believe you can banish ghosts by destroying haunts."

"It is partly true," Vic clarified. "Haunts are like large mementos—a place with considerable history that gives it a kind of connection to Limbo. Ghosts can seek refuge in them and not have to worry about losing as much stygia while they are here. But in a place like New Orleans with so much history and a large number of people passing on over the centuries, it'll be a damn long time before they can take them all down. Not to mention all that history you would throw away. They aren't all dilapidated buildings and no-name warehouses."

A loud bang in the backyard made everyone jump. "What was that?" the young detective asked and looked at Marco. "Do you guys have a dog or something out there?"

"Nah, only the garden and shed," he replied. "It sounds like the door flew open or something."

"Should we investigate?" Johnny asked Vic.

The ghost nodded. "To be safe, yes. I would say it might have been the wind but that never proves to be the case. I'll stay with Annie."

He nodded and stood and Marco followed. "I'll come with ya."

"I appreciate it," he replied as the man took a bat off a stand on the wall. It was well maintained and looked like it could have been from the fifties so was perhaps an heirloom or something. The two of them walked into the back yard, passed the garden, and approached the shed. The door was wide open, the wind had begun to pick up, and a light sprinkling of rain had started.

The young detective drew his dagger and his companion held the bat up as they walked cautiously forward. Johnny was the first to peek inside and determined easily that there was little place to hide. A pathway through the middle was clear but tools and other objects lined the walls and sides. "I see nothing here," he stated and lowered his blade. "Does anything look out of the ordinary to you?"

"Nah," Marco said but paused when he looked at a part of a wall where a rack was hanging. "Hey, wait—our ax is gone."

"Your ax?" Johnny asked before another noise drew their attention. Music could now be heard from the house.

"Hey, what's wrong with your radio?" Vic asked as the sound system activated. It played a high-energy jazz number at first before it began to slow to a crawling, creepy drone.

"I don't know," Annie responded and frowned at it as the lights in the house began to flicker. "I don't have my phone plugged in so it shouldn't play anything or even be on."

More banging issued from the front of the house this time, outside the front door. The ghost detective turned, drew his pistol, and held an arm out to tell Annie to back away. "It looks like we got here just in time," he muttered and pulled the hammer back. "Sometimes, I hate being right."

CHAPTER THIRTEEN

A hefty kick to the front door cracked it. Vic approached as Annie ran into a room, opened a closet, and searched for something. The second kick broke the door off the frame and a large figure in a tattered coat and cowl stood in the entrance, holding a sharpened ax.

"Hello again, you ugly bastard." The ghost detective sneered as he fired several shots. All were strikes but unlike the time on the road, they didn't seem to affect him at all. "Ah, shit."

The brute approached but staggered following a loud boom that shredded his coat. Vic turned to see Annie with a shotgun. "Are those exorcist rounds or buckshot?"

"Birdshot!" she hollered over the rain and the ringing in her ears.

"Birdshot? Why bother?" he asked as the intruder regained his balance.

"You always use birdshot as a warning shot." She held the gun again up. "This one is buckshot, though." She fired and it slammed into the attacker and knocked him on his back.

"This one is different—definitely possessed," the ghost noted and they watched him intently as he sat silently and picked the ax up. "Dammit, where's Johnny?"

"Get back to the house!" Johnny yelled and he and Marco raced toward it. By the time they reached the back steps, however, the door had slammed shut. The rain fell heavily now and he pulled on the door. "It's stuck!"

The resident pushed him aside and tried to pull it himself but to no avail. "I just fixed the damn thing! To hell with it. We'll bust it down!" he decided and took a step back.

"Can't we simply go around?"

"No time—on three!" the man ordered and they prepared to kick the door down. "Three!" They kicked at the same time and hurled the door off the frame. Marco rushed inside as the killer stood with slow determination. "Get away from my sister, asshole!" he shouted and raised his bat, which lit up with blue phantasma.

"What the hell?" Johnny muttered as the man pounded the bat into the killer's chest and flung him down the hall. A spirit manifested in a swirl of dark mist and left the body briefly before it forced itself in again.

"Johnny, it's possessed!" Vic shouted and threw him the revolver. "Take him out!"

He caught the gun and ordered Annie and Marco to move before he fanned the hammer and fired as many shots as he could. Each one struck home and the spirit inside appeared briefly before it ducked inside again. This one was stubborn and lunged into a charge aimed directly at Annie.

Marco leapt in front of him and swung the bat into his head, but the brute caught him by the throat and slammed him into the wall. Johnny ran forward and continued to fire the pistol as he drew his dagger. The killer swung his ax and caught him in the shoulder. The blade sliced through his jacket and blood sprayed onto the ceiling. The young detective hissed in pain before a kick catapulted him down the hall and he dropped the gun.

A similar cut appeared on Vic's shoulder as he came up behind the attacker and reached into his back to grasp the spirit within. His ghostly hand coiled around the spirit and he realized this was no ordinary ghost. He tried to pull it out of the body but it would not budge.

Annie darted in from the side and held the shotgun point-blank to the side of the intruder's head, but he took hold of it and pushed it up as she fired. He pulled it out of her hands and batted her aside before he grasped Vic's arm, pulled him off, and hurled him away.

Marco had found his feet and approached the killer, his bat prepared like he was about to hit a home run. When he swung, the attacker met him with what was most likely their ax that he had stolen. The blade met the wood and should have cut through easily. Instead, the two weapons clashed and struggled against one another while blue phantasma illuminated around the bat again.

"I'll send you back to Hell with a cracked skull, you bastard!" the man threatened, pushed away from his adversary, and swung wildly. He hit him in the ribs and shoulder before the killer raised an arm to block the other blows and swiped with his ax. The blow caught Marco in the leg and as he fell to one knee, his attacker's boot struck him in the face to leave him sprawled on the floor with a broken nose.

Almost in slow motion, the brute lifted his ax over the young man's head, but bullets entered his back and a couple of shots dislodged the weapon from his hands. The killer glanced over his shoulder at Johnny, who fired from the floor. When he turned away, his ax was swung at him by Vic, who buried it into his chest and flung him into the wall.

Seemingly unaffected by the impact, he grasped Vic's ribcage as he pulled the ax out, swung it into a downward arc, and hacked into the ghost's chest. He was able to pull away before it did any real damage to his form, but Johnny uttered a pained grunt as he looked at his shirt and found that more blood appeared on his chest, and his vision began to waver.

"What the hell?" the ghost detective muttered. He checked his wound, which was only a slight scratch across his bones.

Annie had begun to stir and the killer marched to her, grasped her by the leg, and hauled her closer to him before he hoisted her over his shoulder.

"Let go of her!" Marco demanded and tried to stand, but his wounded leg was unable to support him and he toppled each time.

Vic rushed forward and attempted to rip the spirit from the body again but was backhanded out of the way. As he turned toward the door, another shot rang out but not from Johnny. This one came from the entrance and the brute stopped in his tracks and looked at a bullet hole going through the ax wound the ghost detective had inflicted.

He fell to his knees and dropped Annie before he collapsed. As his body turned to dust, an orb of white-and-black phantasma appeared. More shots were fired but it darted to the wall and disappeared through it.

"Dammit!" a familiar voice yelled and Valerie ran to Annie and examined her. "Are you all right?"

"I'm fine," the other woman assured her and leaned against the wall. "Check the others."

"Hey, how you feeling, kid?" Vic asked as he helped Johnny to sit.

"I'm still a breather, so all right so far." He wheezed and tried to clear his head. "Who saved our asses?"

The new figure knelt to help him up as his vision steadied and his eyes finally cleared enough to see. "Valerie?"

She nodded. "I got your text and wanted to check in personally." She looked at the damage and bloodstains. "You've caused more ruckus in a few hours than I've seen in a week. I'm beginning to think you might be bad luck."

"Well, given the situation, I think I'm simply in the wrong places at the wrong time," he muttered and dropped his head back against the wall. "Or the right time. It's hard to tell, honestly."

CHAPTER FOURTEEN

"Agh, that hurts!" Marco yelped as he applied alcohol to the wound on his leg with a cotton pad.

"You're telling me." Johnny winced as he tended the wound on his shoulder. "At least that ax was sharp. I barely felt it when it sliced through me."

"No kidding." The other man reached for the medical tape. "But if that was our ax he took from the shed, it wouldn't be that sharp. I'm surprised it wasn't rusted. We barely use it and it has been sitting out there for years."

"How about now?" Vic asked and held it up. The two men looked at what appeared to be a normal tree-felling ax, if slightly weathered.

Marco blinked a few times to clear his eyes. "That is ours, but there's no way it's the same one that brute used," he said in surprise. "I didn't get a great look at it during all that commotion but from what I did see and feel, it was way stronger than that."

"You're an empath, right?" the ghost detective asked and lowered the weapon to hang at his side. "What you did with the bat isn't normal for someone who is only a specter."

He nodded as he continued to dress his leg. "Yeah, I guess so. That blue stuff appears around ghosts and if I have a weapon—but only some weapons, though." He pulled a strip of tape and threw the roll to Johnny. "Like the bat, my old bike chain, and the pair of brass knuckles my uncle gave me. It's a neat trick and keeps some of the douchebag spooks away from me."

"It looks like something similar to a ghost's memento," Vic commented. "Or at least those who use weapons as a memento. Our pal here seems to have an ax fixation but normally, they bring their mementos with them and don't have to take them from someone's yard." He tossed the ax to him. "When the spirit disappeared, it returned to normal."

Marco looked at it and shook his head. "This has been a weird day, man." He clicked his tongue and looked at Vic. "Should I be touching this?"

"It is your ax," Johnny replied, his focus on his shoulder "Your prints would be on there anyway. Besides we have an actual officer here to vouch for us. Speaking of which, I have to talk to her and check on Annie. Do you wanna come with, Marco?"

The man nodded. "Yeah, let's—ah!" he hissed in pain as he tried to stand and fell back on the chair. "Ah, dammit… I'll be there. Give me a minute."

Vic nodded. "I've taken big cuts to the leg and they ain't fun when you try to put weight on it. Take your time. She's all right." He left the two to recover and stepped into one of the bedrooms where the two women were talking.

"Are you sure you can't think of a reason someone would target you?" the young officer asked and Annie shook her head.

"No, not at all, especially some...thing like that." She looked at her and Vic. "What the hell was it?"

Valerie looked at the ghost detective. "Honestly, I've got nothing. It didn't appear to be any type of ghost I'm familiar with."

"It wouldn't be." Vic looked at his hands. "When I tried to pull it out of the skin, it felt unnatural—something I thought I would never feel again given what I am." He put his hands in his jacket pockets. "I'm familiar with phantoms, wraiths, geist, demons, vamps, shades, zombies, and even kelpie and oni and more exotic fare. I've never seen anything like this. It doesn't fit any description."

The officer sighed and frowned in thought. "Was it the same one you saw on the road?"

He tilted his head. "It looked the same but this one was a spirit possessing a physical body. When we fought him on the road, it was a spirit strong enough to act like it had a physical body, but my shots still hurt it." He looked at her gun. "I need to talk to Johnny about getting actual exorcist rounds."

Valerie looked at the marks on his chest. "Are you all right? I'm not exactly sure what we can do to heal a ghost."

"Whiskey is as good as anything," Vic muttered and leaned against the doorjamb. "I wish I could drown my sorrows in liquor but over the years, the bastards learned how to swim."

She chuckled as she rubbed Annie's back and looked at

him. "Do you still feel pain in the afterlife? If you don't mind me asking."

"Kind of...but not like you experience in life," he told her. "It's more of a sense of nothingness. When you get a deep wound in life, you can feel the wind blowing through it. If you are hurt as a ghost, it means your soul is getting torn apart. While you can walk through things that would kill you in life, enough damage to a ghost means...well, Oblivion. Until it heals, you have this hole or space in you that you have to deal with." He rubbed the back of his skull. "Johnny has to take the brunt of it, unfortunately. He still has blood to spill."

"So what's the deal with the two of you?" Valerie asked. "I have some ghosts I know and some people have ghost friends or friends who have passed away who they see during special events or whatnot. But from what I've seen, you two are joined at the hip."

"Yeah..." He drifted away and stared out of the door to where Johnny and Marco were talking. "We're probably gonna be working together while we're in town, so I guess I can fill you in a little. And Annie will probably have to answer a slew of questions after a while, so fair is fair." He shut the door. "It's not my place to tell you the whole story. Johnny can give you the details some other time. But when the kid was an actual kid—I'm talking thirteen—he was pulled into the ghost world."

"Pulled?" Valerie questioned. "How does that happen? I've heard of people who stumble on portals or something like that but never anyone being forced into the ghost world unless they are dead."

"I have no clue," he admitted. "From what he told me at

the time and what he remembers to this day, he stayed up late watching TV, drifted off to sleep for a while, and when he woke up, he was in the ghost world. He thought he was dreaming at first. I don't blame him. I thought the same thing when I arrived." He tilted his head back as he sorted through his memories. "What is crazy is he ended up in a building I was looking into for a case. It was near what we call the 'Big Dark' in the afterlife. It has a more official name—some Latin thing or another—but that's what everyone born in a year with four digits calls it."

"Abaddon?" Valerie suggested.

Vic pointed to her and nodded. "That's it, yeah. It doesn't sound Latin, though."

"It's Hebrew," Annie stated. "It's from the Bible and means an abyss."

"Well, it's certainly accurate," he responded thoughtfully. "The Bible has basically become a thesaurus nowadays, huh? Anyway, the Big Dark is this void of nothing. If a black hole could die—and not in the scientific mumbo jumbo way—but simply croak, it would be the Big Dark. You fall in and probably only God knows what happens to you. Most say you fall forever or are obliterated. Certainly, no one has returned outside of ghost folklore, although I suppose that would have more credence nowadays."

He stopped and adjusted his cap. "Sorry...sidetracked. Anyway, the Big Dark messes with phantasma, stygia, and all the ghostly magical BS you probably kind of know about. I've never heard of a ghost of any type that can bring a human into the afterlife outside of a reaper, and those dudes are basically robots so they wouldn't have anything to do with this. But if someone else was capable of it, being able to do it near the Big Dark is frightening."

"Did you ever find out why he was brought there in the first place?" Valerie asked.

The ghost shook his head and sighed. "Nah. Johnny and I have been looking into it ever since we met but we've still come up short. Not to slight the kid, but while he is special by normal terms, I can't see him being special enough to be singled out like he was. Although maybe he wasn't and whatever brought him in was only looking for a snack.

"I happened to see him wandering the halls and I can't tell you who was more surprised to see who." He clenched his teeth and shook his head. "Then something...a long-armed, shadowy bastard with a ghoulish look lunged out of the dark and grabbed him, dug its nails into him, and started to drain him—blood, soul, and everything. I've never seen anything like it."

Vic patted his gun and scowled. "I blasted it away and it scampered into the building with a wild shriek. A banshee would be jealous of the racket it made. When I went to him, his body and soul were damaged. I didn't know what would happen to him—a living being killed in the afterlife? Would he turn into a ghost on the spot? Would he disappear? I honestly didn't want to find out either way. For the first time in a long damn time, I simply prayed and hoped I could think of something that could save the kid. After a while, I did—a bonding."

"Bonding?" Valerie recognized the term. "That's when there's a connection between souls right?"

He nodded. "It's not as romantic as most make it seem. There can be bonding between a living and dead person if their relationship was close in life, but ghosts can bond with whoever. It can be used rather maliciously by tough guys trying to keep tabs on their underlings and such but bonded ghosts can help each other out. Like if they get scuffed, they can give some of their phantasma to each other to help the healing process speed up.

"Again, I wasn't sure if it would work on a living person, but the kid was in the ghost world at the time so it was better than merely watching him croak. It would heal his soul, at least." He extended a hand to illustrate his explanation. "I placed my hand on his chest and told him what I was trying to do. All he could do was nod but it was enough. I tried to patch him up and did the best I could. He ended up falling asleep and in another first in a long time, so did I. When we woke we were back in the realm of the living, much to my shock. I still haven't paid a visit to the guy who gave me the gig to go over there. He's probably still pissed."

"And you've been together ever since," Valerie surmised. "His parents didn't have anything to say about all this?"

"It's not my place to talk about the family life," Vic said with a wave of his hand. "But it took a while to settle. He was the one who wanted to get into this business, and after I realized I couldn't go back to the ghost world—well, I could, but I would always pass out and reappear next to him, and he would get sick if I was gone too long. Well, to become a mentor wasn't exactly a dream of mine but it's worked out well enough."

"Wow, that's...wow," Annie muttered as if still trying to take it in.

The young officer snickered and shook her head. "So what does that make you? What does that make Johnny?"

"Technically, it makes Johnny a revenant—a living ghost," he answered. "Although only kind of. Revenants are super-rare and generally are made when someone has a traumatic enough experience to die but their will to live and desire for something—be it revenge or to say goodbye to their loved one—is so damn strong that they continue to live in their technically dead body until they are utterly destroyed or complete their mission. But Johnny is something of an oddity." He chuckled. "Some of the fine ladies and gentleman at the places where we get gigs even gave him a nickname, Rev. Johnny."

Valerie nodded, impressed. "It's not a bad nickname."

"I don't think he's too fond of it, to be honest." At a knock on the door, Vic opened it and Johnny helped Marco to limp into the room. "Do you feel better?"

"I'm not gonna die of blood loss yet," his partner responded as he helped Marco to sit next to his sister before he collapsed on the bed behind them. "Although I'm very lightheaded. Is that bad?"

"Eh, don't worry about it." The ghost looked around. "Now that the group is all here, let's go over the facts. Even if it's only to have some clue where to start."

CHAPTER FIFTEEN

Valerie sat on the couch next to Johnny and read the letter he had found. Vic and Marco were checking on Annie, who sat on another sofa nearby, but she seemed more worried about her brother's injuries than her own.

"I'm fine, Ann," he assured her and touched his nose gingerly. "I need to set this, though."

She went to touch his broken nose and winced when he did. "It hurts bad, huh? If we go to a hospital we can get you some—"

"Scooch aside for a second," the ghost ordered as he moved closer to Marco. "It could be worse but I'll bet it's painful."

"You'd win that bet." Marco sucked a sharp breath in as he tried to correct his nose with shaking hands. "Dammit, I've done this before it shouldn't be so—aaagghh!" His shout was one of pain and surprise when Vic pressed his thumbs against the bridge of his nose and pushed it into place. Annie looked at him with shock and her brother with concern. "*Merda!* God, that hurt." He sniffed, wrinkled his nose for a moment, and nodded. "Thanks."

"You're welcome," Vic said with a nod as he put his hands in his jacket pockets and drifted to Johnny and Val. "So, what are you looking for, exactly? Do you think there's invisible ink or something?"

"I'm trying a fresh pair of eyes, Vic," his partner said and sank deeper into the sofa. "Does anything jump out at you, Valerie?"

"Well…the ax is certainly appropriate." She tapped the start of the message. "But this intro and the location—'hottest Hell'—gives me pause. I remember something about it."

The ghost detective shrugged. "I thought it was only the usual psycho babble. Hottest hell, darkest depths…most of these nutcases have a theatrical streak. It would be quite an accomplishment if this guy got a letter from actual Hell. For all the craziness of the afterlife, I've never heard of someone getting out of the big furnace."

Valerie took her phone out and began to search the web. "I'm not saying that's where our perp is from but the line is familiar." She tapped it in and went silent for a moment. "Are you kidding me?"

Johnny tried to look over her shoulder. "What's up?"

She put her phone down and hung her head. "God, I hope it's a copycat."

"Again, what's up?" Vic asked. "What did you find?"

When she looked up, all eyes were on her and she frowned as she entered something else into her phone. "Are any of you familiar with the Axman of New Orleans?"

Johnny was not and when he looked at Vic's quizzical

expression, he assumed he did not know about him either. But when he turned to Annie and Marco, their gobs-macked faces made him realize that to anyone from New Orleans, the name was infamous. "I can't say that I do but give us the short version."

"He was a serial killer in the early twentieth century. Some compared him to Jack the Ripper."

"Not a very distinctive comparison," Vic commented and caught her frown. "What? How many serial killers who use bladed weapons are compared to the Ripper? Hell, some of them didn't even use bladed weapons."

"There is something else in common too," Annie stated and rubbed her arms in discomfort. "They were both thought to be ghosts or demons at one point."

The young detective nodded and thought about the era. "It makes sense. The late nineteenth to early twentieth century was when the ghost world was becoming widely known. All the pandemonium from back then and mixing that with suspicious killings probably made many people think like that."

"He didn't use his weapons in his crimes," Valerie added. "Except maybe a chisel to break into homes. He would always take something from the property—a straight razor or more commonly, an ax."

Vic tapped his chin in thought. "It certainly fits with our friend's MO and it would explain the ability to use any old ax as a memento. He's attached to the item in general, not a particular one."

The officer flipped her phone and handed it to Johnny. "This was a letter—perhaps the only letter—he sent to the papers." He took the phone and read the letter as Vic moved behind him.

Hell, March 13, 1919

Esteemed Mortals of New Orleans:
They have never caught me and they never will. They have never seen me, for I am invisible, even as the ether that surrounds your Earth. I am not a human being but a spirit and a demon from the hottest Hell. I am what you Orleanians and your foolish police call the Axman.

When I see fit, I shall come and claim other victims. I alone know who they shall be. I shall leave no clue except my bloody ax, besmeared with the blood and brains of he whom I have sent below to keep me company.

If you wish, you may tell the police to be careful to not rile me. Of course, I am a reasonable spirit. I take no offense at the way they have conducted their investigations in the past. In fact, they have been so utterly stupid as to not only amuse me but also His Satanic Majesty, Francis Josef, etc. But tell them to beware. Let them not try to discover what I am, for it would be better that they were never born than to incur the wrath of the Axman. I don't think there is any need for such a warning, for I feel sure the police will always avoid me as they have in the past. They are wise and know how to keep away from all harm.

Undoubtedly, you Orleanians think of me as a most horrible murderer, which I am, but I could be much worse if I wanted to. If I wished, I could pay a visit to your city every night. At will, I could slay thousands of your best citizens—and the worst—for I am in close relationship with the Angel of Death.

Now, to be exact, at 12:15 earthly time next Tuesday night,

I will pass over New Orleans. In my infinite mercy, I make a little proposition to you people. Here it is.

I am very fond of jazz music, and I swear by all the devils in the nether regions that every person shall be spared in whose home a jazz band is in full swing at the time I have mentioned. If everyone has a jazz band going, well then, so much the better for you people. One thing is certain, however. Some of your people who do not jazz it out on that specific Tuesday night, if there be any, will get the ax.

Well, as I am cold and crave the warmth of my native Tartarus and it is about time I leave your earthly home, I will cease my discourse. I hope you will publish this that it may go well with you, I have been, am, and will be the worst spirit that ever existed, either in fact or realm of fancy.

~The Axman

Vic chuckled. "It's well written for a psychopath."

"That's what caught your attention?" Johnny muttered and handed Valerie her phone. "What's with the jazz thing at the end? Did that happen?"

"Oh, yeah. By all accounts, every jazz club was filled that night," Marco confirmed and gestured to himself and Annie "Most houses held jazz parties too. The Axman is infamous around here. Maybe not everyone knows the specifics but New Orleans, for all our parties and good spirits, can be macabre and we don't let a story like that go away."

Annie huddled on the couch, deep in thought. "Vic, when the radio turned on, was that jazz? Do you recall?"

The ghost scratched his skull. "Uh...it could have been. I remember it was slowed and full of static." He looked at

Johnny. "Do you remember if anything was playing on the radio when we ran into him on the way here?"

His partner shook his head and looked at the Maggios. "I can't say but I do remember that the guy who was killed on the road was also Italian."

"Frank Rossi," Vic recalled. "Hmm...who did the Axman kill in his day?"

"Italians," Valerie responded without even checking her phone. "Italian-Americans and immigrants were the majority of his victims. It made many think the mob was involved somehow."

"It could have simply been a racist with time to kill," Marco muttered before he caught himself. "Wait, that wasn't supposed to be a pun."

"It happens to the best of us, kid," the ghost detective assured him and focused on the officer. "Well, I guess it could be a start. Although I agree with Val that there is a good chance it's simply a copycat, it could be an apparition."

"I think we've established that it's a ghost, man." Marco sighed.

Johnny shook his head. "Apparitions are technically made of the same stuff ghosts are, but they are little more than puppets. If someone's hate is strong enough or if their legend grows to such a level that they are on everyone's mind, an apparition could appear and act in a way they would."

"But that doesn't make sense," Annie interjected. "If that's what it is, why would it appear now? He would have been more well-known in the mid-twentieth century, not a century later."

"Yeah, not to mention that if it's the whole 'hatred' scenario, it again seems like it should have reacted earlier," Marco pointed out.

"It's only a thought." Johnny leaned his head against his fist. "So the guy on the road was Italian, at least partly, and so is Annie. But not all his victims have been Italian. Jessy certainly wasn't unless she has an interesting family tree."

"She wasn't. She was creole," Annie confirmed and the thought of her lost friend made her clench her arms tightly around her waist.

"And in something of a twist, none of the Axman's victims were black," Valerie added. "We've had two black victims, two Italian if you include Annie—three, I guess, with the guy on the road—one Vietnamese, and one of mixed ancestry including Native American. He hasn't seemed very selective until now."

"Maybe his early killings were a way to get power somehow." Johnny thought back to Frank Rossi and the descriptions of the other killings. "He seems to be able to drain the soul, life force, or whatever of his victims."

"Wait, what?" Marco leaned forward and Annie gasped.

Vic looked at them. "That reminds me. Something interesting about this attack was that he tried to carry Annie off, not suck her dry like his other victims."

Johnny registered the confusion and worry in the siblings' eyes. "It probably means he's looking for some-thing more specific now and whatever that is, he might have found it in Annie."

Marco looked at his sister. "Annie? What could he want with her?"

The two partners took a moment to communicate

silently with each other before the young detective shrugged. "I'm sorry, man. We couldn't tell you that right now."

"We can't tell you what we don't know," Vic added apologetically and placed a fist over his chest. "But I promise you we will find out."

Valerie stood and prepared to make a call. "I can tell you this," she began as she moved to the door. "You will need protection."

CHAPTER SIXTEEN

Johnny crushed his cigarette under his boot and scowled at the front doors of the precinct. "I still say we should have dropped them at our hotel."

"You think they'll be safer at a chain hotel than with the cops?" Vic asked as he people-watched on the corner and tipped his hat at a kid who gaped at him while he and his mother crossed the street.

"If this guy is after Annie, wouldn't he assume that the next place they would go would be to the cops?" he asked and looked over his shoulder. "Did you ever see the first Terminator?"

"I don't think so. You'll have to show me." The ghost turned and floated beside him. "But even if he made that deduction, what would he do? Try to blitz his way in?"

Johnny ran a hand over the wound on his shoulder. "He seemed to take on the four of us just fine."

"True, but what finally knocked him on his ass was a shot from Val's gun and there should be more than enough of those in there... Well, I guess that depends on how well-financed they are." He tapped his chin as he studied the building. "We might have softened him up for her, but those things still pack a punch. Modern tech is catching up to the ghost stuff."

"Or it could be your old pistol is finally showing its age." Johnny patted the knife on his belt. "Although it would be nice for each of us to have a gun, just in case."

"Val mentioned something about letting us use her spare," Vic told him. "After we give it a test run, maybe we can see if we can find a normal black market and get one. It would probably be cheaper than the real deals at the Limbo market."

"Not to mention we likely won't be allowed into the Limbo market for quite some time." He paused and turned his head slowly to his partner. "When exactly do you think we'll have a test run for this gun?"

The ghost shrugged. "Maybe soon. I have an idea of where we should look next."

"And that would be—"

His partner raised a hand to interrupt him. "Hold up a second. Val's back." Johnny took a few steps forward as she came down the steps, turned toward them, and nodded.

She carried a small black bag, handed it to the young detective, and stopped him from unzipping it. "My backup pistol is in there," she stated. "Along with a few other things to help you. But try to take a look out of a public place."

"Appreciated." He held the bag under his arm. "Will Annie and Marco be all right?"

"They'll stay the night here, then be moved into a hotel." She looked over her shoulder. "Probably not too far from the building. Maybe the Hilton."

"Swanky," Vic commented. "Are you rolling with us?"

"I need to return to the crime scene." She pressed the remote in her pocket that unlocked her car. "I only came here to drop them off and debrief. Where are you going?"

Johnny shrugged. "I don't have a clue. Vic seems on to something, though."

The ghost nodded. "It's more familiar territory for me. We'll go creeping."

"Haunts?" his partner asked.

"We still need more info, kid," he explained. "And with most witnesses dead, you are more likely to know as much about this guy as any breather. So we'll have to talk to the undead and see what they know."

He nodded. "Where would we start? There are so many of those in New Orleans."

"The Carnivale," Vic revealed. "The place where Dwayne showed up. If that is one of the crossways in the city, it gets considerable traffic to and from Limbo. There might even be a chance that our new 'buddy' came in from there."

Valerie frowned. "It's not a bad idea but you should know that we don't have many informants in the dead side of things. The ghost population around here is fairly insular."

"The criminal ghost population you mean?" he asked.

She nodded. "I suppose to be more specific, sure."

"It's an important distinction," he pointed out. "You have to remember that ghosts still have all their human feelings and thoughts. You're a human who can't understand them and a cop. It's not a great combination for casual conversation, especially with the 'underworld.'" He emphasized "underworld" with air quotes.

"I'll keep that in mind." She sighed. "Do you need anything else? I have to go."

Johnny extended a hand and she shook it briskly. "We should be good. Thanks for your help. We'll keep you in the loop."

"Appreciated. Try to not get yourselves killed—or you at least, Jonathan," she said with a smile before she departed.

He frowned. "If I wanted people to call me by my full name, I would use it." He glared at Vic, who simply slid his hands into his pockets and drifted off.

"Hey, she would have worked it out for herself. What else would Johnny be short for?" He wandered to the street and noticed a couple of ghosts chatting nearby. "I'll get directions to the bar."

"Uh-huh." The young detective sighed as he looked for a cab. "Let's hurry. I want to see what goodies she left us."

Once they had left the metropolitan area, Johnny finally unzipped the bag. "So we have the gun, a small medkit, a vial of stygia, a map of the city, and this." He took a circular device out. "Wasn't this what she used at the Limbo market?"

"The ether blockade," Vic said with a nod. "That's useful. I gotta say they are well equipped in the NOPD."

He placed the gun in his holster and the rest of the

items in various pockets. "What they have in gadgets, we make up for in skill."

"That's the spirit, kid," his partner responded. "Although I could be spirit enough for us."

The young detective rolled his eyes. "You can keep the boomer jokes to yourself, Vic."

"Boomer?" the ghost muttered. "I was born in the silent generation, kid."

"Well, you didn't take it to heart." He chuckled, peered out the window, and frowned at the buildings that grew increasingly decrepit. "Haunts indeed."

"Take your eye patch off," Vic instructed. "Have a look at life on the other side."

Johnny complied. Dozens of ghosts wandered the area, some inside homes and living as families or roommates while others drifted around looking for company. "There are certainly more around here than in the city, at least out in the open." He noticed a smaller ghost seated on a swing under a tree with no one around her. "It seems like a lonely life. Why stay here or come back instead of going to Limbo?"

"Everyone has their reasons, Johnny," his partner replied in a flat tone. "Some can't get over their death. Others don't feel at home over there like they do here. In the end, some will realize it's for the best that they head to Limbo while others would rather be obliterated."

"Even the religious ones?"

Vic snickered. "Especially the religious ones. In all the religions that talk about Purgatory or the like, when has it even been a good thing?"

"Limbo isn't exactly Purgatory. The big jail is literally called that," Johnny pointed out.

"True." The ghost detective nodded. "But it isn't exactly Heaven or Paradise either, is it?" He pointed out the window. "It isn't all bad and for some, it can be a fresh start."

The young man looked at a male and female ghost playing with a child ghost as they passed. It was sweet in a macabre way. "I suppose so."

They continued the drive in silence while dark clouds began to roll above. Johnny tensed given that their last encounters had begun with dark clouds, but he relaxed somewhat when a gentle rain began to fall.

The cab driver pulled up at the Carnivale, which was on a mostly abandoned road—at least to the living. A couple of restaurants and shops were filled with ghosts going about their business. "All right, we're here. I'm not sure why and not sure I wanna know," the driver said and turned to Johnny. "That'll be sixty-seven dollars and—" His eyes widened when he noticed his passenger's glowing eye.

The young detective smiled and handed him seventy dollars. "Keep the change." He nodded to him and opened the door, stepped out with Vic, and closed it behind him before the driver accelerated away. The area was lively and he could hear the sounds of laughter and live music from within—Jazz, appropriately enough. He took his phone out and checked the time. "It's only five-forty."

"What use is time to us?" Vic asked with a smirk. "We don't sleep."

"Do you think we might bump into Louis Armstrong in one of these places?" he asked.

The ghost shook his head. "Nah. All the dead enter-tainers generally stay in Limbo. There is more money that way and there are fans there." He smiled as he took his pack of cigarettes out. "I got to see him before I met you. He's still one of the best doing it."

Johnny dug for the lighter and handed it to him. "Well, I guess when my time comes, at least it'll be entertaining."

His partner lit his cigarette and pocketed both the pack and lighter. "Think about that later. We still have a job to do."

"Right," he agreed as they headed to the entrance. "What are the chances I might be able to get something to drink here?"

"At a ghost bar?" Vic laughed. "Slim to none, kid."

"Yeah, I thought so." He sighed and cracked his fingers before he pulled the door open. "Ah, well. I suppose one of us should stay sober."

CHAPTER SEVENTEEN

When they entered, they were confronted by smoke, cheers from a large section where a game was playing on an old TV, and a jazz band in full swing with dancers near the stage.

"Man, they cater to a big crowd, huh?" Johnny commented. He gestured unobtrusively to a group of ghosts dressed in pinstriped suits with women in flapper outfits. "And generations."

"It takes considerable work to set up a place like this." Vic looked toward the bar as he took a drag. "This means there tends to be some of them strictly for ghosts. It's better for us in this instance as it means fewer places to check."

The young detective began to move to the bar. "How is that better? Doesn't having fewer places to check mean we have fewer chances to find something?"

"Maybe, but someone has to have seen something. With these being the most popular places, we have a better chance to get something out of them." The ghost retrieved his bag of coins from his jacket as a couple wandered away from the bar and they took their places. "Let me handle this, kid."

"It's fine by me," he muttered, aware that several sets of eyes had focused on him. "Maybe I'll go mingle."

"Yeah, do that. See if you can get something out of them," Vic instructed as he waved at a bartender. "And play up the whole exotic scenario. They'll love that."

"Most do and some a little too much. Do you remember that guy who wanted to buy me from you?" he asked as he got off his seat.

"Well, don't talk to guys like that—stranger danger and all that. Be mindful." His partner waved him off and went to talk to some of the ghosts who still stared at him.

The bartender approached. "Hey, pal. What are you having?"

"Whiskey, our stuff and the good stuff too," he said and placed a doubloon on the counter.

The man took it and examined the red ruby in the center. "You could probably get a bottle of it for this."

"Then keep it coming. We might be here a while." The bartender nodded and turned to take a bottle off the wall. As he did so, the ghost detective took out a stack of ten of the same doubloons and placed them on the bar. "While I'm here, I need something else—some information."

"Information? What kind? Directions or something?" The man turned with the bottle and a shot glass and his jaw dropped when he saw the stack of coins.

"The kind that is hard to come by." He looked around and took another drag. "Is your boss in?"

"Uh, yeah. Hold on a sec." He poured a shot quickly and

left the bottle as he stepped out of the bar area and into the back. Vic jingled his bag and sighed at the somewhat depleted contents before he put it away. A ghost snoozed next to him with his head on the counter. He checked the mug clutched in the drunk's hand. It was still half-full but the ten or so mugs in front of him indicated that he wouldn't get anything out of him, and the chatty couple next to him were too enamored with each other to bother with for now. Still, as long as the owner paid half a mind to his patrons, he had a good chance.

He shifted his attention to the bartender who approached beside a large orange-hued ghost with a twirled black mustache. The proprietor wore a simple white dress shirt and black vest and slacks but they were certainly made of nice material. After pointing Vic out to his boss, the bartender returned to his duties and the orange ghost nodded and drifted closer.

"I heard you need some information," he began, his voice rough—probably a smoker in life and if the cigar in his vest pocket was any indication, death too. His gaze settled on the coins on the counter. "What kind of information is worth this much?"

"Are you looking a gift horse in the mouth?" Vic poured himself another shot and gestured toward the owner with the bottle to offer him some. The boss nodded, took a shot glass off the shelf, and waited while it was filled. "I need information about some strange goings-on around the city."

"Stranger than NOLA normally is?" the boss asked and downed the shot. "If she were a lady, she'd be a pretty thing but crazy too."

Vic laughed. "No kidding." He swallowed his second shot and tasted some spicy notes. "I'm talking strange for us and the breathers. The killings that have been going on."

The orange ghost froze for a second and inclined his head with a frown. "What makes you think I or anyone here knows anything about that?"

"I can't say that I do, but it's worth a try." He reached for the coins. "I thought in a place like this with so many people coming by and a good owner who always keeps his ear out, there might be something passing through that could be of use." He began to drag the coins away. "But if not, I can go and try—"

His companion stopped his hand and leaned closer. "Why are you looking into this?"

"It's work-related," he answered. "I'm a detective. My name's Vic."

The boss' eyes brightened for a second. "Vic? Vic Kane from Chicago?"

Vic's eyes widened in surprise. "You know me from life?"

The other ghost shook his head. "Not personally but you did some work for my cousin back in the day. Julio Garcia."

He laughed. "No kidding? Yeah, I remember Julio. His bar was one of my favorites to drink at."

"That case you worked?" The ghost released his hand. "Getting the dirt the mafia had on him and destroying it helped the whole family, man. It let him expand and brought money in. That's how I ended up opening this place in life."

"And you were able to keep it open in death?" Vic was surprised. "How did you manage that."

The boss smirked. "Well, we had a good reputation by the end but unfortunately, it was lost in a fire during a gang fight in the street. A Molotov or something started it. I ended up dying in the flames but I took all the knowledge I acquired by running the business and had some connections in the afterlife who helped set me up again. I think I might be doing better dead than I did alive." He proffered his hand. "Well, I guess I at least know you aren't some snitch or anything. My name's Romeo."

He took his hand and they shook. "Pleasure, Romeo. That's a strong handshake you have there." He slid the coins into place again.

Romeo picked a few up and let them drop. "Just because I look like a skeleton doesn't mean I gotta be one, you know?" He chuckled as he spread the coins, confirmed that all of them had the red diamonds, and whistled. "Damn. Seriously, man, do you honestly think information is worth all this?"

Vic adjusted his hat. "Well, given what's been going on and the fact that no official action has been taken by the Agency up here or the Wild Hunt dead side, I'm beginning to think there's some kind of cover-up."

"There could be," the orange ghost muttered. "But I don't think it's all that complicated. Nothing from the big boys at least."

"The mob?" he asked and gestured with his head to some of the guys in suits. "They have a fairly strong hold on this town again, don't they?"

Romeo nodded. "More the ghost side of things, obviously, but they can get things done on the living side. They might know more than you or I but I don't think this was their plan or anything. I think they are trying to keep things as quiet as possible so the big boys don't show up themselves and take them on at the same time."

The detective chuckled and poured another glass before he finished his cigarette and stamped it out in an ashtray. "I guess they didn't get this far by being complete idiots. Still, I'd have to assume that even if someone had information, they'd be hesitant to speak about it given its potential to backfire and coin has a way of calming the nerves, kind of like liquor." He took the other ghost's glass and poured another shot. "Would you care for some more?"

Silence reigned for a moment while the proprietor counted the coins and sighed before he placed them in his pocket and downed the shot. "This is more about paying the debt but I won't look a gift horse in the mouth." He smiled wryly. "What do you need?"

"Anything you have about the killer," Vic responded. "And to specify, the one who leaves the breathers looking like husks."

"It's not only the breathers," Romeo stated and leaned closer. "They only started dealing with it two months ago, but before that—say three months and change—many of our people went as well and it wasn't anything to do with the mob or gangs. I have patrons from all types of 'completely legitimate' enterprises and they seemed as spooked as anyone else."

"Obliterated?" Vic asked. "How many?"

"At least twenty."

"Twenty?" Startled, he raised his voice a little and his companion caught his hand to hold him down.

"Yeah, keep it cool, man. You already saw that some of the patrons are of the 'questions later' type." The proprietor smoothed the detective's jacket. "And those twenty are only the ones we know about. They were mafia guys, gang members, and a couple of business types. A family went missing. I've heard no word on them but they haven't been found."

"When they were obliterated, were their fragments found?" Vic asked.

Romeo rubbed the back of his neck. "That's the thing. From what I heard, they were in pieces but not the kind we typically think of when they burst apart before they fade away. They found actual parts."

The ghost detective frowned. "That's harsh, but unless you are brand new to being a ghost, you can eventually recover from even injuries like that."

"Not in the state they were in, man." The orange ghost shuddered. "I never saw one but heard the details. They were found in pieces, broken or cut through with what was probably an ax."

Vic nodded. "That sounds right."

"But they wouldn't reform. By the time they were found, they had lost the light in their eyes and the shine on their bones and would simply crack and turn into wisps of ether in most cases."

"So you couldn't even touch them then. Hell." He poured another shot. "Were there any witnesses?"

Romeo held two fingers up. "Only two, but both

reported the same thing. The victims were killed by a ghost but nothing like they've ever seen before."

"Description?"

The proprietor took down a bottle of dark liquid off the shelf behind him. "They said he was the color of the night, like this." He shook the bottle. "They probably wouldn't have seen him if it wasn't for the white haze that came off him."

"White haze?" Vic thought back to the spirit they had fought earlier. "I don't know of any ghost that has that."

"Neither do I." The orange ghost folded his arms and looked around the bar and lounge. "There's a pool running for what it turns out to be. Demon has the most votes." He looked curiously at him. "What's your take? Could it be a demon?"

He raised his glass. "It could be. Demons come in many forms. They share some traits but most are unique." He downed the drink and flipped the glass. "It might seem crazy but I hope it is that. I at least know how to deal with a demon."

Romeo chuckled. "Prayer?"

Vic looked at him. "Some say that works. I prefer getting my hands on blessed bullets and shooting until it stops moving."

CHAPTER EIGHTEEN

"Great, it was nice meeting you and I'll get back to that offer for my skin some other time." Johnny shuffled quickly to Vic, took the seat next to him, and hung his head. "Yeah, it seems everyone in here is one of 'those guys.'" He sighed and stretched a hand out for the pack. "Please tell me you found something. I got jack."

"Indeed I did." His partner handed him the pack and lighter and pointed to Romeo. "Johnny, meet Romeo, the fine boss and owner of Carnivale."

"Johnny?" The orange ghost looked at him as he lit a cigarette. "That eye...are you Rev. Johnny?"

He nodded as he took a drag and put the pack down. "Mmmhmm," he mumbled. "It's nice to meet you. I guess it's good to be recognized from time to time— Wait, what have you heard?"

Romeo looked at Vic. "So that means you were the one who brought him back to life using your soul?"

"More like stopped him from dying," the ghost detective

clarified. "And I'm honestly not sure how that all worked out. It's still a work in progress."

"It's been almost eight years," Johnny remarked and studied the bar hopefully, even though he knew he'd be disappointed. His partner was right and he hadn't expected to find anything he could drink. Although technically, he could drink what was meant for ghosts given what he was, even the fumes from some of it made him lightheaded. He wasn't desperate enough to try it yet. "So what do you have for us, Mr. Romeo?"

"I told Vic most of what I know already," the man replied. "The only other thing I have for you is that you aren't the only ones on the hunt. The mafia, gangs, regular ghosts turned vigilantes, and hell, even some of the breathers are getting in on it. Hordes of people are after this guy although not openly."

"Is that so?" He looked at his partner. "Do you think we have enough to claim that finder's fee before it's too late?"

The ghost detective nodded and undid the buttons on his coat. "Yeah, especially with the weapon on hand."

"The weapon? What weapon? The ax?" he asked and frowned quizzically at him. "Where did you hide that? You don't even have an ass to shove it in."

Vic shook his head, opened his jacket, and pulled his shirt up to reveal his ribcage and the ax hidden there. "You have to get inventive sometimes."

"Oh, wow." Johnny put his glove on and poked the weapon. "That must be uncomfortable. No wonder you've walked around straighter than usual."

Romeo stared at it. "Wait, that's the killer's ax?"

Now, it was the ghost detective's turn to tell him to

calm down. "Not this one specifically. He doesn't seem to use his own weapon and takes them from wherever he is. It seems axes are a memento with him. He turns them from old, busted tools left in the shed to something that could belong in an executioner's private collection."

He buttoned his coat, took a card from his pocket, and handed it to the proprietor. "You might want to toss all your axes into a safe. Corkscrews too—you know, just in case. That has our number. Call us if anything comes up or you have something new to tell us."

The other ghost took the card and looked at it before he slipped it into his vest pocket and patted it. The two partners were about to leave when Vic turned quickly to the bar, snatched the remaining whiskey, and brought it with him. "Hey, I paid for it so might as well finish it."

"I wasn't going to say anything," Johnny told him as he pushed open the doors. "I'm used to it." When they stepped outside, it was still drizzling and a very light fog had begun to form. "So what now? Did you learn anything interesting?"

"Well, besides the fact that most of the info isn't getting out of the city because of mafia intervention and other nonsense, it seems this guy is a boogieman to both the living and dead." The ghost detective unscrewed the cap and took a swig from the bottle. "For now, let's head to the hotel and think it over. We should go to Limbo tomorrow morning and see if we can't get that finder's fee. Hopefully, it'll get attention after that."

Johnny nodded. "I'm with you. I'll look at the books and find a crossway to Big Daddy's." He looked around and frowned. "Ah, hell. How are we supposed to get back into town? It's not like there are cab drivers in the haunts." Vic placed two fingers in his mouth and gave a loud, repeated whistle. "How is that possible with no lips?"

"I'm gifted," the ghost stated and took another quick swig before he capped the bottle. "And there are cab drivers here, just not living ones."

Before he had a chance to ask what he was talking about, a black cab pulled up behind them. The young detective turned, walked up to it, and peered inside. The cab driver wore dark glasses, a scarf around his mouth despite it being summer, and a large coat with an afro that was clearly a wig. He pointed and looked at Vic. "Mannequin?" he asked and his partner nodded as he drifted past. "Man, I thought that was something we came up with."

"I came up with," the ghost corrected and opened the taxi door. "And where do you think I got the idea? Get in here and stop staring. It's rude."

Valerie took her gloves off as she exited the house. A crowd had gathered and the other officers tried to hold them back with assurances that there was nothing to see. This was true given that she had taken what remained of the attacker to the precinct when she took Annie and Marco there. They had found more traces of phantasma but she assumed that when they ran it, they wouldn't find anything, exactly like all the other times.

She sighed and glanced in the other direction at nothing but a long field of uncut grass and hedges behind a fence. Not quite sure why, she strolled forward to lean against the fence and her gaze traced the large phone lines that cut across the plains while dark clouds drifted in.

When she looked down to ease her neck, something caught her eye and she frowned at an odd shimmer in the brush. She stood on her toes to get a better look, but there was too much foliage in the way. Intrigued, she hopped the fence and put her gloves on quickly as she strode closer.

Whatever this was, it was not something she had seen before. For a moment, she thought the dark sludge was simply mud and her tired mind was messing with her, but a closer inspection changed her mind. This was inky-black and the shimmer came from dots of white—something within it. She took a vial out and collected some of it, capped it, and prepared to return to give it to an analyst but saw more a little farther down. When she reached that batch, she realized that a trail of this substance led deeper into the weeds and straight across the plains.

In the back of her mind, she knew she needed to call it in but when she looked at the liquid—the same color as the spirit that had fled from the home after she shot its body—she knew this could be a phantasma trail. After another look at the substance on one of the bushes, she wasn't so sure that was all. If this was phantasma, it was...diseased.

She ran hastily to the other officers, located one of the scientists, and showed her the vial. "Take this back with you."

"Why? What is it?" The woman looked at the contents. "Mud? No, it's too inky."

"Don't you see the white spots?" she asked.

"White spots?" The analyst examined the vial again.

"No, I can't say I do. But your eyes are much better than most specters so maybe the lab will come up with something." She placed it into a container and sealed it. "Where did you find it?"

Valerie pointed to the side of the house. "In the grass over the fence. Do you think we can get a search team?"

The scientist shook her head. "It's not my call but we're stretched thin right now, Val. I'll make sure to examine this and get back to you before—hey, where are you going?"

"I'm going to go check something. Get back to the precinct." She hopped the fence again and retrieved her flashlight. It was getting dark fairly quickly. She jogged a short distance and identified more of the substance as she proceeded. It seemed to cross the entire plains to a swamp in the far distance. She nodded, took a map out, and marked the area before she returned to her car. This would be a long night for her.

CHAPTER NINETEEN

It took Valerie some time to drive to the swamp and when she arrived, she had to hop over the guard rails onto the plains to find any sign of the black substance she had seen earlier. Fortunately, she was now able to see the white very clearly in the dark of night and as she'd suspected, it led her deeper into the swamp.

She popped her trunk, put her wet boots on, and traded her jacket for a slicker and a beanie to tuck her hair into. The little warning voice in her head that insisted she should come back in the morning made her pause for a moment, but she didn't want to risk losing a lead. Her mind made up, she shut the trunk and headed into the swamp using the lights on her gun and vest.

Although she tried to keep to the main track as much as she could, the substance trailed through the muck and she was forced to follow. Fireflies helped with the light, along with a few lamps stuck in the ground by the rangers or maintenance teams, but the deeper she got, the more she worried about hearing banjos and pig squeals.

The amount of substance decreased noticeably, not helped by the fact that it was now in and sometimes obscured by the swampy water and possibly moved with the currents. Finally, she stepped through some tall weeds and stopped when her gaze located a small shack in the distance with a single light or lamp barely illuminating the interior. She doused her lights and pressed forward and when she reached the entrance, she saw a small spot of the substance on the door frame. This logically suggested the end of her trail, and she leaned against the wall and readied herself to break in but hesitated when she heard crying.

She crept cautiously around the side of the shack and found a small space between the planks to peer inside. A man was gagged and tied to a chair and the lone electric lamp flickered beside him. Well, she had her probable cause, at least.

Valerie hurried to the front door, kicked it in, and checked the kitchen and the only other room in the shack before she focused on the man.

"It's okay, you're safe now," she assured him as she removed the gag and drew her knife to cut the ropes. "Can you tell me what happened?"

"I-I don't know," he stammered. "I was walking in the park and o-only blackness and then...I woke up here. Some ghost stood over me and said I was next b-but wouldn't say what I was next for."

"A ghost?" she asked and severed the last binding on his hands. "Are you a specter?"

"I-I guess. I can only see them sometimes but this guy was as clear as day. Can we get out of here before he gets back? He—"

"It's a little late for that, I'm afraid." The victim's next words died in his throat and Valerie spun with her gun ready. She aimed it at a green-hued ghost that had appeared from nowhere with the black substance running over his bones. He had a long gray beard and wore a flannel shirt and jeans along with a look of rage. His glare at Valerie chilled her. "How the hell did you get here, bitch?"

Her only response was to shoot him in the chest and the impact hurled him into the other room. She was about to turn and cut through the ropes around the man's feet but a bellow of fury preempted her attempt. The ghost was already on his feet and now swung a hatchet at her. She ducked instinctively before she dove through him, spun, and fired.

The ghost dodged the shots and flung his weapon, and it embedded itself in the wall above her. He turned to the man who was trying to crawl away and cackled. "Well, it looks like you're starting early, boy!"

Valerie fired again but it was too late. He lunged into the man and disappeared into his body. She stood, aimed at the man, and waited for him to turn and reveal the shimmering, ghostly eyes of someone recently possessed. Confused, she frowned when nothing happened.

In the silence that lasted for several moments, she wondered if the victim was able to fight the possession. He remained utterly motionless until, with no warning, he began to flail violently. His frenzy knocked the lamp over and it shattered, and he pulled his legs free of the chair and broke it in the process.

When she activated the flashlight attachment on her

gun, her eyes widened in disbelief. The man seemed to mutate while she watched. His muscles bulged, his skin turned ashen-gray, and his hands seemed to grow to twice the size while black veins showed through his skin.

When he turned to her, his eyes shined and he grinned wickedly. "Is something wrong, little lady?" he asked, his voice the same as the ghost's now. "You haven't seen something like this before, have you?"

He lunged at her and bulldozed through the door frame. As she fell, she yanked the hatchet off the wall and swung it into his leg, but for all the force she put into it, it seemed to make a mark no bigger than a paper cut. The giant lifted a leg to crush her but she managed to grasp the front doorframe and tucked in as she pulled herself away a second before his leg pounded through the flooring.

Valerie was able to stand and jump down the stairs into the swamp. She opened a small case on her belt to reveal bullets with a silver fog inside. The monstrosity didn't remove his foot from the floor. He merely continued his chase and destroyed the timber along his path.

Calmly, she opened a side compartment on her gun, loaded one of the bullets, and shut it quickly to aim at her adversary. He hurled the hatchet at her again but she simply moved her head and it whistled past before she fired the ether bullet. It shattered as it left the barrel and launched the gray smoke at her target. When it struck the head, the ghost flew out and the body seized up and fell.

She ran to the victim. Ether bullets were meant to be used on recent possessions and should knock the ghost out and free the host without harming them. In this case, however, the man's body began to return to normal but simply continued to wither. The gray skin did not revert to human flesh and began to crack apart. Whatever this ghost had done during the transformation, there was no going back.

"I'm so sorry," she whispered before she focused on the shack and rushed forward to find her quarry.

He had crawled into the original room and his body faded steadily. "Damn you!" He hissed in fury and turned to face her. "You have no idea who you are fucking with!"

"I don't care to know," she responded, her weapon aimed at his head as she took some stygia bindings out. "But many at the precinct would probably love to know what you've been up to these last couple of months."

The ghost looked confused for a moment, then smiled and ended with a weary chuckle. "Months? Try weeks." His laughter grew. "It don't matter. Oblivion is probably better than Hell anyway. And at least I know I can go with you on the list."

"The list? What list? Who are you working for?" she demanded.

He rasped a laugh. "Someone who will bring about one hell of a party soon. He's gonna change the way the entire world works." The ghost snatched one of the broken chair legs and studied the sharp end. "He sees everything we do and he has you now. I know he'll make sure you suffer."

She was ready when he lunged at her and she blasted him in the head and forced him back. He growled and tried again and she fired three shots, all to the chest. The ghost contorted and his body began to shatter and spill his phantasma and the black sludge over the floor.

"I'll be happier in nothingness than you are in life or

death," he said and cackled crazily. "Because death won't be the end for any of you, I promise." His last remains disintegrated and turned into phantasma, and she was left alone in the dark.

The young officer holstered her weapon, walked out of the shack, and took a moment to sit. She wrapped her arms around her legs and drew a shaky breath. When she'd composed herself, she stood and turned her radio on.

"Hello, dispatch? This is Officer Simone. I need a team at my position." She looked at the shack and the decaying body. "Send everyone you can and make it fast."

Valerie signed off and retrieved her phone. It had cracked but she tried to turn it on and scowled at the empty battery icon. She sighed and put it away. The next time she met the out-of-town detectives, she would have something new to share, at least.

CHAPTER TWENTY

Vic looked at the manhole cover while Johnny double-checked a map and used his crystal pendulum to verify the location. The ghost looked at his partner and chuckled dryly. "Do you wanna head into town and get some rain boots? Or are you still hoping you're wrong? It would be the first time for that."

The pendulum swung around a position the young detective had marked on the map and he sighed, put it away, and stood as he closed the map. "Why the hell did it end up here?"

"This is merely the one nearby." His companion gestured to their repaired car. "We have the wheels back so maybe you want to look around more. There could be something better in Baton Rouge."

Johnny frowned at him as he shoved the map into the pocket on the inside of his jacket. "You know that crossing points to the same location aren't that close. We'd be lucky if there was one in Texas or in Arkans—oh. You're screwing with me, aren't you?"

The ghost detective shrugged but his playful smirk betrayed his intentions. "Maybe I'm simply holding out hope." He knelt and took hold of the lid. "But if that is the case, we should probably get moving, shouldn't we?" When he lifted it, the young man looked inside and backed away quickly when the smell hit him.

"I guess we can't wait a couple of days for it to potentially move, can we?" He thought about it for a moment. "Technically, I can pass through any area as long as I 'cross' through it. We can go back to that gas station and try one of their doors—there are cabs in Limbo, right?"

"True, but depending on where we end up, that could cost a chunk of coin. Plus, we don't know where we'd end up on the way back. Probably not too far given our experiments, but if we come through twenty miles away and we gotta get here on foot… Well, we just got the car back. Do you wanna get it towed already?"

Johnny sighed, took his jacket off, and returned to the vehicle to throw it in the back. "They can't smell in Limbo, can they?"

Vic shrugged. "Not normally stuff from the living world, but hey, it might be 'cause it ain't strong enough."

The young detective rolled his sleeves up and shook his head as he began to descend. "Fantastic."

His partner floated behind him and replaced the cover. "Now, when we get down, show some hustle, all right? I don't wanna stay down here any longer than you do."

"Why does it matter to you? It's not like you can get splashed as long as you aren't corporeal."

"True, but I have to stay corporeal to keep this ax in me.

And I have this thing about rats. Oh, and plus, this is Louisiana so there might be 'gators down here."

Johnny retched. "Wait, are you for real?"

Vic laughed and it echoed through the sewers. "Like I said, hustle!" A moment of silence followed. "Wait—what will you use to cross? Unless you wanna dive into the...uh, water, don't you need your jacket?"

The silence stretched on before the young man groaned. "Dammit. I'll be back."

His partner sighed and the sound of a lighter being flicked was heard. "I can't wait for the day you are finally a professional."

"Uh, Vic? I don't think you want to light that down here."

"Why's tha—" The flame flared and there was a sudden bang as Johnny laughed.

When the two finally appeared in Limbo, they were about six blocks away from Big Daddy's and Vic still tried to dust the soot off his skull. "All right, let's get this done. Hopefully, no one claimed it before we got here."

"The odds are probably in our favor," Johnny told him as they walked to the dealer's shop. "From what we heard, every ghost organization and gang in New Orleans is trying to keep it under wraps, including the cops. We didn't hear about any other bounty hunters looking for it."

"Which is odd if you think about it." The ghost undid his jacket and took the ax out of his ribs. "There are always bounty hunters in New Orleans—hell, some set up shop for their entire lives there—but we've heard nothing about their involvement?"

"Maybe it is above their paygrade," Johnny suggested as he pulled the doors open. "Or they are paid off. I'm sure some of them deal with the mobs."

They both greeted the ghost at the door. "Hey, Saul." Vic rested the ax over his shoulder. "Is Angie in?" Saul lowered his newspaper and nodded across the lobby. They waved goodbye as they headed to where Angie was doing her nails. "When did you get those?"

"Do you like 'em?" she asked and held them out smugly. "I had some time off after seeing you two and spent some of it at the parlor. They only cost me a couple of yellow doubloons and they last for decades."

"Well, you have claws now. It certainly fits." She scowled at him as he dropped the ax on her desk. "We have some evidence for a case and are here for the finder's fee."

Angie gawked at the weapon for a moment and adjusted her glasses before she picked it up and examined it. "What is this?" she asked when she noticed the odd phantasma on it. "I ain't seen nothing like this."

"That sounds like it's worth something," Johnny pointed out.

Vic nodded, took his cap off, and scratched his scalp. "A large number of somethings. What do you say, Angie? That was used by a ghost of some kind. Exactly what can't be determined right now but he's at least on the same level as a wraith. He's possibly killed dozens of humans and ghosts alike so far. At least they want this guy turned in, right?"

She studied the ax for a moment longer and set it down.

"I don't know what the hell you boys brought in but it is spooky, I can tell you that."

"And that's coming from a ghost." Johnny's quip drew a chuckle from Vic as he put his cap on.

"I'll look up what this could be worth." She began typing on her keyboard. "Can you give me any more details? Because so far, I could put this as a possible escapee with probable homicides."

The ghost detective frowned. "Well…that sounds like it lowers the price." His frown turned to a scowl when she nodded. "Look, we've fought this joker, some kind of ghost we haven't seen before. That's rare, darling! That has to be worth something."

"I guess you do have proof of that," she conceded and shifted her gaze to the ax and the odd phantasma. "That'll bring in a horde of interested parties so you could probably get a nice score. Let me punch it in. This is New Orleans, right?"

"Correct," Johnny confirmed. She typed again before a buzzer sounded over the speakers. "What was that?"

"I was blocked from my computer," she replied, her voice shocked before it changed to anger. "What in the hell?" As she asked this question, two large ghosts approached and looked at Vic and Johnny.

"Yous the guys looking into that finder's fee?" one asked. They were at least a couple of feet taller than Vic and had the same translucent skin as Dwayne did, which meant they were well fed on stygia. The width and girth of their arms and torsos confirmed that.

"Yeah, we's the guys," the ghost detective responded and fixed them with a calm look. "Why?"

"Big Daddy wants to see ya," the other said and thumbed toward the back. "Come on."

The first guard snatched the ax off Angie's desk and the group moved to the main office as she cried, "Hey, Rico! I need technical support!"

The partners were guided to a door at the back that revealed a set of stairs into the basement. "Let's go," the first guard ordered and pushed Johnny forward onto the steps.

As they descended, he leaned toward his partner. "I can't tell if this is a good thing or not."

"They don't make a good impression, do they?" Vic whispered and glanced over his shoulder at the two large ghosts. "These guys are certainly taken care of better than Saul and most of the others. They must be a couple of Big Daddy's personal guards."

"Something must be going on. Angie was blocked immediately after she put all the info in."

"Then I guess it's a good thing we're heading to the source, ain't it?"

The young detective squinted. "Is it, though? I don't know Big Daddy's exact history, but all these gig dealers were toughs of some kind in life, right? This feels more like a situation where no one will ever see us again."

"They didn't take our weapons, so that's a good sign." The ghost detective nodded ahead at a pair of ornate doors. "I guess we'll find out in a minute."

The partners took a door each, pushed them open, and entered a room that looked like it came out of a mansion. Aside from the black silk walls and plush purple furniture, female ghosts lounged everywhere, all with enough stygia to fill their forms out under scanty clothing.

Their attention was immediately drawn to the large, oak desk in the middle and the figure behind it. As large as both guards put together, he wore a very nice purple suit and smoked a cigar. His skin was dark-purple and he looked at them from under a wide-brimmed black hat and smiled.

"Well, now. Look who we have here—Victor Kane and the good boy Rev. Johnny!" His voice resounded in the room.

The guards pushed them forward and Johnny could feel all eyes on them as they approached the desk.

Big Daddy appeared to become even larger as they moved closer. He beckoned them forward. "Come on in, fellas. It looks like we got things to discuss."

CHAPTER TWENTY-ONE

In front of the large desk were several elevated chairs. Vic floated up with no issue but Johnny was forced to hop, grasp the seat, and pull himself up.

"Would you hurry?" his partner demanded when he was finally high enough to turn and sit properly. "You're embarrassing yourself."

The young detective waved dismissively at him, retrieved the pack of cigarettes, and took one out.

"Hold on there a second," Big Daddy instructed and placed a black box with gold designs on the desktop. "I don't want anyone to leave my office and say I'm not a good host." He opened the box to reveal a dozen cigars, each with a silver stamp on them. "So, do you care for some cigars?"

Vic took a few and the cutter, examined one, and nodded appreciatively.

"Thanks, but are those meant for ghosts?" Johnny asked and lit his cigarette before he handed the lighter to his partner. "I can't smoke them."

"Is that right?" Big Daddy chortled and closed the box. "I've wondered how that works. So revenants can't use supernatural items?"

"More like can't imbibe," the ghost detective corrected and lit the cigar. "He can use my gun and other things. I can't speak for other revenants, but he can't have any food, drink, or anything like that. It makes him vomit. He's tried a few different things in the name of research but is less likely to keep it down and more likely to put himself down if you catch my drift."

The boss laughed along with some of the others in the crowd. He handed the cigar box to a guard, pointed at another box, and told him to bring it to him.

"Well, since I have you gentleman here, I suppose I should tell you why." He took a long drag of his cigar and when his guard brought what he'd asked for, he took it and placed it on the desk. "I saw that you've been doing good in New Orleans. I was born there, you know." He opened the case, smirked, and nodded before he looked at them. "I left when I was grown but it will always have a special place in my heart so I like to keep a watch on what's going on over there."

"Then you should be interested in what we found," Vic replied and took a puff of his cigar. "Right?"

"Oh, certainly, and I am extremely thankful that you looked into it." He flipped the case and presented it to them. Two large sacks of doubloons made Vic's eyes shine and Johnny's enlarge. "This is your finder's fee and something a little extra."

"A little extra?" the young detective asked as his partner dug through the bags. "What's the kick for?"

Big Daddy craned his neck, his smile gone. "Let's go with a request fee for you to stop looking into this matter."

This made Vic look up from his treasure counting. "Why's that?"

The purple ghost clasped his hands together and leaned forward across the desk. His large head dominated their view. "Is it not enough that I asked politely?"

"It certainly could be, but if you care so much about New Orleans, wouldn't you want this taken care of? Especially since your company will probably get a large payday from the officials if you claim the bounty."

Big Daddy's gaze darted toward the ghost detective. "I thank you for looking out for the wellbeing of my company—"

"Well, we do good business here," he interjected.

"And I do indeed care about New Orleans. This is why I and several others on this side have been working with other fine organizations on the other side to deal with this matter."

"And that has worked out fantastically so far," Johnny muttered and the boss's gaze now moved toward him.

"I'll admit, things could be in better shape right now. But having a frenzy and an army of bounty hunters and ghost specialists suddenly swarming the city is not beneficial right now."

The young man scratched his chin. "And why would that be?"

Big Daddy finally leaned back after he'd puffed a large amount of smoke in their faces. "Because it looks like it might be what that bastard wants."

"*That* bastard?" Vic asked as Johnny thought this over.

"It seems like you have a good idea who is causing all this ruckus."

Their host scoffed and knocked the ash of his cigar into the ashtray. "And you don't, detective?"

"We have a theory, but the most we have to go on is a fugitive who was never identified." He closed the bags. "I suppose we could go check the athenaeum for New Orleans residents and what they did in life, but if that bastard somehow made it to Limbo instead of going straight to Hell... Well, the whole point of Limbo is to give second chances. A normal book of life wouldn't mention if he or she was the Axman of New Orleans."

"He wants more power," Johnny muttered and caught their attention. "That's obvious, but he's not getting the power he wants from the normal residents of New Orleans —or at least not as much as he wants."

Big Daddy nodded. "That was a freebie. But what you both should know before you dive into two-bit conspiracy nonsense is that this isn't merely something that mid-level cats like me and the mob are trying to bury. You should think about that. If you fuck up, who gives a damn about what happens to you?"

"So this extra coin"—the ghost detective lifted one of the bags—"is hush money so we look the other way and don't talk."

"That would certainly be something I'd prefer," the boss said flatly, finished his cigar, and stamped it out in the ashtray. "But like I said, there's a little extra request fee."

"Uh-huh." The detectives looked at one another before Vic passed the bags to Johnny as he leaned forward against the desk. "Do you want to give us any other pieces of advice? Like why these high-level figures would be interested in keeping this quiet and who they might be? They must be important people for someone like yourself to say you are merely mid-level."

Big Daddy leaned back and cracked his knuckles, which sounded like small explosives detonating. "Don't let a little humility fool you. I act like a badass because I am one, but there are many ways to reach my level." He opened a drawer and took out another large cigar and a pair of clippers. "And I did it through business savvy, connections, and my bounty hunting career."

He thumbed at some framed photos of a noticeably smaller and alive Big Daddy, a tall and muscular man with dark skin, shaved head, and large guns who held possessed artifacts or stood over the remains of crypto creatures. "Both in life and death, when I was called Firewalker Marsan."

"Because you always took the hottest and most dangerous cases," Vic finished. "You have that poster in reception that tells your story. It also says you came back as a revenant to finish the guy who ended your life."

The boss chuckled and shrugged. "What can I say? It's mostly true with a flourish here and there. People like a good story."

"I agree, and this will be a hell of a story when we catch this guy."

Big Daddy frowned. "Are you still going after him?"

Vic pointed toward Johnny. "I still gotta talk it over with my partner, but we're in this now. You understand as a former bounty hunter. You bail on a gig and while you might live, your rep takes the hit." He put his half-smoked cigar out in the ashtray.

With a sigh, the purple ghost clipped the front of his new cigar. "You are setting yourselves up for all kinds of trouble. And while this is going on, I can't provide you with new cases as long as you keep this up." He looked at the bags he had given them. "And I'll need those."

The ghost detective shrugged and gestured with his head. Johnny frowned and threw the large bags onto the table. "Fine. I look forward to doing business again when we catch this bastard." The young detective dropped down from his seat as his partner floated to him.

"You stir up too much trouble and you will have targets on your head!" Big Daddy warned as he reached for the bags. "Hell, you might have them already."

When he grasped the bags and pulled them forward, he noticed that they seemed lighter than when he'd first picked them up. He tried to open them but they had been tied with a complex knot. Irritated, he tore them both open and scowled. One had a bunched-up map to make it look fuller and an empty sack had been shoved into the other. He looked up and Vic waved at him before he disappeared inside Johnny, who opened the door.

"You bastards!" Big Daddy roared and two guards nearby ran toward the door as it closed. When they threw it open, the partners were gone.

The purple ghost leaned back, lit his cigar, and took a deep drag. He let a funnel of smoke pour out of his mouth before he chuckled and elbowed the guard on his right. "Do you think I played it right?"

"I think you did great," his employee replied with a nod and a smirk.

The boss smiled around the cigar in his mouth. "They'll get the job done—or die trying to at least—and it can't be traced to us. Hopefully, it keeps that wily jackass happy." He shook his head. "You know, it kind of makes me want to get back in the game myself."

"Will you go after the guy too, boss?" the guard asked.

Big Daddy laughed and almost dropped his cigar. "This psycho? Hell no. I'll leave it to the young bloods because us old guys can't seem to catch shit right now."

CHAPTER TWENTY-TWO

When Johnny and Vic arrived in the real world, they walked out of a rather dirty bathroom and took a moment to look behind them with distaste.

"Hey, how did you get in there?" someone asked and they turned to a young, skinny guy in overalls, cap, and gloves who stared angrily at them. "Dammit. Did I forget to lock the door again? The bathroom is for paying customers only!" A toilet flushed and all three looked toward the sound. "What the hell? Dale, are you in there?"

"Yeah, man. Gimme a second!" a voice called as the faucet turned on.

Johnny realized that they were at the gas station, which meant they were about a thirty or forty-minute walk from the car. He looked at the attendant, who had taken his hat off and now scratched his head. "So that's where he's been. Dammit. Is Dale hiring those toots again?"

"Toot?" Vic chuckled. "What's a toot?"

The young detective grimaced and walked away. "Don't worry about it."

Still caught between bewilderment and displeasure, the attendant watched him go before he turned as Dale exited the bathroom and locked it with his key. "Well, at least you're getting ones that look good now," he remarked as he headed toward the gas station. "He could have used a shower though." His colleague stared at him with a look of confusion.

Johnny strode through the tall grass to the car and checked it for marks or signs of entry before he unlocked it and slid inside. He checked his phone and frowned. "Oh, I got a text from Val."

Vic appeared in the passenger's seat. "What does it say?"

He took a moment to read it. "Something happened last night. She's asking us to meet her at the hotel where Annie and Marco are and sent the address."

"It works for me. We need to compare notes anyway." The ghost opened the glove compartment and retrieved an empty sack. "It's always good to have a spare," he said as he began to dump the stolen coins inside. "How much did you manage to take while I distracted him?"

His partner took out a few bundles of cash. "It looks like enough to keep us going as long as we don't make too many big purchases." He flipped through one of the bundles. "I can never get the conversion right."

"Why? It's all colors." Vic held up one with a red jewel in the middle. "The lowest amount starts at white, then yellow, and orange. Green and blue are worth a decent amount, then you got red and purple which is worth a lot. Black jewels are worth the most."

Johnny stretched into the back seat, undid a section in the middle, and took a case out. "I'm aware of that. I mean the conversion when I bring it into the living side and it changes to cash." He opened the case, which contained a few thousand dollars, and packed the extra within. "I mean what it changes to when we cross always seems a little different."

"Eh, sometimes you get lucky and at other times, not so much. I'm not exactly sure how that changes either. Usually, bounty hunters have to exchange doubloons at a topside gig dealer if they get their job in Limbo."

"The perks of being a revenant, I guess." He closed the case and sealed it in its hiding place. "All right, let's head out." He turned the car on and let the engine roar for a moment. "You know, I missed this sound yesterday."

Vic chuckled and cut the end off another cigar as they left the forest and returned to New Orleans.

When they knocked at the door, Valerie checked the peephole before she opened it.

"Finally, It's almost evening," she stated as she let them enter and closed the door behind them. "Where have you been?"

Johnny tossed his go-bag on the bed, fell on it, and waved at Marco and Annie who were seated on the other bed. "We had to deal with some ghost stuff." He pushed his eyepatch up and rubbed his eyes. "Which I suppose applies to almost every day of my life for the last seven or eight years."

"And we had to drive back after going out some ways," Vic continued and pointed at his partner. "Plus the kid needed a shower. I know it sounds frivolous but be glad he took one."

The young officer sat on top of the desk in the room. "Speaking of ghost stuff, I obliterated one last night."

The young detective turned and looked at her. "Wait, what?"

"Yeah, man. It was wild by the sound of it," Marco said as he stretched his arm. "But from what you were saying, you don't think it was our guy?"

Valerie shook her head and took her phone out. "No, but he seems to be working for whoever is." She tossed the device to Johnny and Vic floated closer to see. "The guy I eliminated was Tommy Lynn Sells, a serial killer born in California but who was a drifter. He had victims in Illinois, Texas, Kentucky, and others and was put to death in twenty-fourteen."

"Only seven years ago?" The young detective looked concerned as he handed the phone to his partner and looked at her. "The report said he had some mental illnesses in life that might stop him from being sent straight to Hell but he would be under watch in Limbo. There's no way he could be out of Purgatory by now and he sure as hell wouldn't get a pass to come here."

"Ciro found a way over," Vic reminded him and gave Valerie her phone. "It wouldn't be a shock if other degenerates could do the same. But I have to agree with Johnny when it comes to him. He should still be in Purgatory."

She looked at the murderer's picture again. "I assume that whoever got him out and brought him over is the same guy he seemed to hold in such high regard." She flipped through the pictures. "I followed a trail of phantasma—weird stuff like black goo with a white wispy substance running through it."

"It sounds like what we heard about at the bar," Johnny commented.

The ghost nodded and his eyes narrowed. "And it sounds like the same color as the spirit maniac we've run into who keeps leaving the ax. Did this guy have the same color?"

Valerie shook her head and passed him the phone, which showed a picture of a vial of the substance. "No, he was a normal green color. But he had the stuff running through him somehow. I would say his veins if he had any, but he was mostly skeletal with a light amount of flesh. That wasn't the most terrifying part, though. I think I know what attacked us." She bunched her fists in anger. "He had a hostage in a shack. I tried to cut him loose but he attacked me and then dove into him."

"Possession?" Johnny asked. "Vile guys like that can overwhelm the host. They start to feel their feelings and memories and that can—"

"Worse than that," she interjected. "When he entered him, he...uh, changed—began to transform. His body became bigger, had the eyes of a ghost, and his skin color changed. He probably looked like the being who attacked Marco and Annie would have looked if we could have taken that cloak and hood off before he turned to dust."

"Were you able to save him?" Vic asked and looked up

from the phone to see her shake her head again. "That's a damn shame. I know you tried your best."

"I had ether bullets with me and shot him directly in the head with one. It knocked the ghost from him but...well, the body began to wither."

"Were there any remains or did it turn to dust like the last one?"

She relaxed her fists and looked at them for a moment before she clasped her hands together. "It turned to mush. We recovered most of it and the people in the labs have found traces to confirm that it's human— blood and bone fragments and the like—but no one has ever seen anything like it."

The ghost detective removed his hat and scratched his skull. "From what we've heard, the mafia and some Limbo organizations have tried to deal with this on the quiet. It partially explains why bigger organizations haven't come in, but from the hints we've received, it seems some players involved in this mess are bigger than we have imagined."

"He's also feeding," Johnny told them. "He was killing ghosts before he targeted humans and sucked them dry to empower himself. That's another reason why they are trying to keep this contained. They don't want a horde of powerful bounty hunters both living and dead trying to claim the bounty and fueling this asshole through their efforts."

"At this point, I think I'd prefer it if we did have an army at our back." Valerie groaned. "But I get it and as much as it annoys me, it probably is for the best right now. But the evidence indicates that this is a team or maybe a cult. Some in the precinct want to say this is the end of it, but because I've told them it isn't, they aren't making it public, at least for now."

"When will they give you your hero's medal?" Johnny quipped.

She rolled her eyes and folded her arms. "Honestly, they are pissed about me going in there without backup, along with the fact that I've shown up twice to these incidents and my little adventure at the market got back to them. They want me to lay low for now."

"Typical," Vic muttered, put his hat on again, and shoved his hands into his pockets. "Ah, well. They'll play ball once the shit truly hits the fan. My current guess is whoever is doing this is a demon—or at least trying to be one. If he achieves it, you can bet your ass that every big agency will flock here to take care of it. And while they might, both the Wild Hunt and the Supernatural Exorcism Agency have a habit of sticking around in places they are called to, and that will spook the ghosts who live here and cause some issues for both living and dead."

Marco bit his lip before he looked at the ghost detective. "You said the mafia was looking into this right? Or running the whole thing?"

"More like trying to take care of it and failing, but yeah. Did something spring to mind?"

The young man sighed and ran a hand through his hair. "Man, our family can be such a stereotype at times." He looked at the two partners. "Do you wanna meet a capo?"

CHAPTER TWENTY-THREE

"Capo?" Johnny asked. "What's a capo?"

"A caporegime," Vic elaborated, his attention fully on Marco. "A captain in the mafia and probably the highest rank a man can get without being an underboss or boss."

"If we're lucky, an underboss might be there too," Marco added and looked at Annie when she pulled his sleeve.

"What are you doing, you idiot?" she asked and glared at him. "You know Uncle Gabriele doesn't want us to go anywhere near there."

He shrugged and jerked his shirt out of her grasp. "Hey, if the mafia is trying to take care of this, we need to at least consider talking to him." He pointed at her. "Besides, do you think he doesn't want to know that the same thing he's probably helping to deal with targeted you?"

She frowned, folded her arms, and looked out the window. "What if he isn't there? You can't simply walk in there and not expect them to take issue with that."

"It's better than sending Johnny and Vic in there alone,"

he reasoned and glanced at them. "But I'm probably getting ahead of myself. The short version is that we've had family members in the mob—yeah, shocker—but not our parents or anything. A couple of uncles, great uncles, and a grandfather as far as I know. Most of them are dead but the New Orleans mob is mostly dead guys right now anyway. I can get you in to talk to them directly, assuming you don't have any connections of your own."

Vic shook his head and glanced at Valerie, who shrugged. "We had a few informants over the years but most disappeared, oddly enough."

The young man chuckled, hopped off the bed, and knelt to retrieve something from under it. "I hear that's a bad habit most informants have. Anyway, my Uncle Gabe got whacked about fifteen years ago—he was double-crossed or something but Dad never elaborated. He came back about five years ago and reclaimed his position. One of their joints is a restaurant in Avondale. It serves good food for what merely started as a front."

He took a slim case out and opened it to reveal his bat. "I'm not sure if they'll help you, but telling them what has been happening ought to light a fire under their ass, at least." He looked at Valerie. "Since you are trying to lay low, do you mind keeping an eye on my sister while I escort them?"

"I'm coming too!" Annie declared and stood quickly. "I don't want you to face them alone."

Marco frowned and shook his head. "Come on, Ann. Think about it. If we tell them the guy is after you, they will keep you there for protection, and you or we are roped into their BS while we wait for this thing to be dealt with. I don't want one of the corpses trying to set you up with their still-living nephew or something either." He looked at Vic. "No offense." This merely got a casual shrug and knowing nod from the detective.

"You are still under police protection," Valerie pointed out and looked at the door where a couple of other cops were stationed. "As the non-primary target, Marco might be able to walk around a little more freely but there would be issues with you heading out."

Annie frowned for a moment before she exhaled a long sigh and fell on the bed. "Do we even know why this guy wants me yet?"

Johnny shook his head. "Sorry. Our best guess is that he has identified you as a possible host like the guy Valerie saw."

The young officer hung her head. "That might be the best-case scenario."

Marco swung his bat a couple of times before he rested it over his shoulders. "Well, it was nice to have this reunion for a few minutes but what do you say? Should we get going?"

Vic nodded and looked at Valerie. "Are you all right staying behind?"

She nodded, moved to the chair at the window, and sat. "Yeah. Like I said, I gotta stay for a little while anyway, but make sure to fill me in when you get back."

"Roger," Johnny promised as he stood and retrieved his bag. "Thanks for the toys by the way."

"Be sure to make good use of them," she replied and looked around the room. "Do you see the remote Annie?"

The trio pulled up at an Italian restaurant after a long drive. The sky was bright orange but the blues of evening swept in rapidly. They got out and Marco positioned the bat over his right shoulder. "All right, follow me."

"Do you plan to walk in there with a bat?" Johnny asked as he made sure his gun was out of view. "Won't that raise suspicion?"

"We're going directly to the back," the young man explained as they approached the entrance. "That will probably annoy them more than the bat." He opened one of the doors and stepped inside.

The interior was white with pictures of family and what the young detective assumed were landscapes of Italy or similar settings. The restaurant was packed with tables full of family-style meals, and loud boisterous laughter echoed.

"Hey, what are you doing in here with that?" a hostess asked. Marco ignored her, looked at a set of stairs, and motioned for his companions to follow. He ascended quickly while the hostess called after them to come back and a couple of waiters and some of the diners looked on in confusion or amusement.

At the top of the stairs, they walked down a hall with red walls and more pictures, although these were in nicer frames. At the end of the hall, Marco waltzed up to the double doors, turned the doorknob on one, and threw it open.

"Hey! Is Gabriele Romano here?" he asked a room full

of suited ghosts and a few living men as well. Some drew guns but hesitated when a voice responded.

"Who wants to— Hey, wait a minute!" From behind a curtained-off section of the room, a ghost emerged with almost translucent blue skin and slicked-back black hair with white tips. He was dressed in a black suit and leather shoes and studied the young visitor as a couple more men stepped out behind him with revolvers. He smiled broadly and held his arms open. "Marco! Well, I'll be damned. How are you doing, nephew?"

Marco relaxed a little and gave his uncle a one-handed hug. "I've been all right, Uncle Gabe. How have you been since I last saw you?"

The capo rolled his eyes. "If you had come by a few months back, I would have said things were just peachy. But we've been dealing with a hell'uva headache for a while now."

He nodded and gestured behind him with his thumb. "Trust me, I'm well aware. I brought some friends who are looking into it."

"Friends?" Gabriele asked quizzically and leaned around him to look at the partners. He threw an arm around his nephew and moved him away a few paces. "What the hell are you doing, kid? You know you can't bring strangers into one of our places of business, not unless they are paying customers."

"It's weird hearing someone else being called kid," Johnny commented and glanced at Vic. "Particularly when it isn't coming from you."

"You do know how old most of these guys are, right?"

his partner asked with a smirk as he took another cigar out.

"We'll buy some oysters or something on the way out," Marco offered. "Look. We know about the killer and the fact that the mob is trying to take care of him."

Gabriele peered at Johnny and Vic before he huddled closer to his nephew. "We're only trying to do right by the community, kid. It's nice of you to think about helping your uncle, but we have this under control."

The young man snorted. "Is that right? So you know he came after Annie?"

"What?" the blue ghost roared, released his nephew, and looked around the room. "Annie was attacked? Why the fuck haven't I been told?!" He pointed to one of the living mafiosos. "Tony, where the fuck are the guys who are supposed to keep an ear open in the streets?"

The guard shrugged and remained silent. His boss' rage began to build and his skin darkened and fists trembled to the point where the young detective decided he'd need another hit of stygia soon.

"Look, Uncle Gabe," Marco began and placed a hand on the ghost's shoulder that made him look at him. He pointed to the partners with his bat. "Those guys over there? They protected us when the killer attacked. Hell, they were there because they came to warn us. They are all right and they are trying to find this guy like you and the rest of the family."

Gabriele continued to shake but he studied them for a moment. "Is that right?" He straightened and waved them forward. His fists were still clenched but he put them in his pockets. "So who the hell are you?" He scowled at them. "Are you with the Agency?"

"Not quite." Vic held his hand with the cigar up. "I realize that revelation must be a shock. Do you care for a cigar?"

The capo took one, ran it under his nose, and nodded. "The good stuff. It's hard to get on this side of things." One of his underlings approached with a cutter and lighter, which he took. He snipped the front. "So what are you? How do you two play into this?"

"We're bounty hunters," Johnny explained and decided it was probably best to leave Vic's former occupation out to be safe. "We came here looking for a gig that would pay well and ended up with something far bigger than that."

"Really?" Gabriele lit the cigar. "I have heard that a couple of bounty hunters might be snooping around. Not like that is any big surprise around here." He took a few puffs off the cigar. "Not bad. So you saw this creep and didn't run as far away from this place as quickly as you could? I guess you have some guts and I can respect that, at least." He pointed to Marco. "Thanks for looking after the kids too."

"It's what we do," Vic responded and tipped his hat. "Sir, we aren't here to mess with any of your business but we ran into this guy even before we met your niece and nephew so we're in this now. We paid a visit to Limbo and the rumors are starting to spread there, even with people trying to keep it under wraps. It won't be long before official action is taken, no matter what you do to keep this quiet."

The capo took a long drag from his cigar and let the

smoke billow from his mouth. "Ain't that the truth?" He began to walk to the curtain. "Come here."

The three followed as the two guards parted the drapes and they entered a smaller room with brown walls and golden accents. He sat on a large couch and poured a glass of stygian wine for himself and Vic, one of which the soldiers handed to the ghost detective while the visitors each sat in a chair.

"I suppose a good deed should be answered in kind." He sipped his wine. "We've been on this freak's case since he showed up," he stated. "Every squad we send out to deal with him either can't find him or end up in pieces, drained of their essence. Nasty stuff." He pointed to another guard and gestured at one of the dressers. "We've put considerable leg work in trying to find this guy but he appears in random places."

"We have reason to believe it's multiple guys—bonded ghosts," Vic told him and sipped his wine. His bones brightened from the stygia.

Gabriele nodded. "So have we." The guard returned with a large envelope and handed it to his boss. He opened the seal and dumped the contents on the table in front of him. Johnny took one of the photos of a large black skeleton with white light shining in its eyes and from its body. "We've found out about some kind of fraternity calling themselves the 'cult of the ax.'"

It certainly sounded familiar and the trio looked at each other. Vic was the first to voice their collective thought. "Capo, have you ever heard of the Axman of New Orleans?"

The blue ghost nodded and took another long drag

from his cigar. "Damn right we have. I guess you are up to speed. We don't know if it is the Axman himself or someone claiming to be him, but he plays into this somehow." He exhaled a lazy trail of smoke. "What I can't understand is how he's so powerful, even if it is him. It's not like the guy was Ted Bundy or nothing. Sure, he has some clout down here and maybe in other places, but if he's some kind of vengeful spirit, his power can only be linked to his infamy, right?"

"Not to mention that no one ever worked out who it was officially," Marco added. "That muddies things, right?"

"Typically," Vic agreed. "But the more I learn about the situation, the more I begin to wonder if we're dealing with something that is not exactly—" Jazz music began to play from the room outside, slowed down and filled with static.

"Hey, what the hell?" Gabriele shouted and thumped a hand on the table. "Keep it down in there. I'm in a meeting!"

"It wasn't us boss!" someone shouted. "It turned on by itself."

The capo snorted and leaned back but his eyes narrowed on his guests. Vic's eyes lit up and Johnny and Marco had paled. "Hey, what's wrong with you guys?" He snickered and took another puff. "Have you seen a ghost?"

Downstairs, the first screams shattered the calm.

CHAPTER TWENTY-FOUR

"Get down there!"

"What is that?"

"Boss, boss!"

Many shouts erupted in the room as the doors were thrown open and both ghosts and humans rushed to the first floor.

"What the hell is going on?" Gabriele demanded as Vic, Johnny, and Marco stood hastily.

"I think he's here, Uncle Gabe," his nephew stated, spun his bat, and stepped through the curtains.

"Who's here?" he demanded as Johnny drew his pistol and followed.

"It looks like you don't have to find him," Vic stated and turned to look at him. "He's come to you."

The ghost capo's eyes flared. "You mean—" The detective nodded and Gabriele pointed to one of his guards. "Get me my gun!"

By the time the two young men reached the stairs, guns were already being fired. Johnny peered through the railings between the stairs as the killer's familiar dark outfit was riddled with holes from both physical bullets and phantasma shots. He counted at least seven patrons dead, but they were still hacked corpses so he hadn't started feeding yet.

"What the hell is he doing here?" Marco demanded and tried to push past before his companion yanked him back. "Do you think he's after me?"

"Maybe." He held his pistol up. "Or it could be all that leg work your uncle was talking about. Maybe he simply got tired of that and came to take care of it."

The mafiosos stopped firing when they ran out of bullets. Some began to reload while others watched in dread as the figure turned and stormed toward them.

"*Figlio di puttana!*" Marco gasped as a couple of the mafia soldiers drew knives and attempted to attack him.

One was a ghost, who got an ax stuck in his ribs that the killer used to swing him and hurl him into another who tried to reload. The second was human and he sank his blade into the attacker's neck, only for him to grasp his hand and crush it in his fist before he lifted him. The man screamed in pain as he was pounded into the floor several times.

With a grunt that became a roar, the monster whipped the body around and slung it at some of the mafiosos who stood in a line and knocked them down. He charged into those still standing, took a hatchet out, and threw it up the stairs, where it struck one of the human soldiers in the neck. Blood spurted onto Johnny, Marco, and a couple of other mob soldiers as the killer began his full onslaught. He cleaved through ghost and living alike with his ax, which was now much bigger than he remembered it being before.

The young detective looked at the gun Valerie had given him and his spectral energy flowed into it. "I guess it is time to test this," he muttered and aimed as the killer was about to bring his ax down on a ghost he had trapped under his boot. He fired at the weapon and while the shot didn't break it, the strike jarred it out of the giant's hand. The ghost glowered at him and produced another before Johnny fired a shot to the head and knocked him back a step, which allowed the ghost to stand.

Marco used this opportunity to leap off the stairs. His blue ether coated the bat as he swung it against the side of the killer's head and upended him. He immediately began to beat the monstrosity. Some mobsters joined him with knives, chairs, kicks, and anything they could get hold of or had on them, and a few others fired rounds into the body.

While he was being pummeled and shot, he remained motionless. As Johnny descended the stairs with his gun still trained on him, white light flashed under his hood. "Shit—get back!" he yelled.

The killer uttered a roar that the young detective had never heard from man, beast, or ghost. He lurched up suddenly and flung many of the mobsters aside before he caught hold of two of the ghosts. Their color drained rapidly and flowed into the creature before he flung their forms aside and they burst into pieces that were immediately obliterated, much to the shock of some present.

Marco reared for another swipe, but as he arced into the hit, the being snagged his bat in mid-strike and dragged it out of his hands. He threw it at Johnny, who ducked so it careened into the wall, then grasped the young man by the neck and lifted him high. His captive kicked at him and struggled to free himself to no avail as he studied him. "You are not the one he needs," he intoned, his voice heavy and muffled. "But he could still make use of you."

"Marco!" Johnny yelled and tried to get a shot at the killer's head but the human was in the way. The sound of a gun being loaded and racked preceded a loud blast before the killer's hand was blown off. Startled, the detective looked behind him to where Gabriele and a few more mafia soldiers held shotguns. The capo's gun smoked.

"You gonna come in here, wreck my place of business, kill my men, and attack my nephew?" he asked, racked the shotgun, and grinned. "I would be steaming mad if it weren't for the fact that you saved us considerable work by bringing yourself here for your execution."

Johnny pulled Marco away and handed him his bat as the giant looked at the new threat. He didn't respond and simply retrieved the severed hand, positioned it where it belonged, and moved his fingers after only a couple of seconds. When he extended the arm, his ax flew to him and he hefted it in both hands as he began to march forward.

"Finish this idiot off, boys!" Gabriele ordered and he, his personal guard, Vic, Johnny, and every mobster still able to fire a gun complied. The normal machinegun and pistol shots did about as well as they had done previously, but the shotguns had an effect. Each blast made the killer halt or forced him back a step or two. His clothes were slowly shredded to reveal dark-gray skin beneath.

When the flesh was stripped away, it revealed a black skeleton with wisps of white seeping from the bullet wounds. The killer sliced into a couple of mobsters who came too close before he bellowed again, swung the blade, and arced it into the floor. A massive crack formed and generated a force wave that thrust back ghost and human alike.

Johnny collided with a box one of the soldiers brought down and looked inside to see explosives. "Did you plan to blow this place?" he asked Gabriele as he pushed to his feet.

"As a last resort," the capo replied as he selected shotgun ammo that was white with black rings and loaded his gun. "I have both real stuff and ethereal. Which do you think works?"

The young detective fumbled in his pocket for the ether barrier device. "Probably both. Get everyone out and we'll blow this asshole to Hell!" The mobster ghost saw the device and nodded as Johnny looked at Vic. He tossed him one of the live grenades and took one of the ether ones before he kicked the box over. The contents tumbled all around the restaurant.

Gabriele helped Marco out of the building while the other guards with shotguns kept the killer at bay. As soon as the last few were at the door, the two partners pulled the pins and lobbed them inside before they ran out. Johnny placed the device on the closed doors and activated it to create a barrier around the restaurant.

Everyone retreated when they saw the killer stride toward the doors. He tried to open one but was stopped by the blockade. They kept their guns trained on him as he began to batter the barrier with his ax and cracks formed. Fortunately, the grenades detonated and set off all the others in the restaurant. Both fiery explosions and bursts of green ethereal energy erupted and consumed him and the restaurant as the barrier broke.

Everyone in the parking lot fell prone to dodge the explosion and shrapnel, which was now coated in the ethereal energy that could have left the ghosts as screwed as the humans.

They stared at the crumbling restaurant, where smoke billowed with hints of green wisps entwined with it. Gabriele laughed, then sighed. "It's a damn shame. That place has been up for decades." He sighed again and looked at Vic. "But we got that son of a bitch, right?"

The ghost detective nodded. "I doubt he was the mastermind, though."

With a shrug, the capo leaned his shotgun against his shoulder. "We'll get him too. At least there is one less of those bastards running—"

"Boss!" one of the soldiers shouted and pointed at the ruins. A dark figure emerged from the smoke, tall and skeletal. A white mist emanated from him and he held what appeared to be a corpse in each hand.

"No way," Marco muttered, his eyes wide.

"Are you kidding me?" Johnny roared and looked at the capo, whose lights had shrunk in his eyes.

"*Diavolo.*"

CHAPTER TWENTY-FIVE

"Hey, wait—go back." Annie requested as they flipped through channels.

"To what?" Val asked and began to reverse the sequence.

"The news. I thought I saw something." She leaned forward on the bed when her companion found the correct channel and they both watched the video from a helicopter feed of a burning building and a dozen people in the parking lot. To specters like them, the couple of dozen ghosts that flickered occasionally were identifiable if not as clearly visible as they would be in a real-time scenario.

"We are at Luca's Italian Cuisine where there has been pandemonium this evening," the announcer began. "Terrified customers and staff had fled the building minutes before the restaurant blew sky high in a fiery blaze. Some other figures can be seen on the ground below. What has caused this calamity is not yet known but the police are on the way. According to our sources, the supernatural department is involved."

Valerie leaned closer, almost out of her chair. "Don't tell me that's—"

"Oh no," Annie whispered as a figure emerged from the smoke.

A bright light shined on Johnny and Marco and they looked up briefly at a helicopter. Police sirens wailed in the distance. "Well, I guess there's no way to keep this quiet now."

"That's no longer in our hands, kid!" Vic said as he pointed his gun at the figure. "He doesn't care about keeping a low profile either."

"Boss, the cops are here!" one of the mafia soldiers reported but Gabriele was too busy looking at the killer to reply.

The being growled as he sank his skeletal fingers into the charred flesh of the corpses. White phantasma seeped into him, accompanied by faint screams. "Is that their souls?" Johnny asked and looked at Vic. "If they were already dead, they should be in Limbo by now."

"It looks like he found a way to trap the souls," his partner surmised and the idea brought a feeling of dread. He pointed his pistol at the killer. "Why are we standing around? Eliminate him before he has a chance to get back to fighting shape!"

He fired his revolver and the young detective followed suit. The other mobsters joined in and Gabriele snapped out of his stupor and fired on the monster as he advanced. Each shot seemed to affect the killer this time, but as he finished draining the corpses and flung them to the side, his skin began to grow again and the lights in his eyes shined brighter.

The capo soon ran out of ammo and he hurled the shotgun at the monster before he yelled, "Fucking bastard!"

Marco ran forward and pulled him back. "Uncle Gabe, come on! Let the cops deal with this. Everyone is running out of shots."

"They had better." He seethed but returned to his cohorts. "What are we paying them for otherwise?"

Almost a dozen cop cars arrived along with two trucks. Many of the cops exited and aimed their pistols and rifles at the monster while others opened the back of the trucks and began to take a large device out of each one.

"Get down on the ground!" a voice ordered over a megaphone. "We will open fire if you do not comply."

"Obliterate that asshole," Gabriele demanded. "He's one of the killers who has been sucking everyone dry."

"Get the cannon set up!" one of the officers shouted. A stationary gun with a large barrel and wires running through it was positioned at the back of one of the trucks and another was quickly unloaded from a second vehicle.

"That looks like something the Agency would use," Johnny mentioned as a stream of ether was pumped into the cannon.

"I guess the tech is starting to trickle down," Vic replied. "We need to get back, kid. He's juiced up again." The killer had regained most of his flesh. When he extended his hand, his ax crashed through the debris and flew into it. He lifted it and roared as a dark-green glow surrounded it.

"Ah, hell—get away!" the ghost detective shouted and

he, Johnny, Marco, and the mobsters scattered quickly. The cops were unaware and began to fire as the weapon impacted the pavement. Cracks splintered through the entire parking lot, flipped a few cars, and hurled all of the officers back.

He surged into a charge and swung his ax wildly as the cops began to fire on him again. Their weapons seemed to have more punch but the being was in a blood frenzy now. He hacked through a car behind which two cops hunkered and sliced one of them as well before he caught hold of the other, snapped his neck, and drained his soul.

"He's repairing himself!" Johnny shouted. "They aren't putting him down. All this is doing is revving him up."

"Dammit!" Gabriele looked at one of the officers in charge. "Get it done! Where are those cannons?" The first was crushed under one of the cars and the other was flipped, but the cables and wiring were still intact. "Get it going. Your peashooters won't do jackshit." He dashed to the cannon and tried to right it himself but cried out in surprise and pain when he jumped back from it and saw dark markings on his skin. "What the hell?"

"It's pumping with ether!" Vic exclaimed. "We can't touch it without it burning us."

Marco hit Johnny on the shoulder. "We got it!" The two young men ran to the weapon as the officers continued to fight—or perhaps more accurately distract—the killer, who hacked through them in a frenzy. They flipped the cannon and found a cop pushing to his knees. "Hey, do you know how this thing works?"

He nodded as they helped him to his feet. "Yeah, it's almost ready." When he moved behind the weapon and flipped a switch, it began to hum as the ether coursed inside. "It's warming up."

"Warming up?" Johnny yelped and they looked at the killer, who advanced relentlessly. "You have thirty seconds at best—fire!"

The cop tried to move the cannon to aim at their adversary but it only turned part way. "It's jammed!" he shouted and tried to push it more to the left. "I can't move it."

Johnny and Marco joined him and pushed against the head to shift it slowly into position. The frenzied monster was now only a few yards away. "Fire, dammit!"

Without argument, the cop hit the trippers and a large discharge of ether, phantasma, and spectral energy launched from the cannon, a cocktail of supernatural devastation. The target roared and arced his ax in defiance. The two young men jumped away and the cannon blast caught him dead on. An eruption of light spread around him, so powerful that Vic and Gabriele leapt aside to avoid it.

When the young detective rolled over, he grimaced at the body of the cop who had fired, his head split open and bleeding on the ground. He focused on the killer. His flesh was gone and he stood motionless, merely a black skeleton again with no lights in his eyes.

"Is it done?" Marco asked and strained to push himself up. "Did he finally croak?"

"He's not moving," he replied cautiously and stood slowly. "He's still in one piece, though." In the next moment, he noticed wisps of white drifting off the officer and toward the killer. Each traveled up his body. "No."

The lights in the ghost's eyes began to flicker and he

turned his skeletal head toward Marco and uttered a growl that sounded like a low roar coming from a dark pit.

"The cannon!" the young man shouted and pointed to the weapon that was now bisected and from which ether leaked steadily. "It's destroyed."

Gabriele looked at the large cable that funneled ether into the device. It was still functional. "Take the kid and get out of here!" he said and looked at Vic before he scowled at the burns on his arm. "I'll finish this bastard off."

"Uncle Gabe, what are you gonna do?" Marco asked and tried to walk forward. Johnny stopped him but he fought against his hold. "Get off me!"

"You get out of here, kid!" the ghost capo instructed as he drew a switchblade and ran to the cable. "Finish the fight for me, all right?"

Vic rushed closer and helped the young detective pull Marco away and to their car at the far end of the parking lot. Gabriele cut the cable and let the ether pour out and burn his ghostly form as he rushed to the killer, who moved slowly toward them. The blue ghost thrust the blade into his adversary's jaw and pried it open before he forced the cable down his throat. "Feed on this you, *pezzo di merda!*" The ether poured into the brute but the cable ruptured and continued to burn and melt the capo's form.

When the monster drove his ax into his chest, he hissed in pain but he did not let go. "I'll see you in Hell and continue to beat your ass for fucking with my family!" he promised. The ether began to pour out of the killer and rend his skin before he uttered a final roar and his body exploded. Gabriele disappeared in the blast as Johnny, Vic, and Marco drove away. The young man looked back with grief and regret.

CHAPTER TWENTY-SIX

The women recognized the voices outside the hotel room door.

"They're back," Annie said as her companion stood. "But it sounds like the guards have stopped them for some reason."

"You're right," the officer agreed and checked the peephole. "I wonder wh—oh." She undid the lock hastily and opened the door. Outside, the two young men leaned on one another, their clothes bloody and cuts and bruising evident on their faces. The guards were baffled and looked at Valerie, who flashed her badge and nodded. "Come on in guys, you look like you could use some rest."

"Thanks, Val." Marco's voice was hoarse and he and Johnny wobbled in. The young detective placed him on one of the beds before he collapsed in a chair. Vic floated out of his body and stretched his arms.

"I had to help get them up here from the parking lot." He glanced at the news on the TV. "So you are up to speed?"

"Mostly." Valerie sat in a chair across from Johnny, reached under it for a first aid kit, and scooched the chair closer to him. "It seems the cops got there a little late. What happened?"

"I don't know how he found us or why he was even there." Johnny took his jacket and shirt off and showed her the wounds on his chest and shoulders. "Dammit. The old wound is bloody again. Anyway, we were talking to Gabriele and suddenly, that murky jazz starts playing again and the next thing we know, the restaurant was under siege by that bastard."

"His ax was bigger," Marco muttered as Annie tended to him. "It looked like something that masked hockey dude would use if he was in Lord of the Rings." He caught his sister's hand and looked at her. "Annie...I'm sorry, but I think Uncle Gabe died taking him out."

She took his hand in hers. "I know, Marco. We saw the blast go off onscreen before it cut for a while." She squeezed his hand and pursed her lips. "Is he gone for good or..."

They both looked at Vic, who opened the door to the patio. "I wish I could tell you. An explosion of ether like that...well, it is possible it simply blew his body up." He took the pack of cigarettes and the last cigar out, then placed the latter on the table as he opened the top of the pack. "He could eventually reform in Limbo if a keeper gets to him in time."

"Keeper?" Marco questioned. "What's that?"

Johnny winced as Valerie applied some alcohol to one of his open wounds. "One of the big boys or girls in Limbo," he explained. "They keep an eye on both the living and dead and make sure nothing is screwing with the system." She placed some gauze over the wound and he held it down. "I haven't seen it myself but sometimes, they can intervene and save a soul or be bargained with to do so."

"Can we get in touch with one?" Marco asked. "Even only to see if my uncle can be saved."

After lighting his cigarette, Vic closed the lighter and took a drag. "It's not easy to get in touch with a keeper unless they want to find you or you have something they want or are in the mood for a laugh." The smoke poured out of his skull. "There is also a chance your uncle was simply blown back into Limbo. He had enough stygia to give him more defense against ether than a normal ghost, but if it blew all that away, he would immediately be pulled back. He might have to serve some time in Purgatory, but at least he wouldn't be obliterated."

The siblings nodded. "Damn, now I wish I had spent more time with the geezer." Marco sighed and stood but his sister tried to keep him down. "I'm fine, Annie. I'll patch myself up but I need to shower." He rolled his shoulders and sighed again. "Hopefully, our parents didn't see the news. We don't need them to worry."

Annie sighed and rubbed her head. "Tell me, is it over now?" She looked at Vic. "Was that the real one?"

He shook his head. "I doubt it. He managed to get hold of Marco for a brief moment and said he wasn't the right one but that he would do."

"The right one?" she asked as her brother entered the bathroom. "Do you think he was talking about me?"

Johnny helped bandage the gauze in place. "Probably.

Have you been able to think of any reason why they would be so obsessed with you?"

The woman frowned. "Not off the top of my head."

"They seem to be on the lookout for a specific kind of specter," Valerie commented and handed Johnny a small bottle of whiskey from the mini bar. When he looked quizzically at her, she pointed to a large gash on his arm before she brandished a needle and thread. "What they are specifically looking for in them I'm not sure yet, but they appear to need them to do their transformation."

The young detective unscrewed the cap on the bottle and swallowed it in one gulp. "Still, they seem fixated on her specifically. Do you think she is better...uh, material?"

She threaded the needle. "There is probably a better way to say that but it could be. We don't seem to know these guys' endgame and that is starting to get to me."

"Well, we need to try something different," Vic muttered, finished his cigarette, and flicked it over the balcony. "Because these guys keep coming and they are getting stronger. We need to get some stronger weapons just in case, and after you finished getting patched up, I say we head to Carnivale and see what the reaction is over there."

"Yeah, sure," Johnny said hesitantly, his focus on the needle as Valerie prepared to stitch him. "Do you have any other suggestions?"

There was a knock at the door and some conversation behind it. "If that is who I think it is, she may have another option." The officer looked at Vic. "Here, finish him for me, would you?" The ghost shrugged and floated forward to take the needle and thread as she stood and moved to the door.

"Hold still, kid," he muttered and leaned closer. "I might be a little shaky after all that chaos earlier."

"Uh...Val, I can wait," the young detective whined as she turned the doorknob.

When she opened the door, she told the guards it was fine and ushered a woman in. She had tanned skin and was dressed in a long red jacket and a red wide-brimmed hat. Her long black hair offset white earrings in the shape of fangs or claws and she carried a striped satchel. She and Valerie greeted each other warmly as they entered the main room. "Guys, meet Aiyana Baptiste, a friend of mine."

"Good evening." She glanced at Johnny and noticed his wounds. "It seems you weren't exaggerating about the severity of the situation."

The young officer shook her head. "Nope. Some shit went down while you were on the way here."

Johnny was struck by her features. She was quite beautiful but also had something emanating from her he could best describe as a glow. Although clearly a specter, she was something else as well. A stab of pain snapped him out of his daze. "Ow!" He yelped and glared at his partner. "This is supposed to heal me, not hurt."

"Sometimes, it hurts to heal, kid," Vic replied calmly and continued his stitch work. "And don't jump like that. I'm more liable to skewer you."

Aiyana approached and knelt beside them. "Pardon me if this is a little forward." She rummaged in her satchel and took a small container out. "But this is a salve I made. You still have some cuts and bruises and it should help."

The young detective took it. "I appreciate it. My name's Johnny and this is my partner Vic Kane." He unscrewed the lid and sniffed the contents, and his eyes widened as he stifled a cough. "That's strong, lady."

"It might burn a little when you apply it," she warned him with a smile. "But as your partner said, it sometimes hurts to heal."

"See? Good advice." Vic chortled as he dug in the first aid box, took a pair of scissors out, and cut the thread. "Did you bring a change of clothes in your go-bag?"

Johnny nodded. He took a small dollop of the salve, placed it on one of his wounds, and immediately hissed in surprise and pain. "Y-yeah... W-wow, that's a...uh, fresh." He rubbed the salve gently into the injury and noticed that the ends of the wound were already beginning to scab over. "What the... This stuff works unnaturally fast."

"It's not entirely natural," Aiyana confirmed. "I'm a shaman by trade. Valerie called me in to help with the investigation and offer my knowledge and abilities."

"A fresh pair of eyes certainly couldn't hurt." Vic proffered his hand. "I'm glad to have you on board."

She nodded and shook his hand. "I hope I can help. I had hoped to be brought on earlier but the police didn't want any outside help so technically, I'll be working with you."

The ghost chuckled and glanced at Valerie. "Smart move, Val."

She shrugged and nodded. "Will you head to the bar now?"

He looked at Johnny as the shower turned off. "Let the kid dunk his head and change, then we'll be off."

"That sounds good." Her phone buzzed and she retrieved it and looked at the message. "We'll probably have to meet tomorrow. They are sending in extra security for the night as a precaution given what happened earlier."

"We'll meet for breakfast," Vic suggested and lobbed his partner's bag at him. "New girl, we're heading to a ghost bar. Do you wanna come?"

Aiyana nodded. "Sure thing. We can trade information on the way."

He clapped briskly. "A go-getter I like that. Like a young version of me."

The young detective stood and headed to the bathroom as Marco came out. "Not really. She doesn't strike me as an alcoholic," he muttered as he stepped inside.

His partner rolled his eyes. "Wise ass," he retorted as the door closed.

CHAPTER TWENTY-SEVEN

Johnny, Vic, and Aiyana were in the car and on their way to Carnivale. "So, Aiyana, tell us about yourself," Johnny said and glanced at her. "I've heard about shamans but never had the chance to work with one."

She dug in her satchel as she replied. "It depends on the tribe, but the numbers of shaman or medicine men dwindled over the centuries, at least until the Veil between humans and spirits opened during the later half of the nineteenth century."

Vic chuckled from the back. "Yeah, they probably became quite in vogue when the breathers threw everything they could at ghosts when that first happened. Druids, witches, and hell, even witch doctors came back in abundance. It must have been a blast."

"Indeed. I've worked with a couple of witches in my travels. Exorcists too, and ghost bounty hunters."

She took a small object out that appeared to be a white trinket of some kind made of carved wood with etchings in it. "What's that?" Johnny asked.

"This is one of my totems," she explained and placed it on the front of the car. "Shamans, witches, druids, and everyone who is able to tap into the power of the spirits are grouped together and called...well, spirit callers. We share some traits, runes, and old phrases that hold power over spirits, but we also have abilities that make us unique. For us shamans, that would be our totems." She held her palm up, closed her eyes, and made a sing-song hum under her breath. The etching on the totem glowed momentarily and a ball of light appeared in front of the car.

"Whoa—hey, what's going on?" Johnny asked and leaned forward to look at it. Although bright, he didn't feel his eyes straining as he focused.

"A demonstration," she explained with a giggle. "This is a spirit guide, one of the more simple totems I can create. It helps me track ghosts although in this case, it is pointless since you already know where to go and I have the general idea of the area even though I haven't been there person-ally before now. But if I have something from the ghost I'm tracking—a piece of their clothes or phantasma—I can put it on the totem and it can find them." She closed her eyes again, snatched the totem, and hummed and the orb disappeared.

"Spirit guide? How do you make something like that?" Vic asked. "What is it made of? Phantasma?"

"It is made of the skills of spirits." She put the totem away. "I suppose that is a little vague for you. We are taught to treat spirits—ghosts as you are more familiar with—differently. You could say that this guide is made from the phantasma of a ghost, but it is better to say that the phantasma used to make it is the essence of that ghost's skills, a tracker in this case."

"That's wild," Johnny said in amazement and returned his gaze hastily to the road. "And I thought my ability was something special. But you shamans can learn these skills? Any of those…uh, spirit callers can?"

She shook her head. "We can be taught to some extent, but there is both the issue of having the skill and the dedication to do so. I cannot speak for the other callers but for shamans, it is having a close connection to the spirits we commune with, formerly human, animal, and elements."

"Animal and elements?" Vic asked thoughtfully. "I do see animal ghosts, although they are rare, but elements? They don't have a life to speak of."

Aiyana nodded. "True, perhaps not in the conventional sense. But that is why we think of ghosts as a whole as spirits. They are the essence of what they formerly were and that can change. The elements were worshiped by many cultures. Who is to say that does not have some effect on them in the realm of spirits?"

He shrugged. "I guess I can kind of see that but to be honest, with how much people like animated chicks and video game characters, I hope to not run into anything like that."

"They are liked, not worshiped," she clarified but paused for a moment to think it over. "Although perhaps it would be cute to see that cartoon bear from my childhood."

The car began to slow. "Well, before we get too far into that idea, we're here." Johnny pointed out the window as Vic straightened and looked out. "Fewer ghosts are walking around now," he continued. "I know it's nighttime but—"

"That makes it more worrisome," his partner stated and tried to peer into some of the stores. "Ghosts are usually more comfortable running around at night."

"Is that the bar?" Aiyana asked and pointed to the lights in the windows. "It still seems to be busy."

"The band is certainly in full swing," Johnny agreed and glanced at Vic. "Maybe most of the ghosts are in there."

"Drinking and partying their worries away?" the ghost detective asked and nodded as two ghosts entered. "That's certainly normal given the situation. Come on. Let's take a look and see if Romeo has anything new."

Johnny nodded and turned the car off, then locked it behind them before they headed inside.

The bar was certainly still packed but there was a new wrinkle. "Look at the restrooms," the young detective yelled over the music as he nodded at the large crowd gathered in front of the doors. "It's not like ghosts get the runs."

"No kidding," his partner muttered and stepped forward when he located their contact. "Romeo's at the bar. Let's go say hi." The other two followed him and he sat and waved at the bar owner. "Hello again, Romeo." He jerked a thumb toward the group at the restrooms. "Did you get a bad batch of beer?"

With a sigh, the orange ghost rested his large hands on the bar. "They are jumping ship," he explained. "The ferryman's portal is gonna move soon. This one has been here for a few months and most don't know when the next one will appear nearby. The closest one to here is in Greensburg."

"Something tells me that will be a popular destination soon for the ghost tourists," Vic joked. He folded his arms and looked around. "Word travels fast. I guess this has to do with the attack on the mob?"

Romeo nodded. "No one had to send a messenger. Most saw it on the news. That was only part of the mob, sure, but for this guy to attack one of their places of business openly? He's not creeping around anymore. Whatever he's looking for, he wants it bad."

"And most of them think he's gunning for them?" Johnny asked as ghosts entered the restroom and didn't return.

"I think most simply don't wanna take the chance," the proprietor reasoned. "I don't blame them. Usually, ghosts don't have nothing to fear unless they cross the mob or some psycho breather with an ether weapon and a grudge. But this guy is a maniac and has already proven that he doesn't have a problem chopping ghosts."

"Guys, plural, by the look of things," the ghost detective corrected. "I know it's only been about a day and a half, but have any of the panicked masses given you something interesting to pass along?"

Romeo opened his mouth to speak but was interrupted by a drunk down the bar. "This is no man...no simple ghost!" he shouted and his words swung between loud and soft. "Do you think this is a wraith or a demon? I say it's worse."

He stumbled off his chair and shambled toward them as the group and few onlookers focused on him. "This must be the work of the devil himself or perhaps one of those demigods—those who don't care about ghosts or humans as long as they get their fill of…hic!" He leaned against the bar and tried to take a bottle from behind the counter before Romeo grasped his hand.

"I think you've had enough," the owner warned.

"Demigods?" Aiyana frowned. "What is he referring to?"

"Probably a keeper of some kind," Johnny suggested and scrutinized the man's clothing. "The guy looks older than Vic. Keepers were generally thought to be demigods or something similar in the early twentieth century. It makes sense since the ones we know of were worshiped as such."

"It's only a drunkard's babbling," Vic muttered. "Like I told the others at the hotel, keepers aren't only known for making deals—although some do, I suppose, for their personal kicks. But I can't imagine any of them would— Are you shitting me?" He glared out the window.

"What?" The young detective followed his focus. Rain now poured down, the winds were picking up, and a radio behind the bar began to play the telltale distorted jazz that heralded the Axman. "This has seriously been the worst damn night."

The two partners drew their guns from their coats while those in the bar gaped at a dark figure behind the door.

CHAPTER TWENTY-EIGHT

The doors were thrown open. Ghosts gasped and some drew weapons, while others vanished through the walls. The dark figure walked in and Johnny noticed an immediate change from the monster he had grown accustomed to seeing. This figure was not large. Despite the large coat and hood covering him, he could tell that he was scrawny and almost emaciated and walked like he had been on the move for days, his steps slow on legs that trembled visibly.

The mood in the room went from shock to panic and confusion. This did not seem to be the same killer from the news and attacks, so was it some kind of gimmick or trick? The young detective began to wonder if this was a new ploy, maybe to lure them closer so he could suck their souls out or disembowel them with razor-sharp claws hidden in his sleeves. As if he had sensed his thought, the figure rested a hand on the table to reveal a skeletal hand with missing fingers before he tried to take another step. He fell and almost flipped the table onto himself where he sprawled on the floor.

If it was a ruse, this was a committed actor.

Vic was the first to move closer. Johnny tried to stop him but Aiyana stepped forward as well and he assumed they intended to try to help the wounded potential psycho. He joined them and Romeo came out from behind the bar and followed, along with a few curious onlookers, including a couple of mobsters with their weapons drawn.

As the ghost detective knelt and flipped the body, they heard a crackling sound like the figure was a heavy smoker and tried to catch his breath after a long run. He removed the hood and startled a few members of the group.

It was a human—or at least humanoid—face but his pale-gray skin was sunken and his eyes were almost black voids except for a thin circle of white along the edges. He raised his head and focused on the group around him. "This...this is the Carnivale, right?" he wheezed, his voice weak and nasally.

"Yeah, it is," Romeo answered and folded his arms. "What the hell happened to you?"

The man let his head fall on the floor and laughed wearily. "I told him...I told him I could make it!" His voice turned to a growl as he closed his eyes and frowned in anger. "Dammit, the greedy bastard simply couldn't wait." He raised his hand as if to pound it into the floor but after he'd lifted it only a few inches, it seemed to fall of its own accord. "He didn't want partners and not even goons. We were backup supplies, after all."

"What are you talking about?" Vic asked. He unbuttoned the top of the jacket and opened it to reveal not only physical wounds on the body but a disturbing glow beneath. "What the hell is wrong with you?"

The man looked wearily at his chest. "He said he was tired of our incompetence and needed to keep the pot full but kept running out of power. We didn't do enough and didn't get enough life out of this city." He laughed but it turned to a pained scowl. "What the hell. I was here for a good time and a little slaughter but by God, I didn't expect it to be this much. This is actual work."

"It looks like he was here to kill," Johnny commented as he stood and put his gun away, "but didn't make it in time. Lucky us."

Aiyana produced a white totem with a flower-shaped marking on it. She placed it on the killer's chest. "This should stabilize him so he doesn't fade away before we get our answers." It lit up and directed white energy into the ghost, but her eyes widened as the energy grew brighter and she pulled it away. "What?"

"Is something wrong?" Vic asked and glanced at her. "I can't say I know if that was good or bad as I'm not familiar with those items."

She gaped at the totem as it began to decay and fall apart in her hands. "That should have healed him but it was like his body simply absorbed the phantasma and chewed through it." She dragged her attention to the injured body. "And no healing was accomplished."

The man laughed dryly. "All you did was feed him a little more," he explained. "I'm already done for. Whether this is Oblivion or my ticket back to Hell, who knows?"

"Back to Hell?" one of the ghosts behind them asked.

"Wait—is he saying he escaped?" Romeo asked in disbelief.

"I had time off for good behavior." He chortled, then

coughed as dark patches appeared on his face and chest. "Well, good behavior to my boss. But he's pissed off with me now."

Vic caught him by the throat, lifted him, and held his gun under his chin. "The guy who hired you is able to pull you bastards out of the furnace?" he demanded. "How many?"

The man looked away for a moment while he counted in his head. "There were at least a dozen of us at first. Now…only scraps, I think. I'm not sure how many are left. Probably only him and his pet." His gaze focused on the ghost detective. "Oh, and Patrick. He was sent to a restaurant outside the city. You might wanna check the news."

"We were the news," Johnny told him. "He's been taken care of."

"Pat got zapped?" he asked and his eyes widened for a moment. "Well, I'll be damned. I guess that's why he suddenly turned so antsy."

"Stop talking in circles, dumbass." Vic glared at him, aimed his revolver at one of his hands, and fired. "If you are dying, I can make sure you feel much more pain before you go if you don't give us answers."

The man raised his hand and peered at the hole in it. "The thing is, I didn't even feel that." He lowered it and smirked. "I guess I still have some of the benefits." He frowned and looked at his chest and his wounds that had now begun to bleed profusely, evidence of the human body he had almost completely possessed. "Well, shit. I'm still dying, though."

"Adrian, get the mop, dammit!" Romeo yelled and one of the employees nodded and disappeared into the back.

The ghost detective frowned and positioned the barrel of the gun against the killer's temple. "Fine, then. Here's a new offer. You tell us what we want to know and I make this quick. You'll probably have a better chance of being obliterated that way and it's better than going back to Hell, ain't it?"

"Well...Hell ain't so bad." He looked at the weapon for a moment. "Sure, the torture ain't comfortable and the digs are spartan." He shrugged and made an effort to smile. "But when you are obliterated, you're gone for good. At least in Hell, I have a chance to come back again as I explained." He drew a wheezing breath. "But I don't think I'll get that lucky. I'll probably not go to Hell or be obliterated. I'm not that lucky."

"Lucky?" Aiyana asked. "What is worse than Hell?"

"Hell ain't no picnic, that's for sure," he agreed and closed his jacket. "I'll try to not stain your nice floors." He looked at the ghost detective. "At least I know what to expect in Hell. When I die now...well, that master of his will probably claim my rotting soul."

"Master?" Vic looked at Johnny and his expression suggested that he didn't like the fact that a new wrinkle had developed. "What master? Yours or your boss'?"

"My boss' boss," he explained. The dark spots on his face grew noticeably. "I barely had love for that bastard when I worked with him—damn slave driver he is—and sure as hell don't care for him now." He rested his head on the floor. "But I have to say, the guy above him—or at least working with him—is a creepy bastard. I killed ten people in life and was labeled a psychotic. Imagine who I'm talking about."

"I'd prefer it if you simply spell it out." Vic grunted impatiently. "If you wanna get back at these guys...well, that's what we're here to do."

"I can't help you much. My boss didn't tell the jobbers his ultimate plan, only his pet and a couple of the early opportunists. I came fairly late to the party." His eyes whitened gradually. "I don't even know his name but he was a big deal around here for a time. They called him the Axman of New Orleans."

"So did we," Johnny replied, relieved that they had found one thing out after all. "What can you tell us about his boss?"

The man coughed and wheezed. "He ain't no simple ghost," he stated and looked around the room. "He's something far greater—something with powers we can never hope to have. He's a keeper."

"A keeper?" Vic gasped. "You're pulling my leg. There is no way a keeper would be involved in something like this. They might bend the rules from time to time but they wouldn't do something like this, not when their punishments are way worse than what we have to deal with."

"I know, right?" He laughed and dark ooze seeped from his mouth. "It's wild but it's true. I only caught a glimpse of him once. He's a weird bastard. One second he's yelling so loud you'd think the entire country could hear it and threatening to destroy everything and the next, he's cracking jokes and demanding dinner. I didn't get a good look at him. He's always covered in darkness of some kind, maybe because I wasn't connected to him like the boss."

Suddenly, he thrust his arm out and caught Vic by the collar. Johnny drew his gun again and everyone else with a weapon trained them on him as he pulled the ghost detective closer. "If you truly want to end this, you gotta make a decision now. You need to decide whether taking him out is worth whatever the hell you think you are getting out of it.

"I don't know his true plan, but it isn't simply killing for kicks. He's looking for someone and when he finds them, he's got something planned that I'm damn sure you haven't seen before. So either get out of the city or get to sathmp atta boge..." His words became gibberish and his eyes widened as he opened his mouth and pieces of his tongue drained out with the black substance.

His pants flattened and dark ooze slid out as his legs disintegrated. A second later, his hand separated from his arm and both turned to mush. He released Vic, lay back, and closed his eyes as his entire body turned black and spasmed for a moment before it melted into one large black pool.

As the investigators stood and backed away, the drunk laughed loudly behind them. They all turned and he raised his glass and shook his head. "See, what did I tell you? I called it!"

CHAPTER TWENTY-NINE

Valerie, Marco, and Annie arrived at the diner for breakfast and a meeting. They were directed to a large circular booth in the corner where the investigators were waiting for them with a large coffee pot and a few empty mugs.

"Morning." Johnny slurped his brew. "We would have ordered you something more specific but we don't know what you prefer."

"Honestly, any coffee would be good right now," the young officer admitted as she sat and sighed. "I didn't get much sleep last night."

"None of us did," Annie muttered and slid into the booth next to Johnny with Marco behind her. "To be honest, the last couple of days has been too rough to sleep."

Her brother poured some coffee in a mug and looked at the dark contents. "It might not be my favorite brand but it'll get the job done." He took a swig and leaned back. "It's a good thing I'm at the end. I can get to the restroom quickly."

"How was the bar?" Valerie asked and poured herself

and Annie a cup. "I had hoped you would text me something at least before we met again."

"We were there for...longer than expected." Johnny sighed. "Speaking of sleep, Aiyana and I only got a couple of hours." He sipped again but lowered his mug when he realized that everyone at the table was looking at him. "What?"

Marco chuckled. "Man, you've only known each other for a few hours and you're already that cozy? You move fast, my man," he said with a wink.

He almost dropped his mug. "What? No, you smartasses. We got back to the motel after we did some interviews at the bar. She got her own room and said she didn't have time to make reservations anywhere before she arrived here."

"It honestly wasn't bad," the shaman added and stirred a spoon in her mug. "I've grown accustomed to camping, so having a decent bed is a plus."

The young detective looked at Vic. "Why did you look so weird? You were there last night."

His partner chuckled. "Well, sure, but when have you known me to pass up an opportunity to have a laugh?"

"Particularly at my expense," he muttered. A waitress stopped at the table and asked if they were ready to order. Except for Vic, everyone placed an order for breakfast and she returned to the kitchen. "Well, since we have that sorted, we should probably fill you in on what we found." He looked around the table and sighed. "Do you remember all that keeper stuff Vic talked about last night?"

"Yes..." Valerie answered hesitantly and realization came to her before the others. "Please don't tell me..."

Vic shrugged. "We could do that for you, certainly, but we'd be lying." He removed his hat and scratched his skull. "One of those freaks showed up at the bar, but he wasn't in good shape. For them that might usually mean that they looked like a normal guy they'd possessed, but this one was dying and looked like a cancer patient with a dash of the black plague."

"He was a killer like the one you told me about V," Aiyana continued. "When questioned, he said he was pulled from Hell and that he was working for the Axman of New Orleans."

This revelation drew sharp intakes of breath from the others. They looked at each other and Marco was the first to speak. "I suppose it is nice to finally check that off the list but seriously, it's not very comforting."

"Wait until we get into the real shit." Vic chuckled. "I assume as a way to make amends and piss his former boss off, he told us as much as he seemed to know. It appears the Axman is working with a keeper of some kind, which I would usually dismiss off the bat. To be honest, I tried to but with all the weirdness that has been going on and the things we do know, it provides a solid explanation." He rested his head against his fist. "Dammit."

"A keeper? But you said they are responsible for looking after life and death. That's their job," Annie pointed out.

Her brother nodded and stretched for the coffee pot. "Yeah, but he also said they aren't above doing favors and party tricks for the right price." He filled his mug and raised a hand. "Refill over here, please!"

"But not something like this," Valerie added. "I probably don't know as much as you do, Vic, but I've researched keepers. Some of them were considered gods at one point or another, right? They did things for their followers in exchange for their worship."

"Yeah, guys like Odin, Ra, Apollo, and Quetzalcoatl are all keepers. They moved away from that because the big guy is kinda *laissez faire* about the whole cycle of life and death." He tapped his finger on the table as a waitress replaced their pot of coffee. "Still, nothing along the likes of this, although we can thank their buffoonery for things like werewolves and vampires. We're still dealing with that crap."

Johnny refilled his mug. "It doesn't make sense that a keeper, even one who's willing to do something like this for kicks, would take the chance in the first place due to the fear of retribution. And if they did, that they would stoop to relying on a ghost for so much of their plan."

"Retribution?" Marco asked. "Who would go after them if they are so powerful?"

"The other keepers," Aiyana answered. "They police one another and vie for power in the domains like any group. Some are noble and others malicious, but they all work to keep the cycle in balance."

"It's in their best interest," Vic continued. "They wanted worshipers to begin with because that's one way to gain access to power for them. From the stories I've heard, they aren't too different from ghosts, although they are made from different stuff. It's said that stygia—the substance that lets us ghosts have form here on the living side—is a watered-down version of what they are made of."

Johnny raised an eyebrow at this. "Wait, seriously? Stygia is diluted keeper blood?"

The detective shrugged. "I couldn't tell you for sure, kid. Ghosts have their folklore exactly like humans, and if you think the old stories you hear can stretch a metaphor..." He rolled his eyes. "Woof."

The waitress brought their meals and the conversation did not immediately resume once she left them to it. Everyone took a few minutes to process everything and think of further questions, but it seemed they had the same one in mind.

Valerie wiped her lips and looked around. "So what's the plan from here?" She looked at Johnny, Vic, and Aiyana. "And do any of you want to back out?"

"From a case?" the young detective asked and looked at Vic. "Hell no. Weird or not, that would be a hit to our rep."

The ghost chuckled as he put his hat on. "Hell, in our business, weird is better." He smiled at Valerie and the siblings. "Besides, I've grown fond of ya. And it's not like any of you have a choice here. It wouldn't feel fair."

"I will stay as well," Aiyana declared. "It is my duty and I will not be so cowardly as to avoid it." She speared some eggs with her fork. "Not only that but to come here and leave after only a day seems like such a waste."

Marco frowned as he finished his mouthful of bacon. "I wish we could back out." He nodded to his sister.

Annie shrugged. "It is what it is, I suppose." She looked at the two detectives. "Were you able to find any reason why they have targeted me and my brother?"

"You specifically," Johnny pointed out and waved his fork in circles at her. "Remember? Marco was not worthy, apparently."

Her brother folded his arms. "Honestly, I would be

inclined to be fine with it if it wasn't for the fact that the creep still seemed to consider me as some kind of consolation prize."

Valerie chuckled and stirred the fruit into her oatmeal. "So you are less worried about the fact that they might still have some plans for you and more upset that they consider you a spare or something?"

The young man nodded feverishly. "I mean…yeah, it's disrespectful."

"Yes, high on the list of sins these guys have committed is the discourteousness of it all," Vic said sarcastically and earned an annoyed look from Marco. "Look, we at least have the players in place even if we don't know the game yet. We have the Axman, who might or might not have at least one crony left. We are still a little in the dark about that, admittedly, but the killer at the bar mentioned a 'pet,' so it's likely. But we have him, his possible pal, and whatever keeper he struck a deal with. While I would like to say that would be enough to get some real help with this"—he looked at Valerie—"I assume most people will react how I did initially and say it's bogus."

The officer nodded. "I'll try to see if anyone will believe me but they haven't seen what we have. Plus, there's the cover-up so I'm not sure how much fruit it will bear."

"We might have better luck in Limbo," Johnny suggested. "While we might still get some crazy looks, the ghosts are more inclined to listen to crazy after all."

Vic nodded and looked around the diner. "Do you see any crossings?"

"In here?" Johnny moved his eyepatch away and gazed

around. "Here, no, but next door has one. Without checking the maps we won't—"

"We can back out if it puts us in a bad location," his partner responded impatiently. "I wanna get in there to see if any of this is finally drawing attention. Limbo is massive, sure, but this dude has killed enough people and there's been enough time to spread it around. I'm as sure as hell that some of the ghosts who ran off last night are hollering about it in the bars. They gotta be."

He nodded and cut into a pancake. "It sounds good. I'll be done in a bit."

The ghost leaned back. "A 'bit' is relative for you." He looked at Marco. "Do you mind running an errand for me?"

"Whatcha need?"

Vic gestured with a nod to the diner entrance. "I brought a stash of doubloons and need you to head to the market and get us some guns—damn hand cannons if you can get them." He took his pistol out and looked at it for a moment before he slid it under the table toward him. "If you need extra cash…uh, make sure you get me something nice."

"Vic! Are you honestly willing to sell that?" Johnny stared at him in shock. "It's your memento."

The ghost nodded. "It's a nice piece and we had good times but unfortunately, for what we're dealing with, it ain't enough." He frowned at Marco. "Make sure she finds a good home, all right? And don't get cheated. Mementos go for a higher price." He nodded to Valerie. "I'd ask her but I assume she's as barred from it as we are—or probably is, at least."

"I haven't been back," she admitted. "I can drive you there and have a friend who can go with you to keep you safe if you want."

"I'm connected to the mob, remember?" Marco chuckled and bit into another strip of bacon. "They won't hassle me and I'll have my bat. It's cool."

"I appreciate it. Valerie might have some recommendations so I'll defer to her. My knowledge of ghost iron is somewhat dated. If you had told me that the cops had better guns than my revolver, I would have laughed in your face until she proved it."

"The police are taking the supernatural seriously now, at least compared to decades ago," she told him. "Besides, it's New Orleans. Spooky stuff is always going on here." A light rain began to patter against the windows and the whole table tensed. They listened to the music playing overhead but it didn't change from the sweet, simple, easy-listening number that drifted softly through the speakers.

Johnny rubbed his temples. "Good Lord. I used to like the sound of rain."

Vic relaxed and chuckled. "I'm merely glad I no longer have a bladder."

CHAPTER THIRTY

The crisp fall breeze drifted through the vine maple trees of the Kisatchie National Forest. A light mist hung above to create a shrouded but hypnotic view of the moonlit trees. It was the perfect scene for romance for some and a chance to explore for others but for one, it was the ideal time to kill.

On the bank of Valentine Lake, nestled among the trees, a man stood and rocked in worn dark leather boots. One hand was tucked inside his black-and-white flannel and fiddled with a strap across his chest. He looked around and his head jerked anxiously but his eyes were alight with excitement as he checked the patch of dirt. It was important that it wasn't too deep. He wanted to be sure they found him sometime soon.

This was his fifth time and tonight felt right. It would be the real beginning of his new life. While it was ironic that another had to end to accomplish that, he saw the humor in it, at least.

He remembered the first time and the supposed accident at his friend's home and wondered if it had truly been inadvertent. The truth was that he hadn't intended to get into an argument about a girl or for the blade to pierce the man's stomach. Not only that but the rapid blood flow had shocked him and he'd simply gaped as the guy's eyes closed for the last time. With that said, however, he also hadn't intended to feel such intense pleasure from it.

The joyous chills had been unexpected in a room that moments before had been filled with insults and bile-laden accusations. They were followed by the rapturous, gurgling sound his buddy made as he collapsed, his eyes wide in astonishment in a face crinkled in pain.

Thinking back, he decided it was odd that the man didn't scream. They usually screamed in the movies and the girl he killed on a marvelous night a week later had shrieked absolute hell. His friend had not. All he'd uttered was a sharp gasp and a throaty gurgle before wondrous, absolute silence descended.

While he hadn't meant to do that, maybe it was fate. After he'd simply drifted through life with no direction and tried to fill the emptiness with seemingly all of humanity's vices, he had forgotten the oldest one of all. Finally, he felt he knew what he could do to give his life some meaning.

It had already begun. News traveled quickly in this town and grisly murders were already happening around the city. Bodies were found in shriveled conditions and the attacks were reportedly preceded by some kind of sizzling noise according to one survivor. He couldn't bring himself to feel regret that the man's second chance at life was all too brief.

New Orleans was uncharacteristically used to the

darker nature of reality if history was anything to go by, but even the most hardened of individuals could be frightened when the scene was macabre enough, the horrors grotesque enough, and the creator unknown. With all that going on, he might as well join the fun, right?

He hadn't intended to have a calling card but after his first intentional kill, he knew what was effective. Insert a sharp object into another person's sternum and pull to the left. It was quick and dirty but efficient, and it happened to leave a crescent-shaped mark on the body like one of the city's nicknames.

Almost nothing had been written or spoken about the first killing, but after the second incident, then a third, people began to put everything together. Well, except the bodies. Only this morning, he had seen a blog that discussed the killings and bequeathed him the title The Blood Moon Slasher. While a little fancy for his taste, it confirmed that he would be rewarded for his new passion and tonight, he would dot the Is and cross the Ts on his name in the history books.

Shuffled steps on gravel caught his attention and pulled him from his reminiscing. He narrowed his gaze on a man who approached the lakeside. It was fairly dark but his hiding place was in close proximity and he could make out a few features.

The man was maybe in his mid to late thirties and wore a brown jacket and dark trousers. He gazed at the lake and the faint moonlight illuminated his face and revealed dark-rimmed glasses and slicked-back brown hair that reached his shoulders. Dark-gloved hands disappeared into his jacket as he took a minute to admire the lake in the stillness of the night. He was probably a late-night hiker and the Slasher couldn't help but smile. It seemed he would get a two-for-one special tonight.

He slid his hood up and unfastened the strap that held his blade. The knife was one he'd inherited from his father —a memento of his fishing days and appropriately, it had been used for gutting. He didn't remove it yet. After the last time, he realized that he enjoyed the shock of the moment when he unveiled it, but he cocked the sheat to the side for easy access under his jacket, left his hiding place behind the trees, and approached the stranger.

"You know, I watched you for a while." The Slasher stopped when the man spoke. Surprisingly, he did not turn and simply stood with his back to him and stared at the water as he continued. "There would have been a time where I admired your patience. It's becoming so rare in your kind nowadays."

The killer looked at him in bewilderment, not sure what he was talking about. He regained his composure quickly, however, and smiled.

"So you know who I am, do you?" The stranger nodded. "Well then, I have to give you your due. You've got balls." He chuckled as he took a few steps to close the distance between them but leave himself enough room to maneuver in case this was a sting.

"Who are you? Some new detective trying to prove himself and put away the latest killer on the block? Or merely some punk looking to get justice for someone I had a little fun with?"

The man turned slightly toward him. His features were hidden in the dark, but an odd light flickered from him—

perhaps reflections of the moonlight on the water. "I suppose I was a little vague there. I should have said our kind."

He grimaced before his eyes widened and he began to laugh. "Oh, I get it! You're one of the freaky fans of people like me—like the Manson family. Are you looking to join the club?" He chuckled and finished his excited statement with a whistle. "You know, I gotta say that I am impressed —with myself, of course. I've only done this a few times and got me a devoted hanger-on so I must have made an impression." He drew the knife and twirled it in his hand. "I wonder if they are talking about me in Limbo too. That might be an awkward run-in one day." Reluctantly, he sheathed the knife again. He rather liked the novelty of having discovered a real fan.

The man turned fully but with his head lowered. "In Limbo? I would not worry about that. In such a place, you will barely be recognizable. You'll be lucky if you'll be noted in the history of the living. I can speak from experience."

The Slasher's blood boiled in an instant and he yanked his blade from the holster with such speed and aggression that it sliced his jacket and shirt. "Listen, you fucking prick! Do you think that because I've only begun my career that I'm some hick who got lucky a few times? Fuck you! I will be remembered and feared for centuries by the time I'm done—a bloody rock-star. All you will be is one of my mutilated building blocks.

"You know, I might have let you live with only a few wounds or some missing fingers so you could spread my name around and jump-start my legacy. Now, I will eviscerate your skinny ass and leave your corpse with so many tears and holes that they will have to stitch you together to try and identify you. They will—gahk!"

The Slasher's words jumbled in his throat and he tasted a metallic liquid. When he raised his hand to his mouth to see what was wrong and why he couldn't seem to speak, his eyes widened. Sweat appeared on his face and trickled to his neck and he realized that his throat had been cut. He looked up but the man was gone.

As he spat the blood out, a clanging noise next to him made him look at the ground. His knife had fallen beside him and more blood trickled onto it from above.

Shaking, he raised the arm that had held it and gaped. His hand was gone, a bloody stump all that remained like it had been severed cleanly by a razor. A moment later, he collapsed and landed hard chest-down but flipped quickly to see both legs gone, amputated above the knee.

He was now in a full-blown panic and used his one remaining arm to drag himself along the shore as a trail of life force seeped from his lost legs. His horrified senses registered something behind him and he looked at the man, who held a razor blade. The terror he felt increased because his attacker's face was visible now and he was no man.

"It seems I was wrong. Silence only makes you even more pathetic," the monster murmured and kicked him. The Slasher recovered and tried to crawl away again. He didn't know what was happening, only that this being was the reason, and he had never feared anyone or anything like this before.

His attacker walked beside him for a while and simply

observed him before he drove his boot into his hand and stopped him. He shrieked a garbled cry, caught his breath, and looked slowly at the dread being. After a long moment, the killer removed his foot from his hand, knelt beside him, and gave him a devilish smile. His face was skeletal and black and a white light wrapped around his head like fire.

"You would never be anything worthwhile and it wasn't worth the trouble to recruit you. He's getting impatient and hungry." He extended a dark, scarred hand and grasped his victim's throat. "Look at you. The moment things don't go as planned, you reveal who you truly are—a pitiful babe with a megalomaniac complex." Light emitted from his hand and the Slasher's body was wracked by pain worse than he could have ever imagined as the light filled his eyes.

"Perhaps those you killed were even more useless than you, but that doesn't automatically make you better. Most people are utterly pointless. They strive for things like stardom, financial riches, or political greatness. It is all worth nothing, whether achieved or not. Why? Because you can't take it with you. We live two lives. I know that now but you will not."

The Slasher's eyes fluttered and the light was all around him. He began to feel cold and empty and everything was fading.

His killer held his hand up and the last thing his victim saw was his porcelain-white hand with dark marks crisscrossed upon it like a dark web that seemed to pulse under the skin.

"Anything we achieve will only matter once this cycle is

broken." With a vicious smile, he lowered his hand. "At least now you can now truly be what you always were —nothing."

Many strange places and historic landmarks exist in New Orleans, but a new one was added on this night. On the shore of Valentine Lake, a gruesome event appeared to have taken place. Bloodstains on the shore and a knife confirmed this, but only one body was found in the trees nearby. The victim couldn't have been killed there, however, and was reported missing miles away. The body only had two deep wounds in the neck, so who and where was the second body?

CHAPTER THIRTY-ONE

Johnny opened his eyes to fireworks or at least the ghostly approximation of them. Orbs of light in different colors— red, green, purple, and even black, oddly enough—burst in the sky to display images of stars, cultural symbols, and pictures of humans dancing in full movement. These were certainly more dynamic than typical fireworks.

"What's going on?" he asked as Vic placed a hand on his shoulder. "Is this some kind of parade?"

His partner watched the lights with amusement. "More like a festival." He scratched the side of his head for a moment before he snapped his fingers. "Oh, right! Today is the Veil Festival."

The young detective looked around and when he realized that they were in the middle of an alley, he moved quickly toward one of the exits. "Veil Festival? That's the one where they celebrate the day the dead returned to Earth right?"

"Well, the day they flooded back to Earth—technically, it's the week since time works a little wonky here," Vic corrected, took his last cigar out, and lit it. "Back in eighteen ninety-eight. A few other parades and parties celebrate ghosts crossing the plains, one for the first one to do it—some Chinese guy about twelve thousand years ago—a couple for Halloween and *Dia de los Muertos*. Those are holdovers from the guys who can't let go of their lives. Honestly, ghosts don't need a big reason to throw a party."

Johnny walked out of the alley to where a stream of multi-colored ghosts in clothes from various eras danced down the street. Vendors sold items, food, and copious amounts of drink as large floats and supernatural constructs moved along the large roads. "They don't need a reason to hold back either."

Vic blew a plume of smoke out and shrugged. "Hey, you only live once, right?"

The young detective responded with a dry, sarcastic laugh as he pushed through the crowded street to a plaza where many were having a meal and chatting about the event. "I don't think anyone here seems too interested in what's going on in New Orleans. Or they are at least distracted enough to not worry about it."

"Ghosts are good about that." His partner tapped his shoulder. "But that guy over there is eyeballing us fairly hard."

A man was seated alone at a table under a large umbrella. An odd purple mist surrounded him, but whether for decoration or the festivities was unclear. He was dressed in a nice suit in a blend of black and rich purples and long royal-purple feathers emerged from his collar. His top hat was drawn low but not enough that bright eyes weren't visible under the shadow.

Johnny studied his face. The guy wasn't a skeleton like most of the ghosts around them but almost appeared so. He had black skin on both his face and hands and had painted his face with a glowing ink that gave it the appearance of a skull. He smiled and beckoned to them.

"Should...uh, should we go say hi?" he asked and looked at Vic. "He seems friendly, I guess, but kind of gives me the skeevies."

His partner shrugged and puffed on his cigar as he wandered closer. "Hey, we came to get information. We probably have to talk to some freaks anyhow so might as well start strong."

The young detective sighed and followed him. They approached the mysterious man's table and he pointed at two chairs in front of him. "I'm so glad you got my invitation," he said with a wide smile and a notable creole accent. "Come, have a seat. Let's have a chat, hmm?"

"Your invitation?" Johnny asked as he pulled a chair back. "That's what you call staring at someone from the other side of the plaza?"

"Didn't you get my message?" He frowned for a moment.

"Were you expecting us?" Vic shrugged. "We didn't get a fancy letter if that's what you're asking."

The man leaned back, still frowning as he swirled his drink in his hand. "You didn't get my message and you still showed up here. It seems fate is being kind to me for once in a long, long time." His smile returned. "Well then, gentleman, let's not let this good moment go to waste, eh? I hear you've been having a wild time in New Orleans."

"You've certainly heard a lot about us," the ghost detective replied a little suspiciously.

"Certainly." He chuckled and sipped his drink. You guys attract attention. A rather interesting pair, are you not?"

"Sure, but we're only fads," Johnny responded. "At least for now. But I think this conversation is getting off on the wrong foot."

The stranger raised an eyebrow as he stroked his chin. "You think so? Why is that?"

The young detective held a finger up. "For one thing, you seem to know a fair amount about us and we know nothing about you."

Vic leaned against the table. "We're not saying anything about your overall hosting skills, but introducing yourself is fairly common."

The man continued to smile but it had shrunk a little. "That's true, but I can't say I'm a common kind of guy." He slid his hand into his jacket and retrieved a small box. "Besides, I didn't want to drag this on too long. I only wanted to say I'm a fan of what you're doing and wanted to help." He placed the box on the table and slid it forward.

The partners stared at it. "Help with what, exactly?" Johnny asked.

"Isn't it obvious?" The man shrugged. "With the problem in New Orleans."

"At least one person seems to care around here." The young detective picked the box up and examined it.

With a dry laugh, the stranger nodded. "Oh yes, indeed, my friends. I care very much about the city and about that demon who is running around there."

"So it is a demon?" Vic asked and tilted his head toward the stranger as he took the cigar out of his jaw.

The man shrugged and dug in his jacket again for a cigar. "I was being more metaphorical, although given the realm we are in, perhaps I should curb that." He raised a finger and a green flame burst out of the tip that he used to light the cigar. "The Axman...he's a tricky little bastard, that one. Although he might be the main problem, he ain't the cause of it."

"We're thinking it's a keeper," the ghost detective ventured. "But we have no idea who."

In reply, their contact nodded and blew out a large billow of smoke, certainly more than a cigar could normally provide. "It seems you are on the right track then. Good." He stretched his hand through the cloud of smoke and tapped the box. "This will help you to bring an end to this chaos. Use it wisely."

Johnny looked at the box and opened it to reveal an odd bullet. It looked like it was made of bone but an eerie glow beneath told him it was more than merely unusual. "What is this? Where did you get it?"

The stranger was almost obscured by the smoke when he took another long drag. "That's not for you to be concerned about, my friend. But don't waste it. They aren't easy to make."

"Make?" Vic frowned. "You made this? It doesn't look like something any ghost can make."

"That would be true." The man laughed loudly and it echoed around the plaza. "Very true." The smoke seeped from his mouth as he spoke and he composed himself and began to disappear into it. "Also, I would make sure that you fire it, Johnny. It will work better. Ghosts trying to hold it…well, it doesn't turn out pretty." The smoke thickened even further so only his silhouette was now visible. "I wish I had more for ya, but that's how things are right now. End this madness. I'll be watching."

"Watching?" Johnny asked and thrust his hand into the smoke. "I've had enough of this sneaking around shit. Who are you?" His hand grasped nothing. He waved it around to disperse the smoke but the stranger was gone. Disgruntled, he leaned back in his chair and stared at the bullet. "Vic, you've spent more time in this place than I have. Is it always this weird?"

His partner put his cigar back in his mouth and puffed a few times before he nodded. "I can't tell if I'm surprised by that or bored. That should be your answer, kid."

CHAPTER THIRTY-TWO

The doorknob jiggled but was rusted and hard to turn so Johnny kicked it open and they left Limbo. They stepped into an abandoned factory and he dusted his jacket off while the ghost floated around. "Well, it's better to end up here than a gas station bathroom, right?"

"I feel like I'll get tetanus merely looking at all this," the young detective bemoaned as he scowled at the rusted railing. "What now?"

Vic took the cigarette pack out and opened it to find it empty. "We need to restock." He sighed, crumpled it, and put it into his jacket pocket. "It wasn't a fruitful investigation. Talking to a hundred monkeys would have been better than a hundred drunk ghosts."

Johnny retrieved the box given to them by the stranger. "Now that you have had some time to think it over, what do you think about this?" he asked and opened it to look at the bullet. "Do you think this is human bone?"

The ghost detective floated closer and studied it. "It's bleached if it is. There is something about it, though." He reached down to pick it up and the bullet glowed with purple light as he inched closer. Quickly, he yanked his hand away and hissed in surprise and pain. "What the hell?"

"What's wrong?" his partner asked and shut the box hastily. "Wait—did that hurt you?"

Vic looked at his hand for a moment. "Yeah... Yeah, it did." He shook his hand. "I almost forgot what that felt like. It burned like a son of a bitch."

"Well, I guess that means it isn't a placebo, at least. I wonder why it didn't hurt you in Limbo?"

He shrugged and leaned against the railing. "Maybe it reacts differently now that we're topside." He sighed and scratched his head. "We might have the means to take him down but do you feel like we're being played?"

Johnny frowned as he folded his arms and leaned against the wall. "Maybe. I think we're pawns in someone's game but we're on the right side."

"I was hoping we were at least knights or rooks." The ghost chuckled darkly.

"It doesn't exactly sit right but so far, the 'investigation' isn't proving very fruitful. Until now, even if we found the guy, we didn't have a plan to eliminate him. And I think the last couple of run-ins with those giant creeps have proven that normal tactics probably won't work."

The ghost turned to him. "You mean where we simply shoot them until they are obliterated?"

He nodded. "The last one required an ether bomb to get rid of it. I'm not sure how many of those are lying around."

His partner remained silent for a time and tapped a finger against the rail. "What we need to do is get him out in the open," he stated finally. "According to that dying soul at the bar, he might only have one henchman left, right?"

"Maybe not even that, although I'm sure he could get more," he replied. "It makes me worried that he'll go dark and build his squad up again before coming back harder."

"Then we need to think of something fast to make sure that doesn't happen."

"Do you have any ideas?" Johnny asked as his phone vibrated. He took it out and looked at the new text. "It's Marco. He and Valerie are finished at the market. They want to meet us and show off the wares they got for us."

"It works for me." The ghost nodded and pointed to the stairs. "I'll continue to think it over on the way. Do we have a destination?"

The young detective strode to the stairs, his attention still on the text. "Val sent coordinates. It looks like a field in the middle of nowhere but fortunately, we already seem to be in nowhere so it's only a couple miles aw—" The flooring beneath him began to groan and snap. He froze for a moment until it settled.

He looked irately at Vic, who simply shrugged. "What do you want me to do about it? Hold your hand?"

Johnny frowned and hugged the walls as he descended the stairs cautiously. "It would certainly make a stupid story. The last great hope for New Orleans dies dicking around in a dilapidated factory."

Vic chuckled. "True, but would make for a funny one in Limbo."

The partners, despite having to walk, were the first to arrive. The sun was beginning to set when Valerie's car pulled up and she and the siblings got out, Marco holding a suitcase.

"Good evening, gentleman!" he said cheerfully as he placed the case on the trunk of the car. "Do you want to come and view my wares?"

Vic chuckled as they approached. "When did he become a carnival barker?"

Johnny shrugged. "Maybe he gets commission."

The young man opened the suitcase and removed two dark guns. "These are exorcist mark three's. One is for Val." He tossed her one. "And one for you, Johnny." He handed the other to him and the young detective examined it. He ejected the magazine and peered at a glowing gray square inside. "While exorcist is a good name, I have to wonder why they needed to make a third version if they lived up to their name."

"These exorcize harder?" Vic quipped and winced when his partner pointed the magazine at him. "That's almost pure ether."

"They are based on Agency weapons," Valerie informed them as she checked the sights on hers. "Well, reverse-engineered from blueprints that were 'borrowed' by a more illicit organization. Either way, they are far better than the gun I gave you."

"We got two at a good deal," Marco revealed proudly. "Also some backup charges. The gun gets its power from the ether core in the mag. It technically replenishes but damn slowly, so you want to carry around a couple of spares, at least." He took out two small cases. "There are three each, just in case. The guns also have compartments on the side to insert special bullets if need be."

The young officer turned toward the field and fired several shots before she removed the magazine and let Johnny peer inside. The core was now slightly dimmer.

"You'd better make your shots count." He looked at his gun as Marco tossed her one of the containers. "I wonder what will happen..." He turned and fired a dozen shots, and when he took his magazine out, his square was still glowing. "Ha!"

Valerie looked incredulously at it. "I'm sorry—what?"

Vic floated closer as the young detective reinserted the core. "Johnny is able to generate ether. The gun is probably siphoning it. That's how he was able to fire my gun despite it being a ghost weapon."

"It's merely one of the bonuses of being a freak," he said with a smile as he nodded to Marco to give Valerie the extra cores. He noticed a slider on the back of the weapon. "Hey, what's this?"

The officer moved the slider on hers up a little. "It increases the power of the shot." She aimed and fired to launch a larger bolt of gray ether. The recoil forced her to step back.

"While it has more of a kick, it drains more energy too." Johnny nodded, flipped his up all the way, and prepared to shoot but she tried to stop him. "Wait, Johnny, I don't think—" He ignored her and a massive bolt of ether fired while he was catapulted back several yards and over the car and finally landed heavily near the street.

The group ran to him. Marco and Vic helped him up and he dusted himself off. "Ow... Well, I guess Vic did say he wanted hand cannons."

His partner chuckled. "Yeah. It makes me wonder what would happen if we fused."

The young detective looked into the distance. "It would probably shoot me well over the city from here."

Marco snapped his fingers. "Which reminds me!" He jogged to the case. "I know you were willing to give up your precious baby pistol."

"That's not how I refer to it," Vic clarified as he came up behind him. "What did you get me to replace her?"

The young man smiled, turned, and presented him with his old pistol. "And here you are!"

"Marco, I said I needed something better." He frowned in confusion. "Could you not find a buyer?"

"Oh, there were numerous potential buyers, but look closer." He wrapped an arm around Vic. "Look at the barrel —both in and outside. It's different, right?"

The ghost took the pistol and realized he was right. The barrel had been altered and there were also differences to both the cylinder and chambers. "You had it modified?"

Marco nodded. "Yeah. I found a guy hiding in the back and had enough to get him to take a look since I got a deal on those other guns. He works fast too and said he was happy to finally work on a classic." He pointed at the field. "According to him, it should have way more punch. I couldn't get it to fire so tell me what you think."

Vic spun the cylinder before he flipped it in and spectral bullets appeared in the chambers. "The bullets have form now." He aimed at the field, fired, and frowned when he noticed a kick from the gun that hadn't been there before. With a dry chuckle, he clapped the young man on the shoulder. "You did good, Marco."

"I have an eye for weapons. It must be hereditary. Well, our show and tell is over. What did you guys find?"

Johnny sighed. "Outside of one strange meeting, not much. We couldn't even find out why a ghost would be fixated on Annie." He gestured to her with an apologetic look. "Anyone with an idea simply gave us what we already knew about other ghost types. Or would go on tangents about prophecies, but unless this eastern-based folklore somehow changed location to New Orleans, I wouldn't say it was very helpful."

"Stranger things have happened but I have to agree in this case." Vic looked at his partner. "But as he said, we had one interesting talk. Show them the bullet."

He nodded, took the box from his jacket, and showed it to the others. "Some creepy dude in Limbo gave this to us. He said it could deal with the Axman when we find him."

Valerie looked at it and attempted to reach for it at first but held off. "I don't get the best vibe from it," she admitted and glanced at him. "Do we have any proof that it works?"

The young detective nodded at his partner. "It hurt him."

"Hurt?" she asked, raised an eyebrow, and focused on Vic. "Like actual pain?" Johnny nodded and she frowned. "Well, that is certainly something, but is there anything else?"

"I could take a look," Aiyana offered and they turned in surprise as she walked closer. "If you would like me to."

"Aiyana? When did you get here?" Vic asked as he looked around. "I don't see another car."

She smiled as she pocketed a totem. "I have my ways. Sorry, I would have arrived with the others but I wanted to see if I could commune with any spirits in the city. Unfortunately, many are too frightened to come out of hiding." She took the box from Johnny but immediately almost dropped it as she gasped. He snatched it before it fell. "This is...this is unlike anything I know."

"That didn't take long," the young detective said as he put the box away.

"Unlike anything you know? In a good or bad way?" Valerie asked.

The shaman took a moment to compose herself. "I cannot say for certain but it is powerful. I only wanted to look into it. I have seen the many powers and spirits of the Veil and this is beyond anything like that. I could feel it reaching for my spirit—my ghost, as it were—as if trying to pull it from me before it was my time."

"In any other situation, that would be creepy," Johnny remarked. "But it sounds like something that could be very useful soon."

Annie stepped forward. "So you have a plan to find him?"

"Eh...not quite," Vic admitted. "I've considered some ideas but nothing that's guaranteed. For now, he seems to be focused on getting power by consuming spirits. Whoever he's working for is getting impatient or needs the phantasma to sustain himself. At least it's a diversion so we probably don't have to worry about him coming after you for now while he busies himself with that."

She nodded and drew a deep breath. "That's what I've been thinking about. I think I know how we can flush him out."

Johnny looked quizzically at her. "Hey, I'm open to all

suggestions unless they are insane—which is admittedly a very high bar to clear."

The young woman glanced at Marco. "Then it will probably need an explanation but let me make the offer first." She gazed at all of them and tried to take a moment to look each one in the eyes before she asked, "What if we gave him what he wants?"

CHAPTER THIRTY-THREE

A mansion loomed atop a hill outside New Orleans. Originally a French-inspired theater created by one of the town's former wealthy socialites, it stood as a testimony to where the originally humble town was headed—a glamourous future led by the many artists and trendsetters who both came from and were moving to the growing city. Then, like so many other seemingly promising starts, it was stopped dead by a recurring theme in the city that many forgot—tragedy.

The residents, with a trace of gallows humor, called it The Creep's Manor. It was a reference both to the building's original owner, Alexander Kreps, and his history as a womanizer in his youth and shut-in later in life. This was caused by a downswing in both his fortunes and personal life, which lead to only occasional sightings of him before the end of his life, which was taken by his hand at the age of forty-seven.

The shadow of death loomed over the city it looked down on, both metaphorically and quite literally as one observer noted. A figure stood on the balcony of the mansion and contemplated the outlandish mass only ten or so miles from him. From his perch, he could see flickers of light in the clouds that appeared and disappeared in bright flashes. Yet, despite a phenomenon that should have caused the streets to erupt in surprise and maybe panic, no one screamed. There were no hysterics and nothing to indicate that the abyss had quite literally appeared and now loomed above. That was because few could truly see it.

It was a great source of amusement to him. The mental hoops people would jump through to retain their sense of normalcy as the world changed around them were almost as admirable as they were idiotic. Those were merely symptoms, however, minor effects of the vortex they could simply shrug off. It was another thing entirely to see it and so few could. Even those who could see into the realm of the dead—those with the eyes of a specter or even the ghosts themselves—didn't have his eyes.

After a while, the figure withdrew into the mansion and walked the halls dilapidated and worn with the years of neglect. After the owner's suicide, no one was willing to buy a property with a morbid history and it faded into memory, another shining star snuffed out and left to the creeping dark. He found that to be a shame. It was quite comfortable to him.

He entered what was once the main theater dimly lit by candles and lights hooked up to generators. A large stage stood vacant and only half the seats remained. He walked onto the stage past large stacks of books, notes, and old maps that had been strewn about.

With a sigh, he sat on a repurposed theater chair and

opened a leather-bound book that leaned against its leg. It was a journal with pages upon pages filled with personal anecdotes and records. He opened it to an empty page, placed a hand on an ink well, and as white phantasma coated it, began to speak.

"May 25th. The woman's name was Mia. She wore a flowing white dress and had her long blonde hair tied back." As he spoke, his words were not written into the journal by any hand or pen. Blobs of ink flew from the well and landed on the page to form the sentences. "She seemed the gentle sort, sweet to others and particularly her elders —the kind to offer a hand in aid with no expectation of reward. I have no doubt that she could have gone to Heaven in the instant of her last breath if she remained such a kind soul to the end."

His chair groaned with age as he leaned back and rested his chin upon his palm. He closed his eyes and recalled the memory. "It's a pity. She would have made a fantastic bride for the right man or woman. However, I was born a new, unstable something that had not yet walked this Earth and I needed the phantasma. It was always said that such kind souls destined for Paradise had stronger souls than the others. I needed that soul to test the theory if nothing else."

He heard a door open at the front of the mansion and the light pitter-patter of rain from a growing storm begin to fall. "I intended to give her a quick death. I had simply come to gather the girl's phantasma and move on but I could not seem to stop myself from...playing with such a unique toy. The moment I will always recall until my new dream begins is the moment where she returned to lucidity

—that brief time while I drained her life from her and the light in her eyes was not yet extinguished."

Footsteps echoed down the hall, approaching the theater. He straightened and closed the tome slowly as he finished. "I would have to say that she was something unique, to be sure. While the rest of the souls have grown quiet, I can still feel her trying to cry out."

His faithful servant approached, clad head to foot in black except for a gray-hooded poncho. He reached the foot of the stage, stopped in front, and bowed to the occupant, who stood from his chair, crossed to the left side of the stage, and descended the stairs.

"Good evening, sir," the new arrival greeted with a bow. "I saw you went out last night. Did you find anything fruitful?"

The man sighed and pulled his focus from the book that still clung to his thoughts. "A couple of souls, including one of some punk in the park who thought he was the next Bundy." He looked at his black, skeletal hand. "Between what I need to continue my work and the supplies for our...benefactor, supply is starting to become a problem."

"With the loss of the others, we cannot harvest as effectively," his henchman noted and straightened from his bow. "Are you sure it was the right decision to drain them?"

He hissed in irritation. "They weren't harvesting enough souls and they were gaining more and more attention. You were the only one among them who pulled your weight." He thumped a hand against the arm of a nearby chair and cracked it. "And even then, that only bought us a limited amount of time. I can feel myself fading—no, worse, I feel like Limbo itself is trying to drag me back.

And I have to feed him as well as keep my powers working." He sighed and looked at his hands again. "We need her, Jack. I need her to put this plan in motion."

The retainer slid his hand into his shirt pocket and produced a picture. "She has proved rather wily, as have her protectors. If we could get our hands on her brother in the meantime, that could sustain you for longer." He handed his boss the picture. "Although I might have found something—or someone—that could aid you."

The Axman took the picture and frowned at a faded photo of a man in a grocery store apron. "Who is this? Why does he look so familiar?" Jack motioned for him to turn the photo. *Louis Besumer, 1917* was written on the back. The Axman flipped the picture again. "Where did you get this, Jack?"

"From an apartment on Conti Street. I was following a young man who worked at a grocery that is still standing since back in the day."

"Besumer?" He began to chuckle. "He was my third—him and his mistress. Only the girl died, though, after pointing the blame every which way but at me. Besumer went to jail for a time too." He laughed and looked at the picture again. "If this kid has a picture of him, he's probably a descendant, right?"

His henchman nodded. "That's what I thought. And if you get your hands on the soul of a descendant, even if it ain't the one you are looking for—"

"I'll have enough to juice me for a while," the Axman finished. "And truly get the terrors going."

"So you've found yourselves a little side plan then, hmm?" a voice asked and echoed throughout the chamber.

Jack froze and twitched in surprise and worry, even in his larger body. The Axman looked around, not nearly as concerned as his lackey, but the lights in his eyes did glimmer for a brief moment. "You wanna fill me in?" They turned as a large, dark figure appeared and towered over them, at least ten feet tall. He folded his arms and lay casually in the air. "Come on. Share with your good friend, oh dreaded Axman."

He bowed deferentially. "It's merely a way to keep myself in this plane, Baron," he explained. "I intend to pay a visit to the descendant of an old 'friend' and claim his soul. It should provide me with enough phantasma for a long while."

"So you can get me what I need as well?" the shadow asked and anger crept into his voice.

"Of course." He nodded at Jack and they both extended their hands toward him. "We have collected more for you since you last visited us." White phantasma poured out of their arms and turned red on contact with the shadow, who now floated upright.

His form began to take a more notable shape and a dark suit with a blood-red shirt and tie appeared. A top-hat-like shape formed on his head. "Oh, that's nice. A little paltry but...ah, I feel some familiar souls in here." He began to laugh and the sound shook the theater. "So, you 'axed' some of your toadies, huh?"

"They weren't a good use of souls," the Axman said mildly. "I decided they would be more beneficial for you and I."

"Good reasoning." A cane appeared in the otherworldly figure's hand and he pointed it at a small television set in the corner. "I wanted to bring something to your attention before you run off again." The screen flickered on and the Axman and Jack walked closer to it. "Why bother with the small fry in a big lake when the big catch is hanging around in a small pond?"

"We have made headway with the investigation concerning the odd disappearances and supernatural murders," a police chief on the screen stated. "We have two witnesses in our protection who survived an attack and are helping us to pinpoint the perpetrator."

"Sir, does this have to do with the Maggios?" a reporter asked. "Their home was attacked a few days ago and there were reports of odd incidents. Their neighbors have said they haven't been back since—"

"We are getting assistance from the Maggios, yes, but that is all we will say on the matter."

"Why would a cop admit that?" Jack demanded. "Can they admit that before a trial?"

The Axman turned to him. "They are baiting us, I would think." He grinned. "Do you think they can take us?"

His retainer shook his head. "Not a chance, boss, especially since we know where she is now. We'll simply bag her and—"

"Although I do agree that they wouldn't normally stand a chance against our collective might, it seems the simple plans haven't worked." He picked up an ax that leaned against the chair. "Maybe because I've underestimated them or overestimated myself. We'll need to plan for any...eventualities."

The dark figure snorted. "Was that humility there, Axman? I didn't know you were capable of such a thing."

The Axman stepped beside Jack and rested the weapon on his shoulder. "I've had a moment to think all this over. That happens when your plans run into some problems. I might not be all that humble but I am clever." He stood in front of his henchman and smiled. "I've sent others out to do my work for too long. It's time that New Orleans remembers the Axman."

Jack nodded and straightened. "Right, boss. When will we go after 'em?"

He placed his hand on his retainer's chest. "It seems they are waiting for us Jack. There's no need to keep them waiting for too long." Jack gasped and clutched his master's shoulders as he gaped at a light that came from his chest. "But first, the Axman will need more phantasma."

CHAPTER THIRTY-FOUR

"I hate this plan." Johnny scowled from the sidelines as Valerie took the stand to talk to the press.

"We couldn't come up with a better one," Vic reminded him from where he currently hid inside him so as to not alert any of the specters on the police force. "Annie is in the most danger and she offered—"

"It doesn't mean any of us were happy about it," Johnny countered and slouched against the wall. "I thought Marco would have a stroke."

The ghost thought of the fiery young man patrolling the door where his sister was while a patient Aiyana supported him. "Yeah, convincing him to go through with it was tougher than convincing the cops to let him walk around with a baseball bat."

"No kidding." The young detective laughed. "All of them are packing but they are constantly worried about the guy with the sports equipment."

"Are you talking to yourself there, bounty hunter?" one of the cops asked as he and his buddy chuckled at his expense. "Is that one of the tricks you use to hunt the ghosts?"

Johnny shrugged. "It's the only way to find intelligent conversation around here." Irate glares from the cops replaced their amusement. "What? It's not like any of you got leads on the guy. If it had been up to you, your two leads would be on the body count instead of helping since you only respond to the distress calls."

"What the hell are you on about?" the other cop retorted. "Officer Simone was on the scene and she eliminated one of the killers on her own."

"Yeah, she's the exception that proves the rule." He placed his hands in his jacket pockets. "And if it weren't for her, you would simply chalk it up to the one guy and call it done, at least until more bodies piled up and you couldn't sweep it under the rug anymore."

They both grunted and walked away. "What the hell is he here for?"

"Officer Simone brought him in. I heard he's been helping with the investigation."

"Whatever. I guess the mascot gets special privileges."

The young detective looked at Valerie, who was still fielding questions. "Mascot?"

"Eh, it's fairly normal in cases like this. Prop up an officer or someone with lower rank to be the face of the investigation— you know, someone to root for," Vic explained. "It also allows Val to return to active duty rather than keeping her on the bench. I'm holding out hope that she'll be able to take the lead in more cases after this."

A patter on the windows warned them that scattered rain had hit the glass. "Assuming all goes well, yeah, same here." He looked around the precinct building. "I remember when you asked me if I had any interest in being a cop. Meeting some of these other guys makes me thankful that I never seriously considered it."

Johnny's shoulders lifted briefly as his partner shrugged inside him. "I'm not sure how much I can speak about them today, given that the last case involved dirty cops, but I had a good stable of guys I could rely on in the Chicago Police Department. While I can't say they were all clean, especially in the fifties, there were diamonds in the rough."

"The rain is picking up." The young detective took the box with the bone bullet out. "I know New Orleans is one of the wetter cities in the states, but this doesn't help my anxiety."

"Given the number of strip clubs in the city, that could be a euphemism and I guess that would help your anxiety," Vic joked but it merely brought a sigh in response. "What? You need to loosen up a little. If this guy does come and bring this place to the ground, you have to be loose to keep your head on a swivel during danger."

"As I've seen what this guy can do, I'm not so sure he can catch me off-guard at this point." He gazed at the speakers. "Especially with his telltale signs."

The ghost clicked his tongue thoughtfully. "You know, I've wondered about that. You know—the rain and the music starting whenever he or rather one of his cronies approaches."

"Is that so?" Johnny asked and scowled as the rain became heavier. "And do you have any theories?"

"I think they might be a mutation of wraiths," Vic told him. "In the same way, the Axman might be some offshoot of demons. It makes sense that he might be able to do something weird with his cronies. A normal wraith passively affects the environment around them, which explains the rain and jazz."

"True, but for something like the music, he would have to have a strong attachment to it in…" He looked at Valerie, who was wrapping up. "In life. She said that was his thing, right?"

"Indeed it was. The thing is, we don't know if it affects him the same way but if it does, we could track those alterations to the weather and music to where he could be hiding out."

"Well, that's something," the young detective conceded. "We'll give this a while and if he doesn't show, I guess you and I can—" His words cut off abruptly when the sounds of piano, trumpets, drumming, saxophone, and jazz began to play through the police precinct speakers. Valerie had stopped talking and looked around with wide eyes. "Please tell me they are simply playing New Orleans classics."

Vic floated out of his body. "Maybe, if it wasn't coming out of the radios as well." He gestured at a group of cops who were checking their radios. "Get the gun ready, kid."

"Everyone needs to leave the building now!" Valerie ordered. The reporters were confused, as were some of the cops, but others rushed around the room and drew their weapons.

Johnny ran to the front entrance and looked out. It was storming but he did not see any monster approaching the station. "Do you think he's coming through the back?" he asked as he took the bone bullet out of the case, opened the chamber on the side of his weapon, and slotted it in.

"I don't see anything out of the ordinary," Vic said and continued to scan the area. "What about you?"

He flipped his eyepatch up and looked at the front of the precinct. "No, nothing, but this can't be—" A cold chill filled his lungs and his skin began to tingle. Intense shadow coalesced on the left of his vision like half of the lights went out and he turned as a cloud of darkness swirled around the presentation hall. The confused murmurs grew into shouts and screams and the reporters and other civilians ran hastily out of the room. Everyone with a weapon trained it on the cloud, but they held off from firing. Most seemed uncertain that they could even hit whatever this was.

"You wished to draw me out? Bring me in?" An angry, raspy voice asked from within the dark substance. "All right, I'm here."

The young detective noticed one of the cameramen still filming. "What are you doing? Get the hell out of here!" Something whistled past his head and glass shattered as the cameraman slumped. What looked like a metal chair leg had passed through his camera and lodged in his head.

"He's talking, Johnny," Vic pointed out and aimed his gun into the dark. "And not that growly nonsense the other guy did. I think this is a new model."

Johnny turned back as the cloud began to harden around something within. "Or it could be the maker."

A slow, snide laugh came from the being and the darkness parted to reveal a figure dressed in a black suit. While tall, he was not nearly as tall or bulky as the monsters they had faced previously. He wore gloves and shoes, but beneath his slouch hat was a dark skull. White phantasma poured out of it and he held a common ax in his hand. He looked around the room for a moment and lifted the weapon above his head.

"You should have heeded my warning from all those years ago," he declared as the ax was slowly coated by the same dark substance he was. "The Axman is back from Tartarus, you fools!" he bellowed before he pounded the blade into the floor as shots were fired.

The ghost detective looked at his partner. "Kid, shoot him!"

He tried to get a shot in but the Axman's attack didn't merely send out a shockwave or crack the floor. At the point of impact, the floor broke open to reveal a chasm that spat phantasma and chilled the room.

"What the hell is tha—" He began to slip and looked down to see that he and a few other officers now stood on a broken surface. A little panicked, he attempted to jump out of the way but the floor ripped open. The last thing he heard besides the surprised yelps from the other officers who fell with him was Valerie calling to him.

CHAPTER THIRTY-FIVE

The Axman roared with laughter as he turned toward the back wall. "Now then, let me find my vessel." He was only able to take one step before he was blasted from behind dozens of times by the remaining officers. With a growl of displeasure, he turned and lashed out with his ax, which should have hit no one as none of the officers were close to him. Valerie caught her breath when a widening arc of dark phantasma began to sweep the room.

"Get down!" she shouted and immediately fell prone along with other specters. Those who could not see ghosts were too preoccupied or confused to understand and they were cut down by the strike. "Dammit!"

The Axman tilted his head as he looked at her. "Hey, you're her friend, aren't you?" he asked and walked slowly toward her. "Or perhaps babysitter is more apt?"

She twisted and fired at him. Her shots halted his advance but if he was in shock or pain, he certainly didn't show it. She increased the power of her next shot but before she could fire, he kicked her hands apart and the shot went into a wall before he stamped his foot on her arm. It appeared that despite the fact that he did not look as strong as the previous monstrosities, this was far from correct. Her arm broke under the weight and she uttered a hiss of pain.

"Get off me!" she demanded and drew her original gun with her free hand. Thankfully, it was pre-filled with ether bullets. "Or I will send you back to Hell one bullet at a time!"

The Axman continued to grind his boot into her arm as he peered at her and laughed. "I would say I admire your courage, lass, but given your position, it reads more like foolishness." He lowered his ax so it was against her neck. "I was able to make this entire city fear me in less than a year when I was alive. Now that they will know that not even death can stop my reign, how do you think they will react? There are far more souls in New Orleans than there were one hundred years ago, both living and dead, and all who fear and reverence me will only feed me." He brought the ax to the side, ready to behead her. "But I could certainly use you for sustenance. The brave last so much longer than the cowards."

A blast rang out and he was knocked off her by only a step, but it was enough for her to roll away and aim both guns at him. "Get out of here, Officer Simone!" the chief demanded as he racked his shotgun. "Make sure the Maggios get out of here!"

She gritted her teeth in frustration and pain but nodded, raced out of the room as the other officers fired, and was able to get to the back of the precinct before she heard more screams. They had a back exit but she knew he would not stop until he had Annie, even if he had to tear through the streets of New Orleans.

And that did not account for whatever had happened to Johnny and Vic.

"Soooon oooof a bbbiiiiiiiittttttcccchhh!" Johnny yelled as he fell through the darkness toward what he was sure was a very painful impact. Vic managed to snag a piece of rebar, caught him by the leg, and strained to hold them both mere moments before the young detective splattered on the ground. "Nice catch, Vic!"

"Yeah, well, I need...to hit...the gym!" He grunted and let go and they both landed hard. The impact hurt but it was far from fatal. The ghost groaned before he tried to get to his feet. "I think I dislocated my wrists and that fall was... Wait—why didn't we simply phase through the ground?"

"I thought you were corporeal," Johnny responded as he stood and looked at his partner. "How else could you have...caught—oh no." They looked up at a decrepit building, hazy with phantasma, and an unnerving sensation traveled through the revenant's body. "We're in Limbo."

Vic ran to a broken window and focused on a massive bank of darkness. Pieces of buildings and the street were drawn slowly into it. "Near the Big Dark as well. The Axman is able to cut portals into Limbo on a whim?"

"I'm not sure how it works, but it would explain how he was able to acquire his cronies if he can do the same to get to Hell," Johnny reasoned and looked for others who had fallen in. "I don't see any of the officers. What happened to them?"

The ghost checked his coat. "They might have been scattered. I don't know how his portals work but I assume they aren't as precise as ours. Given that living beings aren't supposed to be in Limbo in the first place, they will be found by the authorities sooner or later—assuming they survive the fall and don't become citizens." His gaze darted around. "I can't find my gun."

The young detective's eyes widened and he checked his holster and pockets hastily. "Dammit, mine either. We need it, Vic. It has the bullet!"

"Well, yeah. Okay, think for a moment. How long were you holding onto it?"

He shut his eyes. "I had it in a tight grasp just before we fell and I remember still having it maybe a few seconds before you stopped our fall."

His partner noticed a door but continued to look around on the floor as he moved toward it. "Well, it's probably a good thing as that means it wasn't simply tossed out in another part of Limbo, but we still need to find it. Being this close to the Big Dark means it could get pulled in and lost in the abyss, which is only slightly worse than it getting lost in a random place in the afterlife." His eyes shined as he ran to an overturned chair, reached into the bottom of the seat, and held his gun up. "I found mine!"

Johnny sighed as he approached the door and peered out of the small window in the middle. "It's great that you have your baby back and all, but we still need mine and it's slightly...more— Vic, have a look at this."

"What's wrong, kid?" the ghost asked as he looked out

of the window. Standing in the street and staring into the Big Dark was a child ghost, or at least pieces of one. From their angle, it looked like it was missing part of its face and ribs, and while it had two hands, it only had a left arm and right shoulder. "What in the name of Zeus is that?"

The young detective yanked one of the doors open. "Come on. Whatever it is might be gone soon if we don't get it away from the abyss." Vic nodded and they hurried out. Johnny felt the pull of the Big Dark almost immediately. It was a strange sensation. At every step, he felt like he would sink into the ground but his body felt lighter than air and like he would be pulled into the sky at any moment. The sound was also deafening but it was not the bellowing roar of a tornado or the frightening howl of a Limbo storm. It was an ever-present groaning like a giant creature about to swallow him whole.

Vic grasped his shoulder to steady them both and nodded to the kid only a few yards away. His young partner shouted, "Hey, kid! You need to get away from there!"

This seemed like almost pointless advice. How could anyone in Limbo, even a child, not know about the Big Dark? In fact, how had the kid not been pulled away already? He was only several meters away from the edge.

When the child turned toward them, he held Johnny's gun in his hands. A surge of determination and hope surged through him when he saw it and he took another step forward. "Come on, kid! Come closer. That thing will swallow you whole!"

"Johnny!" Vic shouted and the revenant noted the shock

in his voice. "Look at that kid's face, or what's left of it. He looks exactly like…"

The young detective paused to stare for a moment and almost collapsed in shock but the pull of the abyss forced him to focus. What he could see of the ghost's face was very familiar. As a child, he had seen that face in the mirror every morning. "Me?"

Before they could voice any of the questions that rushed in, the ghost began to dissipate, including the gun. The partners both shouted, "No!" at the same time and dove forward. Johnny was able to snag it before it was taken away but now that neither of them was grounded, their confusion and surprise at the fragmented ghost were replaced by a new realization.

They would be lost in the Big Dark.

CHAPTER THIRTY-SIX

"Up the ladder, Ann!" Marco yelled as he and a few officers turned when loud bangs came from above.

Valerie stepped behind him and placed her hand on his shoulder. "You too, Marco."

He pulled himself away from her and held his bat up. "I can do more damage down here. It's a straight passage so he can't jump around. He'll have to face me head-on."

She grasped the back of his shirt and pulled him away from the group. "No, you'll have to face him head-on! I only saw him for a couple of minutes and you will need the room to maneuver, so go protect your sister. Aiyana and I will be right behind you." Marco looked like he wanted to argue, but playing the protection card seemed to work as he merely grunted and hurried up the ladder and out of the hatch with Aiyana behind him. A loud crash indicated that the Axman had broken through. "We need to go."

"You first, Simone," one of the officers stated as he steadied his shotgun. "You are on detail. Get moving!"

Now, she wanted to argue, but if she did there was less

time for others to follow her. She holstered her gun and scrambled up the ladder behind Aiyana. Gunfire could be heard behind her and someone shouted. "Close the hatch and use a blocker!" She gritted her teeth, reluctant to leave anyone, but when she heard pained yelps and screams, she shut the hatch quickly, locked it, and took out an ether blockade. With a scowl, she placed it on top and activated it. "We need to move."

"Where?" Aiyana asked. She gestured to both fleeing and curious pedestrians in the street. "We need to head in a direction where there aren't pe—"

"We don't have the time. Start running!" she ordered and drew her gun. "The rest will get a clue when he starts to make his way down the street."

"Where are Johnny and Vic?" Annie asked. "I thought they were with you—he appeared in the auditorium, right?"

Valerie moved past the others and caught the woman's hand to hurry her along. "Yes, they were. As for where they are now…" She thought back to the glowing crevasse the Axman had ripped open. "I can honestly say I have no idea."

Vic caught hold of a lamppost and Johnny grasped his leg as they were being pulled into the Big Dark. The temporary respite did little good as the lamppost had begun to bend toward it.

"Kid, I can tell you are curious but we can take a swim through the Big Dark some other time."

"I'm honestly not that curious," he retorted and looked at his gun before he tried to hand it to his partner. "Take it and get back, Vic. They need you."

"What the hell are you on about?" the ghost detective demanded when he was able to get his other hand on the post. "A living person needs to fire that shot, remember? And I won't let you hurl yourself into the abyss out of sheer stupidity."

"It's called selflessness, jackass," he countered and ducked as a piece of rock streaked overhead. "And it might sting like hell for you to shoot it, but you're technically living too, or at least have part of my life. Unless you can pull both of us in, I'm merely an anchor."

Vic tried his best, but the drag of the abyss was too strong and he wasn't exactly a mass of muscle. "Come on, Johnny, you can't give up now. You get a fancy new gun and you don't even get to test it? Where's the fun in that?"

He shook his head and uttered a low chuckle. "We're about to be dragged into potential nothingness and all you can think about is new toys to—" He looked at the gun again and focused on the slider on the back. "Vic, get inside me."

"Do what?" his partner asked flatly.

"Now is not the time to make jokes, Vic. Fuse with me. I have an idea." He maxed the slider and showed it to him. "Let's test it." The ghost's eyes shined for a moment before he nodded, turned translucent, and fused into Johnny, who began to drift off the edge again. He turned and held the trigger down. The pistol whined and shook in his hands before he fired and the shot blasted him in the opposite direction. He landed heavily on the street and a second later, Vic reappeared, grasped the leg of an old mailbox and his partner's hand, and dragged them up and away from the pull of the Big Dark.

"Well, I'll be…" He laughed and adjusted his hat. "That worked!"

"No kidding." The young detective rolled his shoulders. "I think that would have dislocated a shoulder on solid ground."

"You can have it looked at later. We need to find a crossing point and get back."

Johnny pointed to the building they came out of. "We have one. The same way we came in."

"That void?" the ghost asked and frowned at the building. "The upper floors are all busted. Do you think we can climb up to it?"

He twirled his gun and smirked. "We don't' need to worry about that, now do we?"

It was chaos on Royal Street as screams and crashes filled the air. For once, cops and street thugs worked together as a dark, ax-wielding monster marched down the street and slaughtered anything in its path. Shots were fired, both with ether bullets and regular ammo, and while one was certainly ineffective, the other didn't fare much better. Aiyana took one of her totems out and clutched it in one hand while she raised the other, and an orb of fire flared in her open palm. She flung it at the Axman and caught him squarely in the chest, and the supernatural flames began to coat his body.

All it seemed to do was surround him in a coat of fire and make him laugh.

"The spirit of fire doesn't even faze him," she said in a shocked tone.

Valerie fired empowered shots although they would only slow him at best. "He's not simply some ghost or phantom. The regular tricks don't work," she bemoaned and glanced at the shaman. "He would need a special ritual or something."

Aiyana nodded. "But we don't even know what he is. I wouldn't know where to begin."

"Yeah," she admitted with frustration. "That's the problem. Johnny had our best bet and I'm not sure if he'll even come back."

"We need to fill him with ether," Marco suggested and held his bat up. "Like my uncle did. We can blow this bastard back to— Hell, look out!" The Axman pounded his weapon on the ground again and released a wave of white phantasma that hurled everyone in its wake away.

Valerie felt a searing pain throughout her body at first but it became an icy chill. She tried to stand but it felt like the life was being dragged from her body. "What is this?" She gasped. "I...I can't stand. Phantasma shouldn't do anything to the living."

A boot landed beside her head. "My essence is far from normal," the Axman said, his voice full of menace. "Exactly like me, and I'm sick of this little cat and mouse game." He walked to Marco, hoisted him up by the neck, and held him in the air. "Come on out, Annie!" he bellowed. "Or I'll make sure your brother and all your friends suffer before I send them to the other side. Their torment may even break their souls before they have a chance."

"Stop!" Annie called and stepped out from behind an overturned car holding a pistol. "Drop him and spare everyone else here. No more killing and I'll come with you."

The brute turned his head toward her and laughed, but not with menace or contempt. It was an honest belly laugh like he had heard a good joke for the first time in a while. "And pray tell me, my dear, why would I do that? There are countless souls here for me to harvest. What's to stop me from doing so and taking you anyway?"

She held the gun to her head. "Because I'll kill myself before you have a chance to do anything." This made him stop chuckling and the lights in his eyes glowed so brightly they almost looked like flames.

"Annie!" Marco cried as Valerie and Aiyana looked on in shock. "Get out of here. We'll—"

"Hold me off?" the Axman interrupted as he slammed the young man into the pavement. Annie pulled the hammer on the revolver back and stepped forward. "You don't need to be so dramatic, girl. I heard you the first time." He released his hostage and stepped toward her. "I have a little anger to work off, is all, because it seemed you found a way to get one over on me."

"So you need me alive?" she questioned and stood firm as he approached. "Valerie told me what you did to the others you took. Is that why you need me? Simply to be another vessel?"

The killer rested his namesake on his shoulder. "*The* vessel, my dear." He knocked the gun from her hand and grasped her by the throat. "But not for me. For something far more special." He lifted her to his decayed face. "We'll create the original sin and make death an antiquated concept." She tried to respond but only chokes and gurgles came out. "Be silent for now. You can ask all your questions later." He looked over his shoulder. "After I get my fill of souls."

She wanted to scream and he wanted to laugh, but neither were able to follow through. A shot rang out in the street, something that had happened often in the last few minutes, but this one seemed different. It almost sounded like a wail. The Axman shuddered for a moment and the lights of his eyes shimmered before he gasped in confusion.

Annie felt his grip loosen and she kicked him in the chest and managed to pull out of his hand to land at his feet. He seemed to be stuck in place and a purple hole glowed in his skull. That glow began to spread and covered his whole head before it flooded to his shoulders, chest, arms, and legs. He turned slowly and it looked like his body began to set with rigor mortis. When he tried to swing his ax, it simply clattered from his hand.

Johnny stood at the end of the street and plumes of purple smoke issued from the barrel of his gun. He stepped forward as Vic surged out of him with his gun at the ready. Their adversary took one more step before he fell to his knees. "So close..." he muttered as he began to turn into purple ash. "But this is not the end," he whispered as his entire body crumbled to dust.

Valerie could feel her limbs again. She stood slowly. Whatever had affected her and the others seemed to pass with the Axman as Marco, Aiyana, and anyone else who had been caught in the wave began to stagger to their feet. "It's nice of you to come back from Hell," she stated.

Johnny and Vic holstered their guns and the ghost looked at her. "That's not exactly where we were." He focused on the pile of ashes. "Hopefully, he's at the depths."

CHAPTER THIRTY-SEVEN

"And we come to our main story this evening. After the supernatural attack at the police precinct from a terror who referred to himself as the 'Axman,' the creature was vanquished by New Orleans Police Department led by Officer Valerie Simone. The Axman is now considered the primary suspect in the unusual killings that have happened over the last few months and the police have vowed to confirm this suspicion and continue the hunt for any missing persons."

Johnny chuckled as he sat on the motel bed and watched the news continue to discuss the events that had happened only hours earlier. "We don't even get credit," Vic muttered and appeared next to the television. "I always wanted a key to the city too. Just to see what the hell it's supposed to open."

"It's only symbolic, Vic. Contestants on reality shows get them sometimes so they can't be worth much." The young detective collapsed on the bed. "Besides, it's better this way—fewer questions. Most people will simply assume the police had special gear to take care of it rather than a revenant detective duo with a special bullet given to them by someone on the other side." He chuckled and wiped his face. "People may know about ghosts nowadays but they still don't want them to ask too many questions."

Vic drifted to lie on the other bed. "Eh, it could be good for business. More people getting spooked means more calls. It might not be super-profitable but you could do several go-nothing gigs at once and make a decent chunk of change with little effort."

Johnny sighed contentedly. "To be honest, that sounds quite nice after all this. We probably can't go back to Big Daddy's for a while, though."

"Not until we can pay him back, at least," his partner agreed and looked at the sack on the desk. "I spent most of my half getting the new guns but you should be good for a while, yeah?"

"I should be. I considered taking some time off to maybe experience New Orleans rather than simply running through it." He turned to look at Vic. "Still, I can't shake the feeling that it's not over."

The ghost leaned up and tilted his head. "I guess we can offer Val help to find any missing people or maybe his lair or wherever he was hiding. The fact that he wanted Annie alive to be more than merely a vessel is creepy. There are certainly questions that still need to be answered but as for the Axman himself—"

"Are we sure that was him?" The young detective sat again to watch the news. "I know he claimed to be, but what if he was something else?"

"A copycat? He seemed dead set on letting the whole

city know it was him, but that was probably to build fear. For demons, fear directed toward them is like fuel. It keeps them going and strengthens them."

Johnny shook his head. "No. We never found his other minion. Could that have been him?"

Vic considered it a moment. "Maybe he drained him like he did the other guy?"

He bit his lip and nodded. "Maybe. He probably needed the juice. We also never found out who he was working for or with."

"Like I said, there are still questions that need answers and we can look into it if you want." The ghost paused for a moment. "Did you feel that?"

Johnny turned cautiously. He did feel something. It was familiar but in a way he had only felt once or twice. He removed his eyepatch and could see a purple light far in the distance beyond the walls of their motel, . "Purple?" he asked and looked at his partner. "Do you think that's our friend from Limbo?"

Vic nodded. "There are some purple ghosts but none I can think of who can do anything like...whatever the hell that is."

He sighed, stood, and retrieved his jacket. "I'll drive."

***

"Oh, turn that off, Henry," his wife Edna requested. "We should head to bed and I don't want that gruesome thing to be in my head while I'm dreaming."

"Sure thing, dear." The grocery manager acquiesced, pressed the power button on the remote, and pushed from his chair. "Something is always happening in New Orleans, isn't it?"

"It certainly feels that way." She sighed although there was some mirth in her voice. "I always tell Maggie and Joan that you are the crazy one between us, but we must both be crazy to have lived here so long."

"It's our birthplace, even with all the craziness," he replied good-naturedly. "Besides, we might have enough luck to outlast the craziness. I've lived here sixty-eight years and never had to deal with any ghost, werewolf, or chupacabra."

"I don't think there are chupacabras in Louisiana, Henry," she pointed out as she removed her robe and slipped into bed.

"Even better." He laughed and lay beside her. "Either way, don't need to worry about whatever that monster was. It's gone now and I promise I wouldn't let any nasty ghost get anywhere near you."

Edna smiled and ran a hand through his hair. "Like I would let anyone get their hands on you—you know I don't share well since the seventies." He chuckled and they kissed and he turned the lights off. The couple went to sleep not long after. The house had been in Henry's family for generations and even when they remodeled, they had made sure to keep it as traditional as they could, although they didn't need to update the shed all that much.

This made it easy for someone to jimmy the lock, open the door, and find an ax inside.

He stalked across the back yard to the door, pulled the screen door open, and looked at the locked door behind it. In the old days, he would have had to punch out one of the sections of the door to unlock it. As much as he would have liked to relive a little nostalgia, he needed to add a new twist to his old story.

Once in the house with no damage to the door or anything else, he walked past the living room and up the stairs. He looked at the pictures decorating the halls and found an older photograph of Henry with his grandfather. While he might not be aware of who he was, her ancestor certainly would be. He wondered if they would find each other in Limbo. They would at least have that to talk about —how a terror from his time came back in his twilight years and that the fear is never truly gone.

The door to their bedroom was open and he could hear the rhythmic breathing of their slumber. He shut it slowly behind him as he crept to Henry's side of the bed and studied them as they slept, completely unaware of the murderer above them. For a while now, he had kept his eye on many elderly couples around the town in case he needed more pieces in his game. He was down his last henchman but Jack had played his part well and although a little too boastful for his liking, it got his name out there again.

He might have been obliterated but his retainer had set the stage. Fear was power, the feeling that hope was fading away and no longer within grasp. He had found it intoxicating when he was alive to have an entire city under his grasp with only a handful of bodies, but now that they knew he was no mere man? And now when they believed he was gone? When he had taken his new form, the intoxicating feeling in life became actual power. The power of fear and the power of souls fueled him and the terror he brought.

But he would not take these souls, not tonight. For now, he needed to make a statement and make sure that the fear would spread, stronger than ever. He was sure the news and police would try to twist it and blame it on a copycat or some other murderer, but people talked and they gravitated toward their worst nightmares. They would know he was not dead and that there was nothing they could do to stop him.

With care and precision, he hovered the ax head over Henry's sleeping form and moved it so that it was over his ear. In life, he'd had victims who lived—always a smudge against his ledger and his infamy. Now, however, he had no worries that he would make a mistake. He raised the ax above his head, held it in both hands, and swung it. A burst of blood spattered the ceiling, the bed, himself, and the side of his wife's face. She awoke, startled, and took a moment to look around and wipe her face when she felt the warm liquid.

In the dark, he would be almost impossible to see, with the exception of his shining eyes. They glimmered in the night and stared hungrily at her. She looked up and her gaze locked with those lights for a moment before she uttered a fearful scream. He appeared behind her, almost in an instant, and looked out the window as lights turned on in a couple of houses across the way. He raised his ax as she turned to face him.

She played her part gratifyingly well.

CHAPTER THIRTY-EIGHT

"Officer Simone, New Orleans Gazette!" a reporter called as Valerie and several other officers tried to leave the building.

"Haven't you people finished all your questions?" she asked, annoyance evident in her voice before she took a breath to calm herself. "How can I help you?"

"Sorry, I had one last question before you go." She held her smartphone up. "With everything going on and such a big supernatural event, why wasn't the Agency called in?"

She sighed and leaned into the impromptu mic. "The Supernatural Exorcism Agency only handle the cases they deem 'important.' We wanted them to assist us early on in the investigation and we received no word from them." She smiled slightly. "It would appear that this was not in their interest. But the supernatural department of the NOPD will always be here to take care of these matters and although neither I nor any of my colleagues wish for something like this to happen again, if it did, perhaps the SEA would at least look into the matter. Thank you." With that, she turned to head to the parking lot as some of the other officers took questions or held the remaining reporters off.

Valerie reached her car with no interruptions from the news crews, but as she pressed the button to unlock her car, she heard footsteps behind her. "Funny, I never heard of the Agency getting any reports from New Orleans." She drew her revolver and aimed it at a man in a white coat with slicked-back blond hair and stubble. "Although I should say that might be an oversight by myself and my compatriots. Hearing that there is nothing going on in New Orleans would be miraculous or simply another way to say too good to be true."

"I take it you're with the Agency, then?" she asked but didn't lower her gun. "What do you want—or rather, why are you here? The problem has been solved."

He slid his hands into his pockets and smiled. "I'm sure you and I and many others would love to believe that, but even if you were only a rookie looking into the supernatural out of morbid curiosity, you would know better than to think anything having to do with the weird and wicked would be cleaned up so easily." He nodded at her gun. "You can put that down now. I'm no ghost so ether wouldn't do much to me outside of the chills."

She lowered it but only slightly. "You are right. I know you are real, which is why this revolver is a Colt Positive Police Special filled with .38 specials. It works extremely well against flesh and bone."

The man nodded, amused. "I certainly agree. It's somewhat antiquated but it looks in good condition." He leaned against one of the empty cars. "Look, officer, I didn't come here to strike the fear of God into you—"

"And that's a good thing. You aren't doing a terribly good job of it," she remarked.

He shrugged. "Be that as it may, I am here on the orders of SEA to look into the matter you and your department handled today."

Valerie finally allowed herself to relax a little. "All right, but why are you talking to me and not my superiors?"

"Oh, your department head and chief are indeed being talked to. I'm part of a small unit that arrived soon after you eliminated the Axman and if it's any consolation, we were already on our way here before everything happened —you know, to help."

She frowned. "You have the opposite of perfect timing."

The man took a pack of cigarettes and a lighter from his pocket. "Fair enough," he admitted and lit one. "Listen, I decided to come to you instead of someone of higher rank because I've seen the reports. You've been working this case harder than most and you got the ball rolling."

That caught her attention. "Wait—reports on me?"

"Yeah." He nodded and took a drag. "Our information gatherers work fast. After we started to look at this after the incident with the Italian restaurant, they found every-thing they could about everyone involved—including your revenant friend Johnny."

The young woman aimed her weapon at him again. "Are you after him?"

He shook his head. "No, not at all. He's made our work easier in some ways. But he is an unusual person, is he not? Keeping an eye on such rare finds is one of the things we do." He took a puff. "Look, we'll take a look around the city to make sure this is well and truly over because someone has been playing with us and we didn't want to play. I hope that it is done for not only our sake but for everyone in the city. Because if it isn't, we'll have to deal with it and I can tell you, with what we've seen, this won't be a simple smash and grab mission."

Valerie lowered her gun again. "And what would that mean for New Orleans, Mister…"

"Agent Donovan." He took the cigarette from his lips. "And it means that New Orleans would be put under 'protective custody' by the Agency." He sighed and looked at her with sympathy. "Tell me, have you ever heard of a place called Savannah in Georgia?"

She looked quizzically at him. "Savannah, Georgia? I can't say that I have. Is that a city in the state or the country?"

He snickered and took another long drag. "Yeah, that's about right."

The two partners finished their drive to the outskirts of the city and the purple light now looked like a flame to them. As they pulled up at the location, however, it died. "It looks like we've arrived," Vic commented as they exited the car.

Johnny looked around but saw only trees and tall grass. "I have nothing," he admitted and folded his arms. "Was that simply some weird phenomenon caused by the— whoa!" A streak of purple phantasma pounded into him. His partner drew his gun and aimed it at the figure that emerged and pressed the young detective against the car.

It was indeed the stranger they had met in Limbo but instead of the cool, easy demeanor he had then, his eyes were now filled with rage. "You got it wrong, you imbeciles!" he yelled. "You wasted the bullet on a hoax—a trickster! The Axman is still here."

"Let him go!" Vic demanded and pulled the hammer back on his gun. "Get away from the kid, you maniac!"

"Hmm," he muttered, eased away from Johnny, and turned to the ghost detective. "Your little peashooter would do nothing to me but I am not here to fight."

"That was one hell of an introduction." The young detective sneered and pushed the man aside as he stepped away from the car.

The figure shook his head and adjusted his hat as it had almost fallen off in the exchange. "I was simply…letting off some stream due to your hijinks."

"Is that what you call it?" Vic lowered his weapon. "Why the hell are you here? Who are you and what do you mean we got it wrong?"

The stranger walked to a tree, leaned against it, and faced away from them. "That 'Axman' you found? He was not the real Axman. He was his little underling masquerading as his boss." One of his hands curled into a fist and the rings rattled against one another. "This Axman is annoyingly clever. You messed his plans up but he thinks on the fly. He found another way to get his power."

"So we obliterated his goon. That's still something," Vic pointed out, then frowned. "Wait, we did obliterate him, right?"

"No, that was never the plan," he stated. "That bullet brought him to me. I made sure to bury him right. Hell would have been too good for him and Oblivion too easy." He looked at one of his hands as it glowed with a purple light. "He was a spirit already so I could have condemned him to Hell or Oblivion. Instead, I filled his grave and trapped him there, forever lost in the darkness with only the wails of other trapped souls to keep him company for eternity." He chuckled with wicked mirth. "He probably thought his boss could save him from his fate in Hell but I'm sure he regrets that decision now."

The two partners considered this and looked questioningly at each other before they asked the same question. "Who the hell are you?"

Finally, the man turned to face them and adjusted his top hat again. "I am a keeper and if you look in the right places in this very city, you will find out who I am. My worshippers aren't as large here as in other places but they are around."

"Can you hold off on the whole mystery nonsense?" Johnny demanded. "It's not helping us and it took us a while to come around to thinking your bullet could maybe help us in the first place. And you can cross over, so why didn't you help us to obliterate him—or even help now for that matter?"

He looked at them snidely, partially amused but mostly annoyed like a king looking at peasants. "We all have our parts to play in the cycle of life and death, boy," he answered solemnly. "And I am potentially making things worse by being here. That's why I set things in motion to get you two here."

Vic almost dropped his gun in surprise. "I'm sorry—run that by me again."

"I got you here," he stated again, much louder this time. "I was the one who put that gig into the system that led you to Sulfur where you discovered the letter that brought you here. It was easy enough with the promise of a big payday, no?"

"But there wasn't a payday. That was us thinking we could make something out of it," Johnny recalled.

The keeper nodded. "It worked out for me. Otherwise, I would have had to be more involved and a keeper should keep their meddling down in the land of the living. It doesn't mean we don't have a little fun, but we know when to cut off." He brought the brim of his hat down over his eyes. "Most of us do, anyway."

"So why bring us in?" the ghost asked. "We're detectives and the kid has only been doing this for a couple of years. This seems like something you would need a group of bounty hunters on—those who don't mind getting messy."

"Because I thought you would be more subtle," he admitted. "And I was desperate. But given your ability to travel freely through the Veil, I thought it would prove useful since this is a fight on both planes."

Johnny shook his head as he tried to take this all in. "All right, fine, you're a great puppeteer. Whatever. If we got it wrong, can't you make us another bullet and we'll take him out when we find the real one?"

The man shook his head. "He'll be prepared now. My essence will no longer be enough."

"The Axman?"

For a long moment, the keeper remained silent before he bared his teeth slightly. "My brother. The only reason other keepers haven't gotten involved is that they don't know he is acting out and they are loath to do so without evidence."

Vic folded his arms. "What? They don't take your word?"

He snorted and looked away. "This is far from the first time he and I have squabbled, but never with these stakes. He is not doing anything out of the ordinary for him, and since he is not exploiting his privileges and powers openly, they pay him no mind as long as he continues his function."

"Not using his powers openly?" Johnny demanded. "How is he not? He had to have been the one to bring the Axman back and—"

"He did not. The Axman did that himself," the keeper interrupted and twirled his hand, and a black-and-gold cane appeared. "My brother found him and saw the opportunity."

"To do what exactly?"

The man looked into the night sky. "My brother has not been happy in his role for some time. He has looked for a way to separate the Veil between life and death."

Vic waved a hand. "I'm not sure if you've noticed me or a good chunk of the population, but that's already happened, buddy."

"There is a tear, but the Veil is not broken," the keeper corrected and pointed his cane at them. "And you two are as much one of those tears as any portal, but that is beside the point." He lowered his cane and closed his eyes. "If this is not corrected soon, all realms will be in chaos— not something I can imagine can be repaired. The Wild Hunt is not on the prowl for now, but if they should come, they will reap every ghost along with the Axman. They will purge New Orleans of every undead spirit as they are called to do. Even innocent spirits with a chance of making it to Paradise or to be reincarnated will be cast into Oblivion." He peered in their direction. "That would include Vic. What would happen, I wonder, if you were severed?"

"All right, we get it!" The ghost detective growled. "Evil keeper doing evil things, fate of the cycle in balance, whatever. How do we stop your brother?"

"My brother? I brought you to deal with the Axman," he replied and purple smoke began to billow around him. "Whatever he is doing allows my brother to exist here without the use of his abilities as a keeper. If you stop him, my brother has no way to remain and I will deal with him."

The partners looked at one another before Johnny nodded and stepped forward. "Fine, we'll work on it. But do you have a backup plan to kill him if your bullets no longer work?"

The smoke wrapped around the keeper as he grinned. "What do you mean? You are my backup plan, my friends." He slammed his cane down and vanished in the smoke. "Do you fancy yourselves detectives rather than bounty hunters? I need you to be both, exactly as you are both alive and a ghost. I believe in you."

They both waved the smoke away and Vic dug into his pocket for a couple of loose cigarettes. "Damn keepers. Now we're in their mess." He handed one to Johnny who looked at it for a moment before he shrugged and took it. The ghost lit both. "Before we proceed—"

"Yeah, I wanna stay," the young detective said firmly. "That's what you wanted to ask, right?"

His partner took a drag and chuckled. "Well, I intended

to ask if you were hungry first and maybe talk about it over dinner, but sure. No hesitation?"

He shook his head. "No, you?"

Vic looked at the sky. "I don't like being roped into someone else's madness, but I should have chosen a different profession if it bothered me that much."

Johnny laughed and focused on the moon. "Yeah, well, we've both had to deal with each other's madness for a while. What's a little more?" His companion didn't answer and he wasn't looking for one. They both simply took this time to stare at the moon and enjoy a moment of peace before it would inevitably turn into chaos.

But hey, they liked it that way.

THE STORY CONTINUES

The story continues with *Axeman: Cycle of Death*, available at Amazon and through Kindle Unlimited.

Claim your copy today!

Thank you for not only reading this book but these author notes here in the back as well.

For those who don't know me, I'm going to drop a little "about me" down below after a few personal thoughts.

When my collaborator pitched this series to me, I can't say I was overwhelmed with enthusiasm. I'm not normally a ghost story-type reader. However, he was willing to write the first few thousand words and flip them to me to see for myself what he was thinking.

Obviously, I became more enthralled once I got a chance to meet Johnny and Vic. Then, his whole idea of the new ghost world did something I hadn't expected. It captivated my attention.

Normally, I'm a character guy. Give me great characters, and I'll follow them anywhere. The world they inhabit isn't as special to me. Therefore, when I started wondering about the world (and I could catch myself doing this as I was reading the first parts of the story), I realized he had done it.

My collaborator had nabbed me with a world. Well done. Well done, indeed!

I could imagine this world in a video game, a tv series, and/or a movie. I find it interesting to think about the ghosts of the past being able to "live" alongside present-day humans, and we'd get to interact with them.

Well, until you get something like the Axeman to have a chat with. That guy is a serious asshole.

I'll see you in the next book. Don't leave us hanging!

A LITTLE BIT ABOUT ME

I wrote my first book *Death Becomes Her* (*The Kurtherian Gambit*) in September/October of 2015 and released it November 2, 2015. I wrote and released the next two books that same month and had three released by the end of November 2015.

So, just under six years ago.

Since then, I've written, collaborated, concepted, and/or created hundreds more in all sorts of genres.

My most successful genre is still my first, Paranormal Sci-Fi, followed quickly by Urban Fantasy. I have multiple pen names I produce under.

Some because I can be a bit crude in my humor at times or raw in my cynicism (Michael Todd). I have one I share with Martha Carr (Judith Berens, and another (not disclosed) that we use as a marketing test pen name.

In general, I just love to tell stories, and with success comes the opportunity to mix two things I love in my life.

Business and stories.

I've wanted to be an entrepreneur since I was a teenager. I was a very *unsuccessful* entrepreneur (I tried many times) until my publishing company LMBPN signed one author in 2015.

Me.

I was the president of the company, and I was the first author published. Funny how it worked out that way.

It was late 2016 before we had additional authors join me for publishing. Now we have a few dozen authors, a few hundred audiobooks by LMBPN published, a few hundred more licensed by six audio companies, and about a thousand titles in our company.

It's been a busy five plus years.

Thanks for reading this story, and talk to you later!

Ad Aeternitatem,

Michael Anderle

BOOKS BY D'ARTAGNAN REY

The Astral Wanderer

A New Light (Book one)

Bloodflowers Bloom (Book two)

The Oblivion Trials (Book three)

The Revenant Files

Back from Hell (Book one)

Axeman: Cycle of Death (coming soon)

Jazz Funeral (Coming soon)

BOOKS BY MICHAEL ANDERLE

Sign up for the LMBPN email list to be notified of new releases and special deals!

https://lmbpn.com/email/

For a complete list of books by Michael Anderle, please visit:

www.lmbpn.com/ma-books/

CONNECT WITH MICHAEL

Connect with Michael Anderle

Website: http://lmbpn.com

Email List: http://lmbpn.com/email/

https://www.facebook.com/LMBPNPublishing

https://twitter.com/MichaelAnderle

https://www.instagram.com/lmbpn_publishing/

https://www.bookbub.com/authors/michael-anderle